THE HIDEAWAY

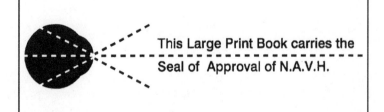

This Large Print Book carries the
Seal of Approval of N.A.V.H.

THE HIDEAWAY

LAUREN K. DENTON

THORNDIKE PRESS

A part of Gale, Cengage Learning

GALE
CENGAGE Learning·

Farmington Hills, Mich • San Francisco • New York • Waterville, Maine
Meriden, Conn • Mason, Ohio • Chicago

GALE
CENGAGE Learning®

Thorndike Press® Large Print Christian Fiction.
The text of this Large Print edition is unabridged.
Other aspects of the book may vary from the original edition.
Set in 16 pt. Plantin.

LIBRARY OF CONGRESS CATALOGING-IN-PUBLICATION DATA

Names: Denton, Lauren K., author.
Title: The Hideaway / by Lauren K. Denton.
Description: Large print edition. | Waterville, Me. : Thorndike Press A part of Gale, Cengage Learning, 2017. | "Thorndike Press® Large Print Christian Fiction. The text of this Large Print edition is unabridged" — Verso title page. | "Published in 2017 by arrangement with Thomas Nelson, Inc., a division of HarperCollins Christian Publishing, Inc." — Verso title page.
Identifiers: LCCN 2017007401| ISBN 9781410499622 (hardcover) | ISBN 1410499626 (hardcover)
Subjects: LCSH: Granddaughters—Fiction. | Grandmothers—Fiction. | Inheritance and succession—Fiction. | Family secrets—Fiction. | Large type books. | Louisiana—Fiction. | GSAFD: Christian fiction.
Classification: LCC PS3604.E5956 H53 2017b | DDC 813/.6—dc23
LC record available at https://lccn.loc.gov/2017007401

Published in 2017 by arrangement with Thomas Nelson, Inc., a division of HarperCollins Christian Publishing, Inc.

Printed in the United States of America
12 13 14 15   21 20 19 18

With great love, thanks, and admiration,
I dedicate this book to my parents,
Randy and Kaye Koffler,
my biggest and earliest fans.

1
MAGS

MARCH

Sunsets in Sweet Bay have always made me feel a little like a child. I think it's all that vast, open water. I expect something to come rising out of the deep at the last minute, something huge and unexpected. I'm always waiting, anticipating. But each night is like the one before — a frenzy of color, the disappearance of the sun, the dusk settling in like an old friend getting comfortable.

Earlier this evening, when I left the house to come out here to the garden, Dot was standing by the microwave waiting for her popcorn while Bert washed his cast-iron skillet with just the right amount of gentleness. Business as usual. We'd had a pleasant dinner — good food, lively conversation — but everyone knows after dinner is my time in the garden. They stopped asking me long ago to join them in their nightly routines —

7

a television drama, a jigsaw puzzle, Glory laying out her quilt squares. Late evenings belong to me and my memories.

I sit here on my old bench, made by hands that once held mine. The bench isn't much, just cedar planks and peeling paint, but it's been a friend, a companion, for almost as long as I've lived in this house. My fingers curl under the edge of the bench, a habit formed over the years. I close my eyes and breathe in deep. So much has happened. Sometimes it hurts to think on it all. Other nights, like this one, the memories are sweet.

Next to me is the latest issue of *Southern Living* that came in the mail today. Sara and her shop are featured on page 50. I like having her photo close. This way, I can pretend she's sitting here next to me. Just as I'm about to open the magazine, I get that hitch in my chest again. A tightness, like a little fist squeezing closed, then a fluttering. Then it's gone.

I reach down and pull off my shoes so I can feel the dirt under my toes. That always makes me feel better. My doctor suggested I wear these ridiculous white orthopedic walkers even though I much prefer my old rubber boots. Good Lord, I loved those things. They were practical, hardworking. Same with the waders and hats. You can't fix a busted boat motor or change the oil in a truck wearing a fussy dress and teetering heels. My Jenny never seemed to mind my getups — she felt right at home in our unconventional life — but Sara was a different story. I saw how she looked at me, like she wondered how in the world her grandmother, not to mention a house as grand as The Hideaway, could have turned out so strange.

I've wondered from time to time whether I should sit Sara down and tell her my story. By the time she moved in with me, she was already at that tender point in every young girl's life where friends' opinions mean more than anything else, and I knew my existence in her life didn't help her climb the ladder of popularity. But I always wished I could find a way to help her see The Hideaway, and me, in a different light.

Truth be told, I think she's a stronger woman now because of who I turned out to be. If I'd remained under my parents' thumbs, always worrying about how others perceived me, I would have been a wispy shadow of a real woman. And I have to think that somehow my refusal to bow to the norms helped shape Sara — even if she hasn't consciously realized it.

Maybe the time is now. She's no longer a

fickle teenager but a grown woman. And a smart one too. She'd do well to know my story, know how it changed me from quiet to bold. Weak to strong. I'll tell her. I'll sit her down and tell her everything. One of these days.

2
SARA

APRIL

I love the smell of New Orleans in the morning. Even now. The city's detractors say it smells like last night's trash or the murky water dripping into the sewer drains, but I know better. It's the smell of fish straight from the Gulf — not stinky, but briny and fresh. It's the aroma of just-baked French bread wafting through the Quarter from Frenchmen Street. It's the powdered sugar riding the breeze from Café du Monde. Sure, there's the tang of beer and smoke and all the sin of Bourbon Street, but when you mix it up together, the scent is exhilarating.

I walked out the front door of my loft at nine fifteen and inhaled the crisp air. It was April, which in New Orleans — and anywhere else in the Deep South — could mean anything from eighty degrees to forty, depending on the whims of God and the

Gulf jet stream. This day had dawned cool and bright.

Instead of slipping into my Audi, I walked to the corner of Canal and Magazine to catch the bus to my shop. It was more of a walk than I preferred to do in wedge heels, but Allyn was always telling me I needed to break out of my routine and "do something unexpected." I smiled. He'd be proud of me for ignoring the time — and my feet — and enjoying the morning. After all, no one would mind if we opened up a little later than usual.

In the Big Easy, businesses were always opening late or closing early for one reason or another. It wasn't the way I preferred to operate, but it was the way of life here, and I'd gotten used to it.

"Hey there, pretty lady," a deep tenor voice called out from the shady depths of Three Georges Jewelers. This George was always trying to hawk CZ jewels and faux baubles to unwitting tourists. I never bought into George's ploys, but I couldn't avoid him. He was too charming.

"Hi, George. Planning to cheat anyone out of their hard-earned dollars today?"

"All day long, my dear. One of these days, you'll have one of my beauties shining on your finger. Send your beaux my way and

I'll set them up with something perfect."

"I'm sure you would, but there is no beau for me today."

"A pretty lady like you? I'm shocked!"

He called everyone a pretty lady. Even some of the men.

I wound my way through the Quarter to where the bus picked up shoppers and business owners and shuttled us to the middle of Magazine Street. Everyone I encountered was in a jovial mood, and I remembered why I fell in love with New Orleans.

As I twisted the key in the lock at Bits and Pieces, balancing a tall to-go cup of coffee in the crook of my elbow, Allyn roared into the driveway on his Harley.

"You're late." He gracefully dismounted the bike. "Pull an all-nighter like me?" His Hollywood starlet shades covered half his face. His hair was orange today.

"No, I didn't, thank you. You're one to talk — you're late too."

"Can't make an entrance if I'm always on time." He hopped up the front steps and grabbed my cup of coffee just before it slipped from my arm.

I pushed the door open and the welcome scent of gardenias drifted past us. We carried a line of hand-poured soy candles in the shop with such pleasing fragrances. Light, not overpowering. I designed Bits and Pieces to make people want to stay for a while. We even kept a Keurig in the back and pralines in a dish by the cash register.

I was in love with everything I'd tucked into the old shotgun house — from restored furniture to antique silver to vintage linen pillows embroidered with the ever-present fleur-de-lis. I'd found much of it at antique markets and estate sales. Even a few garage sales. I didn't limit myself to specializing in one particular type of item — that's why I named it Bits and Pieces. A little bit of everything.

Invigorated by the sunshine and the freshness of the spring air, I propped open the front door and we began the day. I set the music to Madeleine Peyroux while Allyn tinkered with one of the vignettes he'd set up in a side room. In deference to his constant harping that I needed to allow a bit of Southern Goth into the shop — to appeal to the legions of Anne Rice and voodoo fans in the city — I gave him some leeway.

I figured New Orleans had enough mix of high and low, uptown and downtown, that I needed to relax my rules a bit. However, I did draw the line at voodoo dolls. Instead, he scattered tiny white porcelain skulls throughout the shop. Several of my customers bought them to use as unconventional hostess gifts.

The day went on as it usually did. Being the middle of the week, most of the customers breezing in and out were locals. Weekends were for the tourists. A few regular clients had hired me to redecorate their houses, and one popped in to show me photos of sideboards she wanted me to look for the next time I went scavenging. A student from the New Orleans Academy of Fine Art brought by a selection of framed photographs for me to display. Allyn picked up sandwiches from Guy's Po-Boys.

As we neared closing time, Allyn ducked into the back office to check a few voice mails that had slipped in while the shop was busy earlier in the day. After a moment, he motioned to me from the hallway.

"Some lawyer called. He said he needs to talk to you about a Mrs. Van Buren?" He shrugged. "Asked you to call him as soon as you can."

It had been over a week since I'd talked to Mags. We usually talked on Sunday afternoons, but I'd missed our last call because of a water leak at the shop. Instead of hearing the latest Sweet Bay gossip, I'd spent the entire day with buckets, soaked towels, and a cranky repairman. By the time I made it back home and showered, it was too late to call. She left a message on my phone the next morning, but we had yet to catch up with each other.

My customer glanced at me, then at his watch. Not wanting to appear distracted, I shook my head. "I'll have to call him back a little later."

"Sure thing, Boss."

As the customer slowly circled the shop, scratching his chin and considering his purchase, I fought a strange urge to jump in my car and drive back to Sweet Bay to see Mags. I laughed under my breath at the impulsive idea. I couldn't just drop the strings holding my life together and take a break, but I still longed to hear her voice with a force that surprised me.

An hour later, after selling the circa-1896 dining table and packing it into the back of a truck, we finally closed for the day. All I could think about was calling the lawyer. Maybe Mags had gotten herself into hot water with someone in town. I smiled at the thought. It wasn't out of character for my grandmother, but wouldn't she want to tell me about it herself? Or, at the very least,

Dot could have called to fill me in. Why would a lawyer call for something trivial?

Allyn and I stayed in the shop until seven checking the register, straightening furniture, and tidying up in preparation for the next day. I often didn't leave until much later, but I headed out early with him.

"Want a lift back to your place?" he asked when we paused in the driveway. "I have an extra helmet."

"Thanks, but I think I'll take my time getting home. I still have to call the lawyer back."

"Right. What was that all about?"

"It's Mags. Van Buren is her last name."

"Ah, Mags from Sweet Bay, Alabama." Allyn attempted an exaggerated Southern drawl. "Impressive last name for your eccentric little grandmother." He was quiet for a moment. "Lawyers don't usually call with good news, Boss." He fit his helmet over his head.

"I've already thought of that."

"Did she mention anything when you talked to her on Sunday?"

"I missed the call. I was here with Butch and the gaping hole in the roof, remember?" I pinched his elbow, and he pinched me back.

"I still don't understand why you don't go

17

back to Sweet Bay more often. Or why not bring her here for a visit sometime? I make a killer White Russian. Don't old people like those?"

I laughed. "I have no idea if she likes White Russians. And I do visit. I told you all about my Christmas trip — Bert almost burned the tree down trying to decorate it with lit candles. Mags had to douse it with the fire extinguisher. It was total chaos as usual. Our Sunday phone calls work just fine."

"Maybe for you. I bet Mags would love to see your face more often. Who wouldn't?" He patted my cheek and slung one leg over the seat of his motorcycle. "It's not like you have to make a cross-country trip to get there."

I bit the inside of my cheek and glared at him, but he was right. I may have left Mags and my small hometown for the greener pastures of New Orleans, but Mags was my only family — I owed her more than I'd given her.

"Okay, okay, I'll shut up. Go ahead and make your phone call. I'll see you tomorrow." Allyn lifted his helmet to give me a quick kiss on the cheek, revved the engine a few times, and sped away.

Instead of heading for the bus to take me

back to Canal, I took a left on Napoleon and walked toward St. Charles. On the way, I pulled out my cell and thumb-swiped to my voice mailbox. Five or six unanswered messages stared up at me from the bright screen, Mags included. She'd rambled on about nothing in particular so with the ongoing roof problem that week, I hadn't made time to return her call. I touched her name on the screen and the sound of her voice filled the air around me.

As I heard it a second time, the tone of her voice struck me as unusual. I must not have noticed it before because of the chaos surrounding the water leak, but she didn't sound as chipper as she usually did. Just after she gave me a rundown of the squirrels uprooting her geraniums and the bats in the chimney at The Hideaway, she paused and sighed.

"I know it's not a holiday, or even close to one, but I'd love to see you, dear. Sometimes, the sight of your face is all . . . well." She cleared her throat and laughed a little. *"Things are busy over there, I know. It's not like I'm going anywhere, so you just come whenever you can. Don't change your plans for me."*

Her message finished just as I approached the handful of other folks waiting for the streetcar on St. Charles. I sat on a bench away from the group and fiddled with my phone, switching it from hand to hand. I wanted to call Mags — to check on her, to apologize for not calling earlier — but something compelled me to call the lawyer first. I pushed the button, and my stomach knotted as I waited.

"Ah, Ms. Jenkins. Thank you for calling me back. I was just about to walk out the door."

I heard him settling back down in his chair, then a file folder slapped the desk. "I'm Vernon Bains, Mrs. Van Buren's lawyer. Has anyone contacted you?"

"No. What is this about?" I asked, ignoring the gentle sadness in his voice.

"Your grandmother passed away this morning. I'm sorry to be the one to tell you, but Mrs. Ingram didn't feel she could handle speaking about it yet. She asked if I would break the news to you."

I closed my eyes and turned my back to the other people waiting for the streetcar, then covered my eyes with my free hand, pressing my temples until it hurt.

"You'll be happy to know she didn't suffer. She complained of some chest pain, so Dot brought her in to the doctor. They couldn't have known it before, but Mrs. Van

Buren was at the beginning of what turned into a major heart attack. The doctor called for an ambulance, but she died on the way to the hospital. Dot said it looked like she just closed her eyes and fell asleep."

I thought of the streetcar rumbling down the tracks toward me as it picked up and deposited people at various points on the line. Three and a half more minutes and it would stop for me.

I cleared my throat and sat up straighter on the bench. "Thank you for calling, Mr. Bains. I appreciate you letting me know."

"We'll have a reading of the will on Friday afternoon here at my office."

"And where is that?"

"I'm in Mobile. Just across the Bay."

3
SARA

*APRIL*

That night, I took a glass of wine into the courtyard. My building and several others on the block, all duplexes formed out of circa-1850 carriage houses, backed up to a small patio ringed by bougainvillea, sweet jasmine, and palms. Someone had stuck a wrought-iron table and a jumble of chairs in the middle, creating an open area in the lush oasis. On nights when the humidity wasn't 200 percent, a cluster of neighbors and friends of all ages and varying degrees of quirkiness congregated to toast the end of another day.

On this particular evening, Millie and Walt, the couple who lived in the other half of my duplex, were staring each other down across a chessboard. Everyone knew better than to disturb them until one — usually Millie — cried checkmate. I settled down onto a glider and took a slow sip of cabernet.

I had roughly forty hours before I needed to head east on I-10 toward Alabama. I'd have to start early the next morning to move appointments, make phone calls, and write notes for Allyn. He'd probably resent me for assuming he couldn't do my job alone for the week, but I couldn't help it. The shop was my baby, and I didn't take lightly leaving it even for just a few days.

I pulled out my phone to check the time. Eight o'clock, a good time to call. Dinner would be over, and if everything was as it had always been, Bert would be putting the last of the scrubbed pots and pans away. Dot would gather her crossword book and a big bowl of popcorn and retire to the back porch for the evening. Mags would head to her garden in her dirt-caked rubber shoes.

Mags always spent the late evenings there, sitting on one side of a well-worn cedar bench. Not gardening, not reading, just sitting. When I was a child, I'd try to keep her company there, but she always shooed me away, saying she needed to be alone with her memories.

My finger hovered over the number for The Hideaway. What would happen to the house now that Mags was gone? It hadn't been a proper bed-and-breakfast since I was a kid. Could it be again? Should it be?

When I was young, the house had been a fun, if bizarre, playhouse to explore. As I got older, I became more aware of the unusual living arrangements the house offered. It might have been a legitimate B and B at one time, but over the years it had become a senior citizen commune with a revolving door, a long layover for people on their way to Florida retirement glory.

Maybe Dot and Bert would stay on and run the place, although it couldn't have much life left in it. The house had once been a true beauty — Victorian turrets, white gingerbread trim, French doors opening up to a wide wraparound porch — but it had deteriorated over the years. By the time I left for college, it was hard to ignore the peeling paint, dislodged bricks, and window screens covered in wisteria and kudzu.

Even still, no one could deny it had a peculiar charm. Somewhere, in some forgotten, dusty travel guide, The Hideaway was still listed as a "Southern Sight to See." Every summer, some unwitting family would stumble in, bleary from travel, and be shocked to find the B and B was decidedly not what the guide made it out to be. Mags and the others would fuss over them

24

and usher them up to their rooms, excited to have real guests again, convinced it was the start of "the season."

Somewhere in the first couple of days, the guests would inevitably cut their vacation short, saying something had happened at home and they needed to get back. Even though they couldn't wait to leave, something about the place, or the people, would have charmed them. They were always apologetic about leaving. It was a strange conundrum — guests fleeing, sometimes in the middle of the night, but always thanking Mags for her hospitality.

Aside from the true guests who came and went, the B and B was always home to a wild assortment of folks who had checked in years back and never left. Some took jobs at the house, helping with gardening or cooking, and some just lived. Mags's friends Bert and Dot Ingram had been there for decades, and Major and Glory Gregg moved in not long after them. The Hideaway was always a hodgepodge of flabby arms, gray hair, housedresses, and suspenders.

"Good evening, The Hideaway."

I smiled at Dot's familiar voice. "It's Sara."

"Sara, hon. I've been waiting for you to call." She put her hand over the phone and called out in a muffled voice, "It's Sara."

25

Then she said, "Vernon must have called you. I just couldn't bring myself to say it out loud. How are you?"

I sighed and rested my head against the back of the glider. "I'm okay. How are you?"

"Oh, you know. It all just happened so fast." Her voice broke and she paused. "You'd think a seventy-two-year-old woman would have another decade of good living left, if not more. At least a woman like Mags. And her heart of all things. She was healthy as a horse."

"Did she mention anything at all about feeling bad? Had she been having any pain? I didn't have a clue."

"Believe me, I've gone over this a million times in my head," Dot said. "She did mention being a little short of breath a couple times over the last week, but I blamed it on those awful cigarettes she snuck every now and then when she thought we wouldn't notice."

Dot blew her nose. "She'd slowed down a lot since you saw her at Christmas. She just wasn't up to her usual speed, cruising around on her bike and banging through the screen door at all hours. I should have realized something was going on."

Mags had sounded a little weary the last time I talked to her, but I chalked it up to normal fatigue. She was seventy-two, after all.

"She must have had a hint that something was coming though, even if we missed it," Dot said. "Last week, out of nowhere, she said if she ever got really sick, we were under strict orders to pull her out of the hospital and bring her back to the house. She said she'd rather spend her evenings in her garden instead of a cold, sterile hospital room. Can't you just hear her say that? As we pulled down the driveway to go to the doctor this morning, she had the presence of mind to ask Bert to check the garden for berries, because she wanted a slice of his strawberry pie."

Dot's tissue crinkled over the phone.

"There's no way you could have predicted this was coming." I said it as much to myself as to Dot. "I wish somehow I had known though. Maybe I could have done something."

"Not much you can do from three hours away."

"I could've come back for a visit to help."

"She never would have asked you. Regardless of what I think, she wouldn't have wanted to be the reason you left your life there, for any length of time."

"You think differently though?"

Dot sighed. "I just think it was hard for her not to see much of you, even if she never said it."

"But we talked every week. And I came to Sweet Bay as often as I could. It'd have been different if I had more staff at the shop who could take over for me. I only have Allyn."

"I know, I know. You're probably right."

I mentally shushed the voice in my head — maybe it was Allyn's voice, come to think of him — that asked if things really would have been different if I'd had a full roster of staff at my disposal. Would I have gone back more often? I wanted to say yes, but I wasn't sure. I had grown comfortable with the distance between Sweet Bay and me.

"She always told me she understood," I said.

"Sure she did. She was so proud of you over there. She never wanted to be a burden to anyone, especially you. You know Mags. She hardly ever asked for help and she was private until the end."

Of course Mags wouldn't have called me up and begged me to come for a random weekend. That's not who she is — or was. She wanted me to come on my own terms. I just waited too long.

"No sense in worrying over it all now," Dot said. "How could any of us have known? She was Mags — we took it for granted that she'd be around forever."

By the time we finished our call, the courtyard had emptied out. Only Millie and Walt remained, peering at each other and pondering their next moves on the chessboard. I could just barely make out the early evening sounds of Bourbon Street a few blocks away, quiet as a house cat compared to the frenzy that would ensue in the coming hours.

"You're a million miles away," a familiar voice called out. "What's going on?"

Bernard, an artist who lived in one of the duplexes across the courtyard, settled down in the chair next to me. He twisted off the plastic top of a dented Nalgene bottle and took a long sip.

"Just watching Millie and Walt. Married sixty-eight years and still embarrassingly in love."

We watched them in silence for a few moments.

"Gone out with the fellow from the law firm again?" he asked.

"We've gone out a few times." A slow grin crossed Bernard's bearded face. "What's that look for?"

He held up his hands in mock surrender. "I'm not saying a thing. He just appeared to have a fat wallet for someone so young."

Mitch was a lawyer at one of the oldest firms in New Orleans. He made partner when he was thirty, a record in the firm, maybe even in the city. We'd been out a handful of times since he booked the chef's table at Commander's Palace for our first date, but it wasn't exclusive and definitely wasn't serious — which is exactly how it had been with most of the men I'd dated in New Orleans. And I was just fine with that.

"He's nice, believe it or not. He asked me to go with him to some gala tomorrow night, but I have to cancel. I'm going back to Sweet Bay, actually. My grandmother died."

Saying the words out loud gave my new reality — that I was now family-less — a weight I didn't quite know what to do with.

"I'm so sorry. Were you close?"

I hesitated. "We were and we weren't. There was always some part of her she kept away from everyone else, including me."

"So that's where it comes from."

"Where what comes from?"

"You're a private person yourself. Locked up. You don't lay all your cards out like most everyone else around here."

I considered that for a moment. "Maybe Mags and I were more alike than I realized."

"Was she a typical 'fresh-baked cookies and soap operas' kind of grandmother?"

I laughed. "Not quite."

"Mine made the best potato-chip cookies in Butler County, Mississippi."

"Potato-chip cookies?" I rubbed my eyes. "Now, that does sound like something Mags would have cooked up. But no, she wasn't typical, that's for sure. She used to embarrass me like you wouldn't believe."

"Isn't everyone embarrassed by their grandparents to some degree? Come on — potato-chip cookies? No one actually ate them — we just shoved them under our napkins until we could sneak them to the dog."

I smiled and thought of the woman who didn't think twice about picking me up from school in a men's smoking jacket and plastic flip-flops. She walked or biked everywhere she went because of constant floaters in her eyes. When Mom and I would drive her to get her hair done, I always slumped down in my seat. With fuzzy gray curls peeking out from under a bird's-nest hat complete with baby-blue eggs perched on top, Mags was oblivious to my humiliation. At least she pretended to be.

But she was my only true family. Probably my biggest fan. And now she was gone.

I stood and squeezed Bernard's shoulder. "I should get on to bed. Allyn will be giddy at the prospect of running the shop for a few days without me. I need to have his instructions ready to go."

Inside my loft, everything was in its place: overstuffed down pillows on a couple of linen slip-covered couches, vintage silver vases of fresh flowers, a few tasteful pieces of artwork. I'd decorated the loft in the same vein as Bits and Pieces, although I was rarely home long enough to enjoy the flowers or the soft comfort of the couches.

As I went through my usual preparations to get ready for bed, my mind was on Mags. Occasionally, she'd flutter through The Hideaway in a burst of energy, saying she was going to clean out and declutter. She'd poke through closets, check desk drawers, eye various pieces of furniture as if she'd actually have the nerve to get rid of any of it. She never did. It was as if once things — or people — found their way there, she couldn't bear to force them out.

I, on the other hand, hated clutter and chaos, and my home and shop were evidence of that. I hadn't consciously developed a taste so different from what I grew up with, but that's how it turned out.

Across the room my eyes fell on two side

chairs I'd recently refinished but hadn't had the nerve to part with yet. I'd run across them on a rainy Saturday trek to an estate sale at a decadent, moss-covered home on St. Charles. Water dripped from the ceiling into silver buckets discreetly tucked around the opulent parlor of the eight-bedroom, prewar home. Mildewed silk curtains covered the ten-foot-tall windows. A tarnished, silver-encrusted mirror hung in the downstairs powder room. It was shambles like these that had made me fall in love with old, forgotten things in the first place. I came away from the sale toting the pair of French side chairs with busted cane bottoms that now sat in my living room, proud and beautiful. My shop was full of similar rescued and restored beauties.

Maybe I wasn't as different from Mags as I'd thought. I'd spent years all but running from her and The Hideaway, but there I was, inviting other old and tattered things into my life by the armful.

I sat up against the bed pillows and gathered my hair into a braid to keep it neat while I slept. On the bedside table was the bottle of Jo Malone hand lotion I rubbed into my fingers and cuticles, the last item to check off my list before turning off the light. But tonight, I paused with my hand on the chain. Instead of pulling it, I opened the drawer of the small table and reached all the way to the back.

The photo was still there, though I hadn't pulled it out in a while. Mags and my mother smiled up from the yellowed Polaroid, while I, a busy eleven-year-old, laughed at something outside the camera frame and tried to bolt. My mother's hand on my shoulder was a feeble attempt to keep me in place long enough to snap the shot.

I focused on Mags. The ever-present bird's-nest hat was missing, and her hair — salt and pepper, heavy on the salt — was loose around her shoulders. It must have been a day with low humidity, because her hair fell in gentle waves instead of frizzy curls. Her face was soft, and her eyes crinkled into a smile at the corners.

I'd never thought much about Mags as a younger woman, but in this photo, it was easy to peel back the years and see how she must have looked at my age, or even younger. I'd held this photo in my hands many times, but I'd never seen past her fifty-four-year-old face into the person she may have been before my time, before my mom's time even. As far as I knew, she'd always been the same strange, frustratingly dowdy woman I'd always known her to be.

But those eyes. And her smile — it was tilted higher on one side, as if a smirk was in there somewhere, trying to sneak out.

I held the photo a moment longer, then put it back in its place at the back of the drawer and turned off the light. I could feel the storm brewing — my throat burned and my eyes stung. I'd held myself together all day, but with the room dark and quiet, the tension in my chest and sadness welling in my heart overflowed. Tears spilled over my cheeks unchecked and made damp spots on my pillow.

While my chest heaved with quiet sobs, I had a fleeting memory of my grief after my parents' death. It was different back then — not better or worse, just different. A twelve-year-old with a grandmother and four live-in "grandparents" grieves much differently than an adult who knows she's now alone in the world, regardless of how she's tried to tell herself she doesn't really need anyone else.

I rode out the storm until it ended. Exhausted and shaky, I reached over and pulled the photo out again. I propped it up against a book on the table and took a deep breath. The murky yellow glow from a streetlight outside my window illuminated Mags's face in the photo. I sank farther into

the pillows and closed my eyes, content to
know that Mags, wherever she was, was
sending that half smile my way.

4
Mags

JANUARY 1960

I was going to leave him, but he beat me to it. My bags were packed, stuffed into the upstairs closet ready to go when the right moment presented itself, but then I found his note. I couldn't believe he left a note.

Margaret, I have business in Tennessee. I'll be gone a while.

Robert

As if I didn't know what his "business" was. Mother kept telling me to ignore everything. Of course she did. She said if I kept busy at home, doing what I was supposed to do, my husband would end up back under our roof where he belonged. I took her advice through gritted teeth for most of the three years Robert and I had been married, but I just couldn't do it anymore. And I didn't even get the satisfac-

37

tion of leaving him, because he was already gone.

Once everyone found out he'd gone out of town on "business" again, they'd surely think I left to escape the embarrassment, eyes rimmed in red, hair a mess, vowing to do better, to be the wife who would keep him home. But I wasn't worried. No one in that town knew me very well anyway.

After I read the note, I took a pencil from the drawer in the kitchen and poured myself a gin and tonic from the stash Robert never bothered to hide because he never thought I'd want to drink it. I took the drink, pencil, and note into our tidy backyard. I sipped the cocktail, thinking, massaging Robert's note in my fingers. When the glass was empty, I took the pencil and wrote "Good riddance" underneath his words. Then I grabbed a box of matches from next to the grill and lit one. I held the note over the fire until the flames licked the bottom edge of the paper and engulfed it.

I was just about to pull out of the driveway when Daddy careened down the street in his silver Chrysler, landing like a pinball in front of our house, one tire up on the grass. When he climbed out of the car, he was red-faced and out of breath, as if he'd run the whole two blocks from their house instead of driven.

"Margaret, I'm so glad you haven't left."

I hadn't told anyone I was leaving.

"I know you, my dear," he said, as if he'd heard my thoughts. "I knew what you'd do as soon as Robert told me he was going away."

"You talked to him?"

"I was supposed to have a meeting with him at the bank today, but he called and canceled. I saw through the lie right away. If he had business in Tennessee, I would have known about it."

When I opened my mouth to speak, he did instead. "I'm not here to talk you out of it. I just wanted to give you this." He handed me an envelope. "For whatever you need."

"I don't even know where I'm going."

He nodded. "You'll find the right place. When you come back, everything will have straightened itself out. You'll see. Some time away will be good for you."

So he didn't know me that well after all, but I appreciated the effort. I took the envelope. I didn't need to open it to know what was inside. "Yes, the next time you see me, things will be much different."

For one thing, I wouldn't be wearing my

wedding ring, although I hadn't had the nerve to take it off just yet.

He took a step closer to me — still too far away to put his arms around me, but close enough to warrant some sort of physical touch. In the end, he patted my shoulder awkwardly. We stood there, two statues full of emotion, neither able to make the first move. I was always more my father's daughter than I cared to admit. Better than being my mother's daughter though.

After all, it was Daddy standing there in front of me, concerned about me. Mother was probably at home trying to come up with a reason to call me. A new recipe I needed to try for Robert since he was so tired of my tuna casseroles. ("I bet a good juicy Steak Diane would bring him home from the office earlier.") Or maybe she found out I skipped my Camellia Ball dress fitting with Mrs. Trammel, and she wanted to call and chide me. Forget the fact that I was a twenty-two-year-old adult with my own home and husband, and I could make my own dress-fitting appointment if I needed one. Which I didn't.

I opened the car door, tossed my bags in the backseat, and turned back to face Daddy.

"I'll see you soon?" he asked.

I shrugged. Smiled.

"What should I tell your mother?"

I thought for a moment. "Tell her the truth." His version of the truth was all she needed to know.

"Good-bye, Daddy." I lowered myself into the car. He put a hand on the door and helped me close it. It always stuck, something Robert promised many times to fix. The door shut with a dull thud.

Finally.

"I'm gone," I said out loud.

I rolled my windows down when I reached Mobile Bay. Warm air laced with the scent of just-caught fish and soft muddy banks whipped around my face. I ripped out my hair band and let the wind have its way with me.

Along the edges of the Causeway, old men stood in clusters, each holding a cane pole with the line dropped into the marshy waters along the shore. A shrimp boat bearing the name *Miss Carolina* in sweet cursive pulled away from a dock while a deckhand threw nets over the side.

I pushed the gas down a little farther, even though Robert always cautioned me to stay below the speed limits. "There's no need to draw attention to yourself, Margaret."

Funny, he never wanted his *wife* to be the center of attention.

On the other side of the bay, I drove through the familiar towns — Daphne, Montrose, Fairhope — until I reached a deserted road lined with pecan trees and open fields. I'd gone over the bay many times with Mother, shopping for clothes or getting a bite to eat at Central Café. Robert and I stayed a long weekend at the Grand Hotel in the first year of our marriage, back when things were mostly peaceful and I could still close my eyes to his indiscretions. But I'd never been off the main roads and thoroughfares of the quiet "over the bay" communities. This was unfamiliar territory.

The last marker I remembered seeing was one for Sweet Bay. I needed to pee ("Oh, don't be crass," Mother would say) so I began looking for a place to stop. A faded sign directed me to "The Hideaway — the South's Best-Kept Secret." The driveway was long and curved. I assumed there was a house at the end of it, but I couldn't see it through the trees. My heart beat faster the farther I went down the driveway.

When I emerged from the canopy of trees, I put my foot on the brake. A gorgeous old Victorian house sat bathed in the sun's last remaining rays. An old woman stood in

42

front of the house sweeping an Oriental rug with a straw broom and yelling at a feisty black-and-white dog. The dog played a game of chase, darting on and off the rug as the woman worked. They both stopped and turned when they heard me approach.

The woman directed me to a parking spot under a large oak tree. When I opened the door, she asked, "Parker, four nights? I wondered where you were. I thought you may have changed your plans without letting me know."

"Excuse me?"

"Are you Parker? Mrs. Helen Parker? Double for four nights?" She peered around me into the car. "You're by yourself? What do you need the double room for? I have a full house tonight — I could use that double elsewhere if you can take a single."

I could be anyone I wanted to be.

"A single would be fine."

The woman told me to wait in the foyer while she got my key. Inside, people were scattered everywhere. Miles Davis floated from an unseen radio. In the large room to my left, a man sat at an easel in front of a tall window. A few others sat around him, lounging on various couches and chairs. Some smoked, one sipped on brown liquid in a highball glass. They all gestured wildly, pointing to the man's canvas and out the window. The artist laughed and flicked a bit of paint at one of the women.

Down the hall in the kitchen, someone stood at the stove singing. Her back was turned, showing off dark hair hanging all the way down to her bottom.

The woman came back down the hall with a key in her hand.

"I'm Evelyn DeBerry. I'm the owner here, and I'll give you a rundown of the rules." She glanced at my gray-checked Christian Dior dress and black peep-toe heels. "Although it doesn't look like you'll give me any trouble." She smiled at me, then gestured toward the group of people on the couches and rolled her eyes. "Beatniks."

I knew I looked like a dutiful housewife. It was what I was expected to look like, and I'd never questioned it. Not really, anyway. But I was no longer dutiful. I had escaped, and my sense of liberation was powerful. Now, I felt more of a connection with the beret-wearing crowd on the couch than I did with Mrs. DeBerry, who sported pearls and rolled hair like mine, despite the age difference. I could feel the stares from those on the couch. *"Oh, how sweet. June Cleaver in the flesh,"* their smirks seemed to say.

As Mrs. DeBerry rattled off a list of rules,

I looked past her into the living room again. A man I hadn't seen at first sat among the artists. He wore dirty blue jeans and a long-sleeved plaid shirt. No beret, no cigarette, no brown liquid. But his blond hair was long. To his shoulders. For some reason, it caught me so off guard. I had to stop myself from crossing the room to touch it.

As I watched him in my peripheral vision, he turned to me. In response, my whole body turned toward him without my permission. In that never-ending moment, everything about me was reflected in his face — the way I looked on the outside and everything roiling around inside me that didn't match my appearance. It was as if I'd been hollowed out.

Then the moment passed. He gave a small smile, pulling just a corner of his mouth upward, and rejoined the conversation around him. The encounter left me disoriented. I took a deep breath to slow my heart.

"Mrs. Parker, are you okay?"

It took me a moment to realize Mrs. De-Berry was talking to me. "I'm fine."

I struggled to regain my composure. I glanced at the man again. His back was to us now. For all I knew, I had imagined it all.

5
MAGS

Mrs. DeBerry led me upstairs to my room. It was large and filled with stuffy antiques — a mahogany rolltop desk, a Chippendale curio cabinet, and enough occasional tables to hold a dinner party's worth of drinks. Mother would have loved it. Mrs. DeBerry stood at the door waiting, so I thanked her and told her it was lovely. Satisfied, she turned to go, then paused and stuck her head back in the door.

"The arty types just keep filling this place up. The worst part is, they don't pay half the time! They feed me lines about money coming in — I know it's all lies, but the bills keep coming, so I have to take whoever shows up. Henry never would have let this happen . . ." She trailed off, staring out the window.

I longed to finish unpacking, crawl into bed, and disappear for a while, but I didn't want to be rude. I sat on the edge of the bed and waited.

"Let me know if anyone gives you any trouble. Mr. DeBerry may be gone — he passed away last year, God rest his soul — but I'm no pushover. I'll kick them out in a heartbeat if they cause any problems for a regular guest." She smiled at me like we were in this thing together, then left the room.

Mrs. DeBerry had taken one look at me and lumped me in with the "regular" people. I knew I looked the part, but I also knew what stirred deep in my soul. I wasn't "regular" if it meant socializing only with those who had money and the right appearance and peering down my nose at anyone who fell outside the lines. Or if it meant sticking with a marriage that had crushed any dream I ever had about what marriage could be. Not anymore.

The next morning, with nothing to do and no responsibilities, I stayed in bed until nine, then made my way downstairs for breakfast. I took in more of the house than I had seen the night before. It was grand, if a bit run-down. The dust was thick on tabletops and the rugs needed a good airing out. Cigarette smoke hung thick in the air, despite no morning appearance of the crowd from last night.

Outside, Mrs. DeBerry sat at a white wrought-iron table in the backyard overlooking the bay. She nursed a cup of tea, adding to it from a porcelain teapot. Limoges. The same pattern Mother had selected as my wedding china.

I walked down the steps, and Mrs. DeBerry turned.

"Have a seat. I'd love company." She gestured at the extra teacup, as if she'd expected me to appear. "How was your night? The riffraff didn't make too much noise for you, did they?"

"They were fine. I slept well."

"That's good. Sometimes lying in bed at night, listening to them cut up for hours, I think of how it used to be around here. Much more civilized, that's for sure." She sniffed and looked at me out of the corner of her eye. She wanted me to ask. Hearing stories about her more proper and civilized clientele was the last thing I wanted, but I indulged her. I looked out at the water as she spoke.

"We bought this house as our summer home, but Henry decided to open it to paying guests when we realized its income possibilities. It took off immediately. People came from all over the South to stay for weeks at a time. Magazines used to send their editors out here at least once a summer, sometimes twice." She sighed.

"It was perfect — the lawn dotted with ladies in hats and gloves. And such dashing men. Henry would take them out on the boat, and they'd come back windblown and glowing. And the dinners — oh, the times we had. Guests filled the table, and our staff served gumbo with the most succulent shrimp you've ever tasted. Fresh bread. Pies so good they'd make you cry. Mrs. Parker, I wish you could have seen this place then."

I smiled, but it felt stiff on my face. It sounded just like dinner parties at Mother's house, the ones she insisted Robert and I attend, if for no other reason than to show her friends we were a happy couple. "What happened?"

She shrugged. "Henry got sick, and we had to stop taking on so many guests. He'd long stopped working — the house was our only source of income, and it more than paid for what we needed. But with fewer guests, money got tight. We had to let the kitchen staff go, then our cleaning staff. I'm sure your trained eye could see the state the house is in. Our old Bertha would have an apoplectic fit if she saw how I've let things go." She refilled her teacup and mine.

"After Henry died, I needed the money, so I had to be less selective about who I allowed to stay here. Hence, the artists," she said with a flick of her wrist. "I just don't know how long I can keep this up. I can always move back to Mobile, but I've been gone so long, I don't know anyone there anymore. If I did go back, I'd be the outsider, and I assure you, I have no desire for that. Imagine me, an outsider. It's preposterous."

She fanned herself with her hand, then rose from the table. "I need to get on with my day. You enjoy yourself, now. I can't offer you a boat ride, but there are games in the main parlor — the artists break those out later in the day. Heavens above, I don't know how they get by in life. No jobs, no money . . ." She continued her rant as she walked back up the steps and into the house.

Alone, I breathed in the cool air. It was January, but it felt more like early spring. I leaned my head back in my chair, untroubled for the first time since learning of Robert's indiscretions. Sitting in that chair with the sun on my face, miles away from the center of the storm, I finally felt free.

I awoke sometime later to a man sitting at

the table opposite me. I sat bolt upright, patted my hair — an automatic gesture — and smoothed my hands down my dress.

"It's okay. You look fine."

When I chanced a look at him, I realized he was the man from the night before, the one who stood out from the crowd. I hadn't noticed how defined his jaw was, how thick his fringe of eyelashes. He was so close, it was hard to breathe. He seemed to take up all the air in the entire world.

"Pardon me for saying so, but you look a little out of place here," he said.

I looked down at my dress and put my hand up to my hair again. His scrutiny reduced me to half my size.

"I don't think it's me who's out of place," I said, surprising myself. He wore a flannel shirt, dungarees, and scuffed boots. "Where's your black turtleneck and beret?"

He let out a soft laugh. "Touché. Your name's Helen, right?"

I reached up to scratch the back of my neck. The collar of my dress felt warm and too tight. "That's right. Helen Parker."

He stood and held out his hand. "Want to take a walk with me?"

Under the table, my wedding ring sat heavy on my finger. I had yet to take it off. I rubbed the ring with my other fingers,

51

considering his offer. In the end, I took his hand.

And that one little decision changed everything.

6
SARA

APRIL

I spent Friday morning going over last-minute details with Allyn. As I'd suspected, he was ecstatic about having the place to himself.

"No more French café music, for one thing." He walked around the shop, ticking items off on his fingers. "I may move some of these sconces to the back to make room for a few paintings a friend of mine dropped by. Oh, and I saw some great old masks sitting by the curb in front of the Funky Cat last night. I may stop by and see if I can pick them up before the garbage truck comes. They might make a nice vignette somewhere."

"I'm not deeding the shop over to you. I'll be back by next Friday at the latest. I figure that gives me time to go through Mags's things and tie up any loose ends with the lawyer. Don't think I won't notice if this

53

place looks like a Mardi Gras float when I get back."

I thought he'd tease me as he always did about running too tight a ship, but instead he hugged me. He'd been doing that a lot. He sniffed and I pulled back to look at him.

"It's okay, Allyn. Why are you upset?"

"I always wanted to meet her. The way you described her, I thought we might have been kindred spirits or something. Her having African American roommates in the 1960s? In the Deep South? If she loved people on the fringes, she would have loved me. Anyway, she was the last family you had left. Doesn't that make you the slightest bit sad?"

"I'm fine. Really." To avoid meeting his eyes, I turned away and straightened my dress. Allyn eyed me, assessing me. I raised my eyebrows in answer.

"Whatever you say." He looked at his watch. It was a couple hours before I had to leave town. "Get out of here. Finish packing, put on something comfortable, and pick up a large coffee on your way out. When you get to Sweet Bay" — he affected the drawl he liked to associate with Alabama — "call me if you need me. You keep your emotions stuffed in a drawer somewhere, but your grandmother died and you're going home."

Home. I hadn't thought of Sweet Bay as home in over a decade. The word unsettled me a little.

"I can get Rick to come and take over if my services are needed," he continued. Allyn's friend Rick annoyed me — constantly misting his face with lavender water (to keep his complexion young) and boasting about his ability to fit into women's skinny jeans — but he had a killer eye for what customers liked.

I took Allyn's advice and was now zipping across Lake Pontchartrain headed toward Alabama. I rolled down the windows and let the breeze play with my hair and soothe my frantic mind until the car got too warm and my hair began to frizz.

On the way, I mulled over what Allyn had said about burying my emotions. My first reaction was to blow it off and blame it on his constant attempts to psychoanalyze me. But he wasn't the first person to tell me I had a tough exterior. When I'd called Mitch to cancel our date on Saturday night, he called me unreadable.

"You break our date to one of the biggest events I have to go to all year, and you don't even seem sorry about it."

"I told you, my grandmother died. I'll be

wearing my black dress for a much more somber occasion than a fund-raising gala at Galatoire's."

"I don't mean to slight your grandmother's death, but you've hardly mentioned her to me. We've been going out for — I don't know, a little while — and I still can't read you. I don't know what makes you tick or what's important to you."

Maybe Mitch and Bernard were right. Maybe I was too private. But it didn't bother me. Allyn was one of the few people — okay, the only person — who knew what I was really like on the inside. And that wasn't even by my choice. Early in our friendship, he more or less kidnapped me one night after work and whisked me away to a party in a courtyard much like the one behind my loft. We hung out with his friends for hours, talking and laughing. I was more comfortable in the company of his strange, colorful friends than I had been with any other group of people I could remember.

Around midnight, someone popped in an old VHS tape of *Xanadu,* and most everyone flocked to the TV inside. Allyn and I stayed outside and talked. Actually, I did most of the talking, answering every one of his myriad questions about my life and childhood as honestly as I ever had.

The next morning, nursing a grating headache, I opened Bits and Pieces an hour late, much to a snickering Allyn's delight. He admitted there had been a boatload of vodka — cleverly disguised as pineapple juice — in the punch he'd been handing me all night.

"How else was I going to get you talking? I had almost no idea who you were until last night. I never would have pegged you as a former Bourbon Street bartender in hot pants."

I smacked him on the arm and pretended to be put off all day, but he knew better. "You had fun and you know it. You should let your hair down more often. You're much more fun to be around when you're not working so hard to keep all those balls up in the air. Let one fall now and then."

The rest of Louisiana and all of Mississippi passed in a blur of concrete, casino billboards, and occasional lingering hurricane damage. When I crossed the state line into Alabama, something clenched in my stomach. I had no idea what the next few days would hold. Being twelve years old when my parents died, I didn't have to take care of anything related to the business of death. Mags had been there to talk to the doctors, the lawyer, the funeral home. I was insulated from the ugliness of it all, except for the savage hole in my heart. When Mags took to her bed after the funeral, Dot stepped in as my surrogate mother. She sent thank-you notes to those who had sent food, returned casserole dishes, delivered the funeral bouquets to the hospital, and packed lunches for me when I went back to school.

As the only surviving member of our tiny family, I'd likely be responsible for all those particulars. But this time, there wasn't a twelve-year-old child in the mix. She had grown into a thirty-year-old woman more than capable of taking care of the details.

I arrived at Mr. Bains's office ten minutes before our scheduled meeting. I approached the door to his office on the sixth floor with a mix of nerves and determination, certain I'd be walking away with nothing more than a few dusty boxes of old clothes and maybe some items belonging to my parents.

"Excuse me. It's time to . . . um . . . ahem." Mr. Bains cleared his throat to get our attention. Dot, Bert, Glory, and Major had spent the last ten minutes oohing and aahing over me.

"Your hair is so pretty. It's longer since we saw you last." Glory examined a dark lock between her fingers. Her short dreadlocks stood up at jaunty angles. "I just got a new shade of red in last week. Maybe you'll let me try it out on you? Fix you up nice for the funeral."

Glory Gregg was the hairdresser at The Hideaway. At one time she kept the residents' hair in the latest dos deemed acceptable for senior citizens, and a few that would look better on skateboarding teens. Did Ms. Mary Lou ever forgive Glory for the bad dye job that left her hair eggplant purple instead of dusky midnight? Major was Glory's army veteran husband. I never knew if Major was his given name or just his title.

"I'm making Mags's favorite chicken à la king tonight in her honor," Bert, the chief culinary officer, said. All the residents knew they needed permission before entering the kitchen. Bert was soft-spoken and gentle, but the kitchen was his domain and he'd let you know if you overstayed your welcome when he needed to start a meal. "You'll be at the house for dinner, right?"

"Sure she will," Dot said. "I've already gotten the blue room ready for you, dear."

Before I could speak, Mr. Bains stood up behind his desk. "If I could have everyone's attention, we'll get started. This shouldn't take long, but I don't want to waste anyone's time." He looked down at his watch before he sat and opened a slim folder.

"As you all know, I've gathered you here for the reading of the will of Mrs. Margaret Van Buren, better known as Mags. In typical cases, as the estate attorney, I would mail a copy of the will to beneficiaries. However, Mrs. Van Buren specifically requested I gather the five of you to hear the will together. Being a longtime friend of hers, I intend to follow her wishes to the letter."

Instead of speaking of the house itself, Mr. Bains began with a list of mundane items. When he started outlining which kitchen items would go to Bert and which quilts Glory could have, I tuned out. My mind drifted back to the day I became a permanent resident of The Hideaway. My parents had dropped me off so they could do some Christmas shopping. It was only September, but they liked to spread the expenses over a few months rather than end the year in the red. As owners of the only diner in town — famous for their loaded cheeseburger and a darn good catfish pie — they made enough money to pay the bills and keep me in My Little Ponys and then Converse sneakers, but not much extra rattled in their pockets.

It was raining that day. I had curled up in the window seat in the downstairs den, tracing raindrops trailing down the window with my finger, when someone knocked on the door. I paused, waiting to hear movement in the house. No one came, so I rose and peered out the window next to the door.

Sergeant Burnside, the chief of police in Sweet Bay — and a frequent Jenny's Diner customer — stood on the porch shaking water off his cap. As he settled the cap back on his head, he noticed me standing in the window. His eyebrows crunched together and the worry lines on his forehead deepened.

When Mags appeared behind me and opened the door, Sergeant Burnside asked if he could talk to Mags in private. I knew it was something terrible.

A little while later, Dot found me in my room and gave me the details: the rain, my parents' 1975 Volvo, a huge water oak, slick roads, and flashing lights. The police found a toy store shopping bag a hundred feet away, sitting in a horse pasture like someone had set it down and left it for a child to find, like a present.

I hadn't noticed the quiet in the small office overlooking downtown Mobile until Mr. Bains said my name. Now everyone was looking at me.

"I'm sorry. What did you say?" I asked.

He looked down at the paper in front of

him and read.

" 'To my granddaughter, Sara Margaret Jenkins, I bequeath The Hideaway and all its contents, save for those already specified for other people. She is to take possession of the house effective immediately. I request that she use her talents and skills to renovate the house and property to its fullest potential, hiring help as necessary, and live in the house during renovations to keep a close eye on the work. Don't let anyone bungle this job.' Her words, not mine." Mr. Bains looked up at us.

" 'My friends can stay in the house as long as Sara owns it,' " he continued. " 'After renovations are complete, she may do with the house what is in its and her best interest.' "

Mr. Bains rummaged in a desk drawer, then handed me a manila envelope closed with a metal clasp. "Enclosed is a letter she said will explain things in more detail. There's also a copy of the will for your records. I trust any questions you have will be answered fully by the contents therein."

We sat in silence as he gathered his things. "If no one has any questions, I have a four o'clock meeting I need to get to. I'm only a phone call away if you think of anything later."

"Wait, wait." I held my hand up, unable to grasp what he had just unloaded and not ready to be alone with the others and their questions. "That's it? That's all it says?"

"Well, there's the letter . . ." He motioned to the envelope in my still-outstretched hand.

"But I don't understand. I only planned to be in Sweet Bay a week. I can't . . . She's giving me the house?" I looked around at the familiar faces next to me. "Did any of you know about this?"

"Know she'd leave you the house, you mean?" Dot asked. "No. Although I suppose it's silly to think she would have left it to anyone else — especially us."

Bert cleared his throat and Major shifted in his chair. "Silly? What's so silly about it?" Major asked.

"We're old!" Dot said. "Why would Mags leave it to us when we're probably not far behind her? It belongs to Sara, as it should."

"Maybe, but we've all lived there for decades." Major's voice grew louder. "She could have at least given us a say in what happened to the house."

Glory rested her small dark hand on Major's beefy one. "We're lucky Mags made any plans at all. She loved us, so of course she wants to take care of us. She would

never want us turned out on the street."
She glanced at me as if looking for confirmation.

I opened my mouth, then closed it. My mind was a chalkboard wiped clean. My fingers found the edges of the folded letter inside the envelope.

"Thank you, Vernon." Dot stood. "It's time for us all to go home. We'll eat, then we can talk about everything." She looked at me. "We'll see you at the house."

I pried open the manila envelope before I even closed my car door. Aside from the copy of the will Mr. Bains mentioned, there were two sheets of paper. The first sheet was letterhead from First Coastal Bank with an account number stamped at the bottom. The other was Mags's letter. I peered inside the envelope, expecting it to be empty, but it wasn't. I turned the envelope upside down and a key slid into my open hand. It was small, the color of an old penny, and almost weightless.

Dot and the others were still moseying across the parking lot toward their cars. I pulled the letter out and started reading.

Dear Sara,

You're probably wondering why in the world I decided to leave you the bed-and-breakfast — my refuge, my own hideaway for fifty years — when you've spent years building your own life in New Orleans. But aside from my dear roommates, you are my entire family. Who else could I give the house to? I'm sure at least one of them (probably Major) will disagree, but it's my house, my choice.

As Mr. Bains read in the will, my hope is that you will do what you must to make The Hideaway beautiful. It was once, long before I stumbled on it, and it's high time someone restored it to what it should have been all along. I let it go to make a point, but my anger has long since dried up. The place deserves to shine again and you, my dear, are the person to tackle the job. I don't care how you do it, just give the house back its glory. After that, you can do whatever you want with it. If you decide to sell it, please give my friends enough time to make alternate plans.

Don't worry about money. I have an account at First Coastal with your name on it. Use the money to do whatever you need.

To say The Hideaway is important to me is an understatement. I'll go to my grave carrying memories of both sweet, miraculous love and deep, aching loss in my heart, and the house has been a witness to it all. My highest hope is that somehow, it can give you the love and strength it's given me over the years.

I trust your vision for the house and for your future. Just remember the two don't have to be mutually exclusive.

Love,
Mags

7
Mags

JANUARY 1960

His name was William. He told me a little about himself on our walk: woodworker. Had some pieces in local shops and galleries. Good at it, but didn't make much money. Never married.

I gave him similarly scant details about my own life. Society life in Mobile. Balls and parties. Married. Husband huddled up in a chalet with his lover.

"Puts you in a bit of an awkward position, now, doesn't it?" he asked.

"Awkward?" I laughed. "Of all the positions it puts me in, awkward doesn't come to mind."

He just smiled.

"What are you doing here?" I asked. "At The Hideaway, I mean. You don't live here, do you?"

"I do. For the moment, at least. I've moved around with buddies the last few years. We were up in Asheville for a while, then down to Florida. I landed in Sweet Bay last year but just moved in with the charming Mrs. DeBerry a couple of weeks ago."

We walked on. Down the path in front of us, a family piled into a motorboat, arms overflowing with jackets, blankets, and fishing poles.

"And you? What brings you here?"

"I told you. My husband left. So I did too."

"There's more to it than that. There always is."

"You want to hear the whole sad story?"

"I don't have anything else to do or anywhere else to be." He smiled, then his brow creased. "But if it's not something you want to talk about, I understand."

I took a deep breath of the damp, cool air and blew it out. "I think it's okay. Being here makes everything that's happened seem . . . well, a little less crushing. It started before we were even engaged, so I guess you could say we got off on the wrong foot. Robert and I had been going steady for a while when he asked me to be his date to the biggest Mardi Gras ball in Mobile. A mutual friend had seen him downtown weeks earlier outside Zieman's Jewelers, shaking hands with Mr. Zieman himself.

Naturally, I expected a ring to come soon, maybe even the night of the ball."

Just then, the boat with the little family roared to life. We paused and watched the man back the boat out of its spot alongside a covered pier, then zoom off toward deeper waters.

"Let me guess — the ring didn't come," William said, resuming our walk.

"Not exactly. I knew Robert was very popular — especially with the girls — but I chose to ignore the rumors. I was content knowing he'd asked me to be his date when he could have asked anyone. In hindsight, I should have paid a little more attention to those rumors."

"It's always easier to ignore the things we don't really want to know."

"Yes, well, it would have saved me some tears if I'd listened."

In my mind, I saw the twinkling lights hanging from the ballroom rafters as if they were etched in my brain. The men at the ball were in high spirits, drunk on liquor, excitement, and the look of their ladies in floor-length, sparkling gowns. Every so often, Mother would catch my eye and smile like everything was right with the world.

And it was — until AnnaBelle Whitaker entered the room.

"What happened at the ball?" William asked.

I shrugged. "He had a problem being faithful. Even back then."

"So you left."

"It took me a while, but yes. I left."

"And you could have gone anywhere. Gotten in that car and put a thousand miles between you and your cheating husband. But instead you ended up here, walking beside me. Life's a funny thing, isn't it?"

"Funny?" I asked. "I'm not quite sure that's the right word."

I married Robert Van Buren. Handsome Robert, who came home from Korea and wanted to get to know his neighborhood pal again. But by that time, I was a woman, no longer the childhood buddy. He courted me, romanced me, and asked me to the ball, then humiliated me in front of all of Mobile. But I married him anyway! Then he did just what I, and probably everyone else in town, expected him to do — and I kept staying! After all, good wives didn't leave their husbands, however unfaithful they were.

Without warning, a snort of laughter escaped me. William stopped walking and stared at me, but I kept laughing, unconcerned with whether I was being proper. I laughed until my stomach ached and tears dripped from my chin. I wasn't altogether sure whether those tears were from humor or grief.

"Feel better?" he asked when my fit was finally over.

"Tons." I wiped my eyes.

"I think this place will be good for you." He took my hand.

I instinctively tried to pull it away, but then I thought of Robert and AnnaBelle on the dance floor at the ball, his hand on her lower back, both of them oblivious to the openmouthed stares all around them. William's hand was large and warm and it felt good.

"You can hide out while you figure out what to do next. But I should warn you: The Hideaway tends to make people want to stay."

He squeezed my hand, and to my surprise, I squeezed back. Life already felt different.

Before heading back into the house for dinner, William took me to his workshop to show me a table he was building. "I'd love to know what you think about it," he said as we crossed the grass between the house and the small woodshed where he did his work.

I looked up at him in surprise. Robert rarely asked my opinion about anything other than the doneness of a steak or whether the housekeeper had cleaned the kitchen well enough. The simple fact that William wanted to know what I thought about his work sent a spark of longing through my chest.

"You seem like someone who appreciates nice things. It's not perfect, but I think it's kind of nice." He grinned at me and pushed the door open.

A table stood in the center of the room, lit by a single light hanging from a cord in the ceiling. I inhaled sharply. With his rough, calloused hands and joking manner, I'd expected something practical and useful, not such beauty.

The table was long and slim with oak boards stained a rich, dark brown, but the best part was the legs. Delicately carved vines and leaves snaked around each one. I knelt and ran my hand down one leg, my fingers following the shallow curves and twists of the carving.

"This is beautiful." I looked back up at him.

"You sound surprised."

I shook my head. "No, I —"

He laughed. "It's okay. I've heard it before. I learned carving from my grand-father. He used to whittle sticks into little creatures — bears, dogs, cats. I tried it one day on a scrap piece of wood and discovered I was good at it." He shrugged, then looked around the shop. "I didn't realize it was so messy in here until now."

Sawdust covered the floor like dew, and his tools were in disarray on his work surface. In the corner, broken pieces of wood sat in a jumble.

"I can help you straighten up, if you want."

"You don't have to do that. I wouldn't want you to get your clothes dirty."

I raised an eyebrow.

"Suit yourself." He reached behind him and grabbed a broom, then held it out to me. "You can start with this."

We got to work. I swept piles and piles of sawdust — the stuff seemed to multiply the more I swept — while he gathered loose boards and stacked them along one wall. It wasn't long before we both grew warm and William pushed open the door to allow in a breeze. I paused in the open doorway and slipped my feet out of my heels, kicking them to the side.

"You'll ruin those in no time." William pointed at my legs covered in pantyhose. "You might as well take them off too."

"What? My stockings?"

"If you haven't noticed, you're the only one here who wears those things. Well, you and Mrs. DeBerry."

I looked down at my stocking feet. I could see the indentations on the top of my toes where the heels had dug into my skin. My heart beat a little faster as I reached down and pulled the thin silk off, one leg at a time. Then I dropped them in a pile on top of my shoes.

Lord, if Mother could see me now.

With the sweeping finished, I helped him organize his tools in his tool bag and on little hooks stuck into the wall. We worked in easy silence at first, then we began to talk. About his family and mine, about Robert and our marriage.

"I remember the night he arrived home from the war," I said. "My parents and his were having dinner at the Battle House Hotel. Robert had his family's chauffeur bring him to the dinner. Mother said when he pulled her to the side and asked about me, she knew he was going to propose. She burst into my bedroom late that night and told me all about it. She was so excited about the prospect of marrying me off — especially to the Van Buren family."

"What makes them so special?" William asked.

"The Van Burens own Southern National Bank downtown. My father is an executive in the shipping industry. It helps my family to have a friend in the banking business — even better if we're married to them."

"I see. And did the proposal come quickly?"

"Not as quick as Mother would have liked." I smiled. "We'd been friends before, but it wasn't romantic. We had to get to know each other again. But something about him was different, more serious than I remembered."

"I'd imagine war will do that to a man," William said.

"I don't know if it was the war or just that he decided it was time for us to be together. Everyone knew it would happen. I was never too comfortable with the idea that his parents and mine decided a long time ago that we'd be a perfect match for each other. I guess I just let myself be pulled along by everyone's excitement. And the fact that Robert was quite charming didn't hurt matters either."

"Was it ever a perfect match?"

"I suppose in some ways it was. Just not in the way I wanted it to be."

"And what way is that?"

I laughed a little and smoothed my hair with my hands. "My, you are direct, aren't you?"

"I'm just curious about you. That's all."

I didn't answer his question — after all, how could you explain true love, the kind that nurtures and respects, that honors and cherishes? That's what I'd hoped for when I married Robert, even though all the signs pointed to him being unfamiliar with — and uninterested in — that kind of love. But I hardly knew William, and it felt silly to try to explain my heart.

"You wanted to be treasured."

"I-I guess you could say that," I said, stammering. "Instead, I got this life — and a husband — I hardly recognize. It's not what I pictured, that's for sure."

I looked up to where he stood in front of the window, framed by the fading daylight outside. His gaze on me was so intense I had to turn my eyes away. I pushed off from the worktable where I'd been scraping spilled paint off the handle of a hammer. I wasn't sure where to look or what to do with my hands. William crossed the floor toward me. When his fingers touched mine, I closed my eyes and exhaled.

Big and warm, his hand wrapped around mine. I wanted to close the distance between us with one more step, but propriety held me back. He dropped his gaze to our laced fingers. Just as he opened his mouth to speak, someone called from the house.

"Dinner!"

He leaned around me and peered through the window toward the house, then sighed and looked back at me. "I think it's time for us to go," he whispered. He held his elbow out to me. "May I escort you?"

I raised an eyebrow and smiled, then bit it back. I nodded and slipped my arm into his.

Dinner was a loud jumble of laughter and conversation, dishes passed down the long table, a wineglass spilled, chairs scraping against the hardwood floor. I tried to keep up with the conversations as well as I could, but William's steady presence next to me scattered my thoughts. My fingers still tingled where he'd held my hand earlier, and I both wanted him to touch me again and was afraid of what might happen if he did.

After dinner and dessert, guests drifted away from the table, some to the back porch, some to the parlor where easels had been abandoned almost midstroke, and a few to bed. When a couple of women grabbed the remaining plates and dishes and carried them into the kitchen, I pushed my chair back and stood.

"I should probably go help." I gestured to

the open door of the kitchen. I picked up a scraped-clean casserole dish and followed the women out of the dining room. If they thought it strange that a woman they didn't know was helping with the dishes, they didn't say anything.

As I washed and wiped, I tried to calm my frenzied mind and racing heart, but it didn't work. Compared to Robert's charm and swagger, William was substantial and strong. Still confident, but there was no boasting. No bluster. But it was more than that. We'd only spent one afternoon together, and already this man knew me in a way Robert never had. I'd been acknowledged — *seen* — maybe for the first time. The sensation was dizzying.

Fifteen minutes later, I walked out of the kitchen drying my hands on a towel. William still sat at the dining table, alone. At that moment my heart stilled, calm and sure. He smiled and pushed my chair back a few inches with his foot. Instead of sitting down next to him, I turned toward the stairs and began to climb. More than hearing him on the stairs behind me, I felt his presence staying close. When I walked into my bedroom, I left the door open.

The next morning, I woke with the sun on

my face. I'd left the window curtain open to catch the breeze when the room grew warm during the night. I stretched and smiled, remembering, but I froze when William stirred next to me in bed.

Good Lord, Margaret, what have you done?

But then he wrapped his arms around me and pulled me close to him. Whispered into my hair. Kissed my neck. Things Robert never did. In that moment, it was easy to forget the previous three years had even happened.

I felt bold. Eager. Yet I was scared to speak, scared to break the silence between us that felt almost sacred. I waited, a complicated knot of tension and contentment in my chest.

A few minutes later, I couldn't wait any longer. I rolled to my other side and faced him. "I have to tell you something."

"Mmm?"

"My name isn't Helen Parker."

He smiled, his eyes still closed. "I know."

"What do you mean, you know?"

"I saw you through the window when you first arrived here. You hesitated when Mrs. DeBerry asked for your name. I thought, 'Now there's a girl who's running from something. Or someone.' Makes sense that you'd give a different name."

Was that what I was doing? Running? It didn't feel that way. It felt more like I was arriving.

"So what's your name?" he asked.

"Margaret."

"Margaret," he repeated. Just when I thought he'd drifted back to sleep, he spoke again. "Can I call you Maggie? Margaret's a little . . . stuffy."

I laughed. "You can call me whatever you want."

"Okay, Maggie." He propped himself up on one elbow. "Remember what I said yesterday about you being in an awkward position? This is what I meant."

"You'll have to explain that."

"It's awkward because you're going to fall in love with me. Don't laugh, just wait — it'll happen. Then when people hear that you left your husband, they're going to say you're getting back at him by being with me. You'll have to defend yourself to them — prove to them that this is something other than a rebound." He lay back down next to me.

"I am not going to fall in love with you," I said, our faces inches apart.

"You're not?" He moved his lips closer to mine.

"Nope," I murmured.

80

He smiled. "Now it's my turn to tell you something. From the moment I got here, I felt like this was where my life would start. My real life. I've done a lot of things and gone a lot of places, but when I arrived here, something felt different." He reached up and stroked my cheek. "I wasn't sure what to look for, but then you showed up. I think you're what I've been waiting for."

Silence stretched between us, but it wasn't uncomfortable. Rather, it was a space for dreams. For possibility.

8
MAGS

FEBRUARY 1960

William and I quickly became an item. Everyone in the house saw it and no one questioned it. Only Mrs. DeBerry thought it improper.

"Mrs. Parker — or whoever you are — it is 'Mrs.,' isn't it?"

I nodded.

"Mrs. Parker, he's a bum. They're all bums. They don't do anything. You're a young girl. What would your father think?"

"He'd probably be shocked, Mrs. De-Berry. Just like you are. Even I am, a little. But William isn't a bum. You should know that."

She shook her head and walked away, mumbling about ladies and gentlemen and indecent things.

William introduced me to his friends as Maggie. He looked at me when he said it the first time, as if asking for belated permission. I nodded. Maggie felt good. It felt light.

A woman in the house, Daisy, lent me some clothes when she saw me adjusting the waistband of my slim skirt. "Here, this will be more comfortable." She pulled a long tunic dress out of a bag.

I smiled — Mother would definitely not approve. I stopped rolling my hair that day. I let it fall around my shoulders, free and unruly. That night, I shoved my bobby pins, pearl necklace, and foam rollers into a side pocket of my suitcase. I went ahead and dropped my wedding ring down there with them. Lord, it was a sad, expensive little collection.

The days were long, with nothing concrete to mark the passage of time. Most mornings William and I sat among the other guests in the dining room, munching on croissants and idly reading the newspaper. No one had real jobs to hurry off to, so the mood in the house was one of utter relaxation. It wasn't hard to slip into a routine of ease.

As the painters painted, the sculptors sculpted, and the yogis practiced their moves in the grass, I learned the routines of the house and became a part of them. Since I didn't have a creative endeavor to take up my time like everyone else, I wanted a job to do — something to make me feel useful and productive.

Starla, the woman I'd seen in the kitchen the first night I arrived, asked me to help with food preparations. She just needed an extra hand to help pull meals together, but I took it a step further. I made a grocery list every few days with ingredients for each meal plus extra items for the house — toilet paper, matches, soap. I organized the pantry by food type and size. I scoured the oven and cleaned out the refrigerator. As a wedding gift, Mother had hired a woman to clean our house in Mobile twice a week, so I rarely had anything to clean or straighten at home. The hard work felt good, and I relished my sore muscles and dirty fingernails.

William and I spent most evenings sitting on the back porch, huddled together on the glider. He'd massage my feet and tell me stories of working in orange groves in Florida and selling his tables and benches from a roadside shack in Asheville. My privileged prior life was sedate and sheltered compared to William's hard-earned wisdom and tales from the road. I soaked him up, every word, laugh, and touch.

■ ■ ■ ■

He knocked on my door early one morning before the sun was up. He stuck his head in the room when I answered.

"Come with me," he whispered, holding up a mug of coffee. "Outside, five minutes."

Curious, I dressed quickly. Following the aroma of coffee outside, I found him waiting in his truck, the passenger door open for me.

"Where are we going? It's still dark."

"I know. You'll see."

He drove fast down Highway 55. When he turned onto a side street, I grew lost in a maze of dirt roads and creek beds. Finally, we went around a bend and the path opened into a cove overlooking Mobile Bay, isolated except for a blue heron standing on thin legs in the shallow water. It was still dark beneath the cover of trees, but directly in front of us, the sky had exploded in streaks of orange and pink, with violet clouds scattered like pebbles. Just above the waterline, the horizon remained a deep indigo blue. Seagulls gliding in the air provided the only movement other than the quiet waves creeping forward and back along the shore.

We watched the sky change colors without

speaking. At some point during the show, we walked to the edge of the water and sat down, a blanket over our shoulders and our toes just touching the water. I leaned my head on his shoulder.

"What do you think?" he asked once the sky was a solid fluorescent orange.

"It's breathtaking. How did you find this place?"

"It's mine. I bought this plot of land from a buddy who moved to San Francisco. It had been in his family for generations, but he didn't plan to come back and said he didn't need ties here. I've done nothing but move around, and I guess ties are what I'm looking for — something to anchor me to a place I can call my own."

We sat close and still, watching the gulls overhead and the water's gentle movement. In the distance, the double masts of a shrimp boat interrupted the perfect line of the horizon. He took my hand in his and traced the skin on my palm and wrist, up to the crook of my elbow. The light touch sent chills up my arms and down my back. He laced his fingers between mine and I pressed myself into his side. It had been a little more than a month since we met, but already, I felt connected to him in a way I'd never felt with Robert.

"This thing that's happening between us — it's fast." I was scared to say the words out loud, so I whispered them.

"Too fast?" He turned to face me.

I shook my head. "I don't know. I don't even know how this sort of thing works. I've never been with anyone other than Robert, and we'd known each other for years. Is it possible — rational — for us to feel so much so quickly?"

"Sure it's possible. Rational? I don't know and I don't care. I care about us and where we're going."

"How do I know this isn't a rebound, like you said?" I touched the tip of his nose. "And how do I know you're not just taking advantage of the only woman at The Hideaway not dressed in black and ranting about Kerouac or Ginsberg?"

He didn't laugh or even smile. "I'm not taking advantage of you. You know me well enough by now to know that."

"That's the thing — sometimes I feel like I don't know you at all."

"You do know me." He pulled away a bit. "What else do you need to know? My life before you wasn't that interesting, then you showed up and my world cracked open. Isn't that enough?"

"It is — or I want it to be. But you have

87

to understand how it feels to open the door to a world that's entirely unknown to me. And . . ." I stopped. I didn't want to remind him. Or me. As if either of us could forget.

"And what?"

"I'm still married. I have a husband."

"You're right," he said softly, his gaze on the water. "Do you have plans to return to him?"

I shook my head.

"Then this new world — I know it makes you nervous, but isn't it also a little exciting?" He cupped my cheek with his hand. "We can make our future anything we want it to be." The corner of his mouth pulled up — the same half smile he offered as a life preserver the first evening I arrived at The Hideaway.

It almost made me mad — that smile that seemed to belittle my fears of linking my future to someone — and somewhere — else. But at the same time, I wanted to cling to that smile, to wrap myself around the unknown and not ask questions.

"And as for this just being a rebound for you," he continued, "a way to get back at Robert for his lady friend, you'll have to judge that for yourself. I don't think it is though. I think this is . . . something else."

I nodded and he took my hand.

"Let's not mention Robert again. I don't want him to be a part of this," I said.

"Suits me just fine."

I nestled back down beside him under the blanket. He pulled me closer and kissed me.

"I told you, you were going to fall in love with me," he said with a grin.

I pushed him away and laughed. "What makes you think I'm in love with you?"

"You are, aren't you?"

I was a new woman — risky and adventurous. It felt foreign and perfect at the same time.

"I guess you'll have to wait and see."

9
SARA

I pulled down the long gravel driveway in front of The Hideaway and began the slow trek through the trees. When I reached the house, I parked my car under the big oak. Nerves stalled my hand on the car door handle.

My parents' deaths and the lonely years after had left a wound deep in my heart. Although the wound had healed, it was still tender. I didn't let myself think of their deaths often — it was too painful, like pressing on a bruise. Thankfully, my scrambling to open Bits and Pieces and make a name for myself in New Orleans occupied almost all my mental energy. Their absence was always present, but most of the time, I was able to keep it tucked under the surface of my life. I was comfortable with that. I could live with that. But here I was, back at the place where it all happened.

When I finally exited my car, I stood in the driveway holding my suitcase and picking rocks out of my open-toed sandals. I heard the crunch of gravel and turned around to see Major's car slowing to a stop behind me. I waited by the door while the four of them climbed out.

"Go on in," Major said. "You don't need to wait for an invitation."

"I still can't believe y'all leave the doors unlocked."

"It's not New Orleans, honey," Dot said, before kissing me on the cheek and walking past me into the house.

I took a deep breath before following them in.

Major pulled out my chair at the table before I sat down. Dot and Glory must have done a number on him on the ride over from Mobile. He seemed calm, but I could only imagine the rant he probably unleashed in the car. I glanced around, trying to gauge the tension level, as Bert filled our glasses with iced tea.

"We're real glad you're here," Glory said to me, spooning out a serving of green beans.

I laughed a little, but her calm, delicately lined face told me she was serious. "I

91

thought y'all might fight over who got to kick me out the door first."

"You're like a daughter to us," Glory said. "Kicking you out would never cross our minds. All we can do is look to the future of the house, whatever that may be."

Four pairs of eyes shifted in my direction. I took a long sip of tea.

"I meant what I said earlier," Dot said as I set my glass down. "The house belongs to you now, as it should. Mags asked you to take care of this place, and no one could ever argue with her once she got an idea in her head. Regardless of what you decide to do with the house in the end —"

"She's not going to sell the thing, that's for sure," Major's deep voice burst out. "It needs to stay in family hands." He shot to his feet, his chair squeaking on the hardwood, and stomped to the other side of the room. So much for him cooling off in the car.

He stood at the window overlooking the driveway for a long moment before he turned back to us. When he did, most of the anger had drained from his face. "I know we don't deserve the house. Blood's thicker than water, and all that. But after living here so long and being with Mags every day, I'd say we're a little more than just water. Now she's gone and given our house to someone who only visits a couple times a year." He lifted his glasses and rubbed the bridge of his nose. He sighed. "I know it's not *our* house, but it feels that way."

"It does feel that way, but Sara grew up in this house," Dot said. "It's more hers than ours. Mags let us stay here so long out of the kindness of her heart — and because she loved us. But she's not forcing us out. She wouldn't have given the house to Sara if she didn't trust Sara to make the best decision. I agree with her on this."

Silence fell in the room as Major shuffled back to his chair and we all started eating. Forks clinked against plates and a breeze from the open window ruffled the curtains.

Dot looked at Bert and tilted her head toward the kitchen. Bert raised his eyebrows and nodded. "I'll be right back." A moment later, he returned carrying a bottle of wine and a tray of glasses. "Nothing like a little wine to loosen the lips and calm the nerves, right?"

"I think someone's lips are already loose enough," Glory said.

Bert started to laugh but stopped when Major glared at him.

"Okay, let's all just enjoy our dinner," Dot said. "We need to speak words of love to each other and celebrate who Mags was, not second-guess her actions. It's her life, her house, her decision."

I looked down at my lap and smiled. Dot was Mags's best friend in the world. It made sense she would echo what Mags had said in her letter to me.

"Everybody agree?"

We all nodded. Glory winked at me from across the table. I smiled back at her. Everyone watched as Bert uncorked the bottle and poured a couple inches into each glass. His calm movements soothed our frayed nerves. One by one, everyone reached over and took a glass, even Major.

I waited until everyone had taken a sip before I spoke. "It means a lot that Mags trusted me with her home. In all of our conversations, she never said anything about leaving the house to me. If she wanted to surprise me, she did it. I have a lot going on with my shop and —"

"Yes, your shop," Glory said. "Did you see the binder by the couch when you came in? She always kept it in her bedroom, but we brought it out so you could see it. She has every magazine article that has ever mentioned you or Bits and Pieces. She showed that binder to everyone who came through the door. She was so proud of you."

I always told Mags when a magazine writer or reporter came into the shop with a voice recorder and a notebook, telling me we'd been noticed again by another editor somewhere. Sometimes I worried she'd think I was flaunting my success, but she always celebrated with me. I had no idea she'd gone to the trouble of tracking down the magazines and clipping the articles.

"Sara, you have quite a talent and *we*" — Dot bored a hole in Major with her eyes — "think you'll be the perfect person to whip this place into shape. I, for one, am glad for it. A few cans of paint and a hammer or two are just what we need around here."

From the little I'd seen before dinner, painting and hammering were the least of my concerns. If I decided to sell the house — and living three hours away, did I have another choice? — I'd have to do a lot of work just to get it ready for the market. Talking about selling right now was premature, but finding a good contractor wasn't.

"I'll check everything out, put a plan together, and start calling around," I said. "I'm good at cosmetic updates, but I'm no expert on plumbing, wiring, any of that."

"Now, don't get too ahead of yourself, dear," Dot said. "The house doesn't need that much work. She's still a beauty, much like your grandmother. She just needs some spit and polish."

"We'll start there and see how it goes," I said carefully.

"And have you thought of your plans for the house aside from the renovation?" Glory asked.

I knew what she was really asking. "I haven't thought about much, honestly. It's been a quick couple of hours."

"Just give us some warning if you decide to pull the rug out from under us," Major said.

"Mags specifically asked me to do that. Even if she hadn't, you know I wouldn't do that to you."

With dinner mostly over, Bert stood to get the dessert. "Someone dropped off a hummingbird cake this morning. I've been holding myself back all day."

"So many people have been bringing food by," Glory said. "Such kindness."

"I didn't know Mags had so many friends," I said.

"Most everyone in Sweet Bay has been helped by Mags at one time or another," Bert said. "Either that, or their parents were. Anyway, this is what Southern people do, whether they know the deceased or not. You know that." He set the cake down in the center of the table as if he made it himself.

"If it's okay with you, I'm going to pass on dessert," I said. "I think I'll walk around a little before heading upstairs."

"You sure you don't want any? You're not one of those girls who never lets herself eat sweets, are you?" Bert asked. "If nothing else, that's what grief is for. You can stuff yourself silly and blame it on the person who died."

"Bert! That's terrible," Dot said.

"I'm just kidding and Sara knows it. But we do have a counter full of cakes and pies in the kitchen. Someone will have to eat it all."

"I'll have a slice tomorrow," I said as I stood.

"Let us know if you need anything," Dot said. "Your room is all ready, but I may have forgotten something. Feel free to look around, go on down to the dock, whatever you want. The place is yours."

"Sure is," Major said under his breath. "She's got the keys to prove it."

I spent the next hour walking around the house and yard to get a sense of what a renovation would entail. Of course I'd seen the house each time I'd come back for visits,

97

but I hadn't taken a hard look at it with a critical eye.

Inside, it was hard to get a sense of the space because most of the rooms were overstuffed with furniture, as if each person who'd moved into the house over the years had added a treasured chair or table to the mix. The resulting hodgepodge of furniture matched neither each other nor the style of the house. A few pieces stuck out though, and for good reason — an oak pie safe with hand-punched tin covering the bottom shelves, an armoire with delicate scrollwork carved into the pine at the top and bottom, and a corner hutch covered in peeling white paint and doors with squares of wavy glass. These had been in the house for as long as I could remember, but before, they'd just been part of the overall chaos of the house. Now, I saw they bore the handmade, vintage charm so many of my customers craved.

The main living room had floor-to-ceiling curtains that, when opened, revealed beautiful windows reaching almost to the ceiling. I tied the curtains back on their hooks and peered through the salt-crusted glass. Past the lawn, the bay stretched out flat and calm. As I turned to cross through the room, a blur of blue on the floor caught my eye. I knelt and ran my fingers across the splotch of what appeared to be blue paint just inside the front door. I scratched at the edge with my fingernail, but the paint was so old it had almost blended in with the wood.

Across the hall from the living room, the kitchen had last seen an update in the 1980s. The countertops and backsplash still boasted the cheery yellow Mags had loved so much. Laminate cabinets with faux-wood trim and ancient appliances rounded out the dated look. Baskets hung everywhere, adding a country feel that must have been Bert's doing.

Despite this veneer of age, the house had great bones. I couldn't help but feel a ripple of excitement as I walked the wide center hallway from the front door straight through to the porch in the back. Twelve-foot ceilings, tall windows, hardwood floors, curved staircase — these were the things of a designer's dream.

I moved outside to the yard. The house had been built with boards salvaged from an old barn in Virginia, or so the story went that I'd heard as a kid. Mags used to tell me if I looked hard enough, I could find places in the wood where goats had rubbed their horns or chickens had pecked, leaving small holes and dings. I never did find those places, but I spent whole afternoons looking for them. Mags probably told me that story just to occupy me while she worked in her garden, but now, as I looked at the façade of the house, it wouldn't have surprised me if it was true. Most of the wood was pockmarked with holes the diameter of a No. 2 pencil, although they were probably due to industrious carpenter bees, not farm animals.

A thin layer of peeling paint covered the grass at the base of the house. Fungus-green peeked out where the paint had peeled from the weathered wood. Kudzu, that great Southern beast, covered the entire chimney and one upstairs window. On the chimney, crumbly bricks at both the base and top made use of the inside fireplace impossible — or at least dangerous.

Much of what I saw remained exactly as it had been for as long as I could remember. The house had always been a little disheveled, but I was used to it and didn't question it much. Now, standing in the grass facing the house, I wondered about the general sense of deterioration and neglect that covered the house like a shroud. Mags had let the house slip into disarray for a reason — she'd said so in the letter — but any hint of anger in her had been lost on me. Whatever her reason, my fingers itched for a paint scraper, sheet of sandpaper, or bottle of wood glue.

If I didn't have a life in New Orleans and a business to get back to, I knew I could make something of The Hideaway. Mags was right. The beauty was there — it just needed someone with a trained eye and good taste to uncover it. But the project would require a much longer duration in Sweet Bay than I had anticipated. What would happen to Bits and Pieces if I stayed away for too long, unable to offer input on items purchased and sold, decorating decisions, and customers' urgent requests?

Later that night, I sank into bed in the blue room without changing clothes or even washing my face. The crisp sheets were cool against my legs, and a breeze through the open window lifted the curtains. Dot called it the blue room because everything in it was in varying shades of blue — the bedding, curtains, rugs, even the framed prints on the wall. Each of the bedrooms in The Hideaway had its own color scheme — my blue room, the yellow room, the pink room, and a red room that I had always thought was a little creepy.

I bunched up the pillows behind my head and surveyed the room where I spent so many nights as a kid. It still felt familiar despite having spent only a handful of nights here over the last several years. I'd already checked the closet. It still held some of the clothes I hadn't gotten around to packing up and taking back to New Orleans with me. Earlier, I'd run my fingers across the polo shirts and too-small blue jeans.

Despite making a life for myself elsewhere, I felt like the last eight years in New Orleans hadn't even happened. Except now I was Sara Jenkins, owner of Bits and Pieces, with a client list as long as my arm. I wore Nanette Lepore and Tory Burch instead of cutoffs and flip-flops. I'd been intentional for nearly a decade, working my butt off to be successful, but back in the blue room, it felt like nothing had changed, like all my hard work had just been "spit and polish."

Allyn will know what to do. He loved to dole out advice to anyone within earshot whether she asked for it or not. Occasionally, his words of wisdom were too risky (or downright scandalous) for my taste, but underneath the sass, his pointers were always spot-on. Working together for four years, six days a week, eight hours a day gave him the ability to home in on all my insecurities, insufficiencies, and flaws. In a loving way, of course.

Allyn had been with me since the very beginning of Bits and Pieces. He breezed through the door the day before I opened, and all the revelry and cheekiness of New Orleans blew in with him.

"Honey, you better be doing something special here because there are a million and one home décor shops in this city. What's your hook?"

I was busy typing on my laptop, trying to get a press release out to *New Orleans* magazine, when he entered. I'd spent the morning rearranging furniture and dusting in the heat. The AC repair guy was late, and I was sweaty.

"Sorry, we don't open 'til tomorrow." I barely looked up from my work.

"You may open tomorrow, but you won't have any customers with this boring old stuff. You need my stamp on the place."

My fingers paused on the keyboard and I looked up. "I'm sorry, can I help you? If you're looking for a job, I'm not hiring yet. And this stuff isn't boring, it's tasteful."

"What's that you're working on?" He sat next to me and peered at the screen. The smell of his cologne was thick as cake batter.

"A press release, if you must know. Like I said, we open tomorrow."

"Who's the 'we' if it's just you?"

"It's a figure of speech." I closed my laptop and stood. I knew enough of New Orleans by then to know he didn't necessarily mean trouble, but I was still a little wary of this colorful stranger in my shop. The place was full of small items I'd picked up here and there, and he could grab something and run off with it in a heartbeat if he wanted.

"I'm Allyn." He extended his hand. "With a *y*."

"Sara. No *h*. And the shop isn't officially open yet, so if you could come back tomorrow . . ." I stood by the front door and gestured through it with my free arm.

"You need me. I can make this place sing."

"It looks pretty good already, if you ask me." I glanced through the front room I'd so carefully decorated.

"It needs something. More Southern Gothic flair. I'm your man for the job. Or I can be your woman for the job, whichever you prefer."

I raised an eyebrow.

"Just kidding," he said. "But seriously, I'm an out-of-work hairdresser waiting for Hollywood to call, and I have time on my hands." He paused and looked down at his feet. "People used to live in this house, you

104

know. A lot of people. I was one of them, and I know every nook and cranny of the house and the neighborhood. I can help you."

I started to speak but he continued, confident again and grinning. "And anyway, seeing as you're the one writing press releases and shopping for inventory, you're going to need some help. Who's going to make coffee runs? Get the air conditioner fixed? Open up in the morning when you have a late night?" he said with a smirk.

"First off, I've already called the repairman. He's just late. And second, I don't have many late nights, except now that I'm trying to get this place up and running. I would have opened quicker, but it's been a chore getting people to show up on time and do the work. Like this AC." I fanned my gauzy top away from my body in an effort to stir up a breeze. It was June, and the heat was already intense.

"You must be a transplant. We natives know how to get things done. Just give me a shot."

For the first time I took him in from top to bottom. Movie star sunglasses perched on his head. Acid-green hair with blond roots showing. Red tank top tucked into black skinny jeans. Black Chuck Taylors.

"You look like a Christmas nightmare," I said.

"I can get the AC fixed in an hour."

I hired him on the spot, and it was the best decision I could have made. I discovered early on that he was being truthful when he said he'd lived in the house. A decade before, when he was young, scared, and desperate to figure out who he was, he'd run with a slew of other kids from the dirtier parts of the city. Without welcoming homes to return to, they'd lived in the empty house on Magazine Street for months. It became their refuge, and Allyn still felt welcome in the space — hence his attitude of ownership the first day he'd strutted into my shop. I never would have thought we'd still be together four years later. He may have been flamboyant, keeping odd hours and even odder company, but he was a true friend to me.

Backed into a corner, I did the only thing I knew to do. I picked up my phone from the nightstand and called him. I had to shout so he could hear me over the pounding house music.

"Just a minute," Allyn said. "Let me go outside."

"Where are you? That music is terrible."

"No, it's great. You should see the people

here. It's Margaritaville meets Marilyn Manson."

I told him about the will, the house, and what Mags had done. He wasn't as shocked as I'd been.

"Who else would she have left it to? The old folks? You're her family. You obviously care about the place, or you'd have stuck a For Sale sign in the yard the minute you got there."

"I guess so. I just wasn't prepared to come here and start the biggest house-rehabbing project of my career. Especially not in Sweet Bay."

"It doesn't have to be that big, does it? Make a few tasteful changes and bring it up to date. Why the drama?"

"A few tasteful changes wouldn't even scratch the surface of what's necessary to turn this place around. Plus, it *is* Mags's home and she loved the place. I wouldn't feel right doing it halfway. She said it deserved to be beautiful again, and I have to honor that."

"Then there's your answer."

"But I don't live here," I said. "My life — my job — is in New Orleans. I can't stay here and direct a renovation. Dot, Bert, and the Greggs would all be under my feet, trying to micromanage everything. Plus, I miss you."

"Are you done? First, your life here in the city isn't going anywhere. Just because you stay there a little longer than you originally intended —"

"A little longer? This could take months. Lots of them."

"— that doesn't mean you can't pick right back up when you get back," he continued, undeterred by my outburst. "I can manage the shop and Rick can help when things get busy. Plus, it's not like you'll be across the country. Sweet Bay is, what, three hours away? You can come back for an afternoon or a whole day if necessary. It's not a long drive.

"Second, you always talk about how you set people up with beautiful houses and things, then you leave and never get to enjoy the beauty of what you created. The house is yours now. You won't have to hand the keys over and never come back, unless that's what you want to do. Regardless, you'll own the results and you won't have to bow to what anyone else wants. Sounds like a no-brainer to me."

"What am I going to do with a bed-and-breakfast in Sweet Bay even if it is beautiful again? If I keep it, I'll have to hire people to run it, and if I sell it, I'll have my head on a

108

plate carried by Major Gregg." Even I could hear the petulance in my voice.

"I don't know who Major Gregg is, but Mags left the place to you, no one else. Remember, you called for my advice, so listen to it. You have to do this. This is your project, and I think you know it. Yes, it's happening somewhere other than here, but you're good at what you do. And anyway, you need to make peace with Sweet Bay. We'll all be here when you get done."

I was quiet, digesting, listening to the muffled bass and manic voices in the background. I gripped the phone in my hand.

"Third," he said, "I miss you too. If you do this, don't think I won't drive over to check things out. I think I need a little Sweet Bay in my life too."

I laughed. "This town wouldn't know what to do with you. You'd stop people cold."

"Darling, I'd be offended if I didn't."

After the call, I didn't feel total relief, but I did allow that tingle of excitement and anticipation to bubble back up to the surface. I wanted to pull out my computer and notebooks where I'd sketched and mapped out ideas, but my eyelids were heavy. I pulled the blue quilt up to my chin and surrendered.

10
SARA

APRIL

The funeral was a quiet affair, almost an afterthought — no real ceremony, no tearful eulogies, not even a funeral parlor. The five of us just met the funeral director at the cemetery. He shared a few words about the meaning of life and loved ones who had passed on, then pushed a discreet button and the coffin slowly descended into the ground. It was simple, just as Mags wanted it. I found out later that Mags gave Dot clear instructions for her last hurrah.

"You don't have to put me in a pine box, but you get my drift," she'd said. "And don't anyone go crying over me. We've all had enough years together to be happy we knew each other at all. Just skip the hoopla and take me straight to the grave."

Dot couldn't resist adding a couple of extra details. She laid an armload of cheery sunflowers on top of the casket and propped an eight-by-ten framed photo of a smiling Mags on an easel next to our chairs.

I'd never noticed the resemblance between us. In this old photo, it was unmistakable. I had the same dark, unruly curls, although I tamed mine with a flat iron and extra-hold spray. But I saw something else, something in the shape of her light-blue eyes or the slope of her nose. I saw me in there. Even more than I resembled either of my parents.

Mags was young in the photo, early twenties at most. Her curls tumbled out of a messy ponytail and one shirttail hung free. Her eyes crinkled into barely visible laugh lines. I recognized pieces of the Mags I had known, but I'd never seen her smile like that. She was holding her arm up, trying to get the camera away from whoever was taking the photo, but that smile — no one had ever made me feel that way.

As the funeral director spoke of the glorious light (he must have missed his calling as a revival preacher), a small blue car approached a little ways off. A man climbed out of the car, his face shaded under a cap. He stood still and glanced over at us a few times. After a little while, he sat back down in the car and slowly pulled away.

When the service was over, I helped Dot and Glory gather the flowers while Bert and

Major talked to the director. In the hurry to get everyone into their cars and back to the house, I didn't notice the man drive back up to the gravesite. As I pulled out of the cemetery, I saw him in my rearview mirror. He stood by Mags's grave as the cemetery workers carried off our chairs. He brushed his hands against the sides of his pants as if he was dusting something off, then reached over and touched her headstone.

Back at the house, the driveway was already full of cars. Word had spread quickly, and old friends of Mags, some neighbors, mostly former "guests," came to pay their respects. It was a good thing, because the house was stuffed full of food, like Bert predicted.

Mr. Eugene Norman, the glassblower who used to make all the neighbors nervous with his raging furnace in the yard, sent a towering bouquet of lilacs that Dot placed on the table in the entryway. Mr. Crocker, who owned a farm up Highway 22, dropped off a mason jar stuffed with gardenias. Tiny Bernadette Pierce hobbled up the front walk with the help of a gold-tipped cane. Bernadette, or Bernie, as everyone called her, checked in a few weeks after my parents' wreck and stayed a while, long enough for her husband to think she really had moved to Tahiti with the gardener. She moved slowly and painfully up the walkway. I took her arm, fearing she might topple over before she got to the dessert table. The grin on her face when she turned to see who I was proved me wrong.

"The cane is just a prop," she whispered. "I may be eighty-four years young, but I can move just fine. And this." She gestured to the gray bob on her head that wasn't moving in the breeze. "This is a wig. Luis and I may not have gone to Tahiti, but we did get out of Dodge. This is my first time east of the Mississippi since I moved out of The Hideaway and we went to California. My former husband, Harry, is still alive and living somewhere in the South, so I have to be careful." Her eyes were bright and wild. Crazy maybe, like a fox.

Other folks came and went throughout the day, many more than I'd expected. Those who remembered me talked about what a sweet girl I had been, as if I'd turned out to be someone wearing black lipstick and studs in my chin.

"That's not what we mean," Hattie Caldwell said when I joked about it to a small group of ladies gathered on the back porch. "It's just that after all you'd been through, you were still a polite, gracious child. I was a therapist in my former life, and believe me when I say you could have taken many roads after such tragic deaths in the family. From the looks of you, you've taken the right one."

Hattie hadn't been back to the house in at least twenty years, so she may not have known I no longer lived in Sweet Bay. What would she think of the road I'd taken if she knew it had paved my way clear out of Alabama?

That afternoon while most of the guests were out on the porch or sitting around the main parlor, I caught Dot alone in the kitchen. She struggled to open a Tupperware container of pimento cheese. A tray of crackers sat on the counter next to her.

"Dot?"

"Mmm?" She couldn't get the lip of the container to pop up, so I held my hand out and she slid it over to me. "Did you notice the car that pulled up toward the end of the funeral?" I pulled the lid off and handed the Tupperware back to her.

"At the gravesite?" Dot asked, her attention on me now that the pimento cheese was no longer stuck inside frustrating plastic. She dipped a cracker in and took a bite. "I didn't see anyone but us."

"An old man pulled up on the path and

watched us for a few minutes. I didn't recognize him, but I think he was there for Mags."

Bert and Major walked through the kitchen door. Bert put his hand on Dot's back and Major pulled open the fridge.

"Who was where?" Major asked.

"Sara saw an old man at the funeral. Someone who had come to pay respects to Mags."

Dot and Bert exchanged a look, but Major shook his head.

"The obituary said the funeral was family only. That's why everyone else came here." He shut the fridge. "He must have been there for someone else."

I nodded but kept thinking about the man. It sure looked like he was there to pay respects to Mags, so who was he?

Later, after all the guests were gone, I came back downstairs for something to eat. Dot and Bert were on the back porch talking. As I moved around in the kitchen, their quiet voices drifted. I took my plate to the door of the porch and watched them.

They sat next to each other in wicker chairs, hands linked in the empty space between them. I smiled thinking of how these two found love at The Hideaway. The house provided the perfect backdrop to their second shot at love when they both checked in on the same day for solo vacations. Bert's wife had died a few years earlier, and Dot was getting over a messy divorce. When it came time for them to go back to their own lives, they decided to stay. They got married on the dock at sunset six weeks later.

I turned, not wanting to disturb their moment, but my foot bumped an overlooked plate from earlier in the day. Dot turned.

"Hi, dear, come join us. We were just telling old stories." She wiped her eyes with a tissue. "The funeral seems to have dragged up all kinds of memories."

"Are you sure? I can take this upstairs . . ."

"Nonsense. Come sit. This will give us a chance to talk. The day got busier than I expected. I knew Mags had admirers all around, but I didn't know so many would show up. Many of them were older than she was, not that seventy-two is old."

"If it is, I'm ancient," Bert said.

Dot sniffed and swiped his shoulder. "You're not ancient, just well aged."

"Doesn't make it sound any better." He smiled.

I settled into an adjacent chair and took a bite of my ham sandwich.

"We were just talking about Bernie Pierce," Bert said. Dot still had tears in her eyes, so Bert gave her time to gather herself. He gently tipped his rocking chair back and forth. The wooden boards on the porch floor groaned and squeaked. "Do you remember her?"

I nodded. "She's a hard one to forget. The situation always seemed a little scandalous to me — Mags harboring someone who left her husband. Did Bernie actually run off with her gardener?"

"In a nutshell, yes," Bert said. "But it wasn't that simple. Bernie's husband Harry was a bully. He used to knock her around, and one day Mags happened to be outside their house when she heard a ruckus inside."

"Mags claimed she'd been out delivering tomatoes to some of the neighbors, but I think she was just sneaking one of her cigarettes," Dot said.

"She was in the right place at the right time," Bert continued. "Harry shoved Bernie and she fell through the open doorway and onto the front porch. Mags stomped up the front walk, stepped right up to Harry, and thumped him hard right here." Bert pointed to the space between his eyebrows. "Then she did it again for good measure. Harry was so taken aback, he just let her do it. Then she took Bernie's hand and led her down the steps into the front yard. She told Harry that Bernie wouldn't be coming back and if he ever so much as stepped a toe on her property, she'd chase him down with her oyster knife."

Dot laughed. "Mags never would have actually hurt him, but the important thing was Harry didn't know that. Everyone knew Mags could shuck oysters faster than the men down at the docks, so for all Harry knew, she'd shuck out his heart with her little pearl-handled oyster knife."

"Her gardener, Luis, packed up some of her belongings one day and brought them all over here for her," Bert said. "He handed her the bags and a pink rose he'd plucked from someone's yard on the way over. We saw a lot of him after that, and they finally left for California together. We didn't hear from her again. Not until she walked in here today."

"Sounds like Mags was a good friend," I said.

"Sure was," Dot said. "She was the best."

We were quiet a moment until Dot spoke again. "Have you thought any more about your plans for the house?"

"I've had a chance to look around. I have a few ideas. Nothing too drastic yet."

"I just hate to see it change too much. Mags liked it the way it is," Dot said.

"I'm sure she did in some ways, but she left me with specific instructions to fix it up. You have to admit, the house has seen better days. I'm good at my job, but it won't be worth it if I only use a hammer and a can of paint," I said as gently as I could and waited for Dot's reaction. She had become the mouthpiece for the four still living in the house. I wasn't looking for permission, but if I had her blessing, I knew the others would fall in line.

She took a deep breath and looked at Bert. He raised his eyebrows and held his hands up in surrender. "It's your call, honey."

"We all know I don't have a real say in this," Dot said. "The house is yours now to do what you like. Me? I'm partial to the old place being a little rumpled — just like Mags was — but I understand most people wouldn't agree. You do what you need to do to spiff it up, whatever that means. If you think you might sell it when you're done, just try to give us as much warning as you can. I know you have a life to get back to in New Orleans, but remember we have a life here in this place."

"You took your first steps out here on this

porch, did you know that?" Bert asked.

I shook my head.

"That's right," Dot said. "Jenny brought you over here one afternoon before the evening rush at the diner. You'd been on the verge of taking off for a few weeks. She wasn't gone ten minutes before you put one foot in front of the other and toddled clear across the porch. I still remember the look on your little face when you realized what you'd done."

"I've never heard that story," I said.

"An old house can hold on to its memories for only so long," Bert said. "We may hold you hostage at night and spoon-feed you old stories."

"Bert," Dot said firmly. "She does not want to sit around here with a bunch of old folks all night." Dot turned to me. "Mags did ask you to stay at the house while you're in Sweet Bay. Is that your plan?"

"Sure beats the Value Inn on Highway 6," Bert said.

I smiled. "I think I will stay here. Judging by how much work there is to do, it'll be easier if I'm here to at least make sure things start off right. If that's okay with all of you," I said, not wanting to sound, well, like I owned the place.

Dot smiled. "I was hoping you'd stay." She

looked at Bert. "Not so we can smother you in old stories, but so you can get a real sense of the life here. This was your home too. It still is. We all need a place to escape real life sometimes."

My life felt fine to me — no need to escape, thank you — but maybe there was something to what Allyn said about making peace.

11
MAGS

Just before I left for one of my trips to Grimmerson's Grocery for weekly supplies, the doorbell rang. I left my list in the kitchen and walked to the front door. Mrs. DeBerry came out of the living room just as I arrived at the door, and I stood by as she opened it.

A man in a dark suit and sunglasses stood on the porch holding a briefcase. "Are either of you" — he looked down at the piece of paper in his hand — "Mrs. Henry De-Berry?"

I looked at Mrs. DeBerry.

"I am," she said, turning to me. "Could you put the kettle on the stove for me, dear? I'd love a cup of tea."

"Of course." I started down the hall, though curiosity paused my feet by the staircase where I could still hear them talk.

"I've already asked you people to stop

122

coming to the house. The money is coming if you can give me just a little more time."

"Mrs. DeBerry, this is your second notice. You won't get a third. I understand you have several people living under your roof. I'm sure they wouldn't appreciate —"

"Can you step out on the porch, please?" she asked a little too brightly. "Let's just talk out here, why don't we?" She pulled the door behind her, closing me out of the conversation.

Another man like this one had come to the house the week before, but I hadn't thought much about him. I'd asked Mrs. DeBerry later if we were going to have a new guest at the house, and she laughed. "Oh no, he won't be staying here."

I opened the envelope of cash I was about to take to the grocery store, then ran back to the door. I flung it open, only to find the man climbing into his car and Mrs. DeBerry pressing her hands to her flushed cheeks.

I held the envelope out to her. "We can do without a trip to the store this week. We have leftovers, and Starla and I can rework the meals around what we still have in the pantry. You can use this."

"Don't be silly. Everything is fine. I told Mr. Curtis he must have written the wrong name down. Simple as that. You go on to

123

the grocery and be sure to pick up a box of tea bags for me."

Mrs. DeBerry ambled down the hall to her bedroom and closed the door behind her. I went on to the grocery and tried to put the thought of Mr. Curtis out of my head.

When I wasn't helping Starla in the kitchen or cleaning up after the artists, I sat in William's workshop while he worked. His hands carved rough planks of pine and oak into smooth, practical pieces. Kitchen tables. Pie safes. Armoires. Buffet tables. Things Mother would display proudly at the front of the house. I told him so.

He nodded as he pushed a piece of sandpaper down the length of a table leg. Up and down. Slow and steady. "Your life at home sounds a lot different from mine."

"What do you mean?" I asked, not as innocent as I sounded.

"I make the furniture people like your mother show off at parties, but I don't actually go to the parties."

"You're not missing much."

He laughed, just a puff of air from his nose. "What are you doing here?"

"You know why I'm here. I've already told you."

He put the sandpaper down and slapped his hands against his pants to rid them of dust. He marched over to me, grasped me firmly by the shoulders, and lowered his head so we were at equal height. "Tell me why you're *still* here."

"I-I've stayed because of you. Because everything feels different with you. I'm different with you." I pushed his hands off my shoulders. "Why are you asking me this? You were the one who said your life began when you saw me at the front door. Have you changed your mind?"

I paced to the other side of the room to escape the uncomfortable intensity of his gaze, but then his hands were on my shoulders again. He turned me around to face him, his face close to mine. I smelled wood dust, turpentine, and something else distinctly William.

"I'm not going to change my mind. I just want to make sure you know what you're doing. You're giving up a lot to be with me. I'll never be able to give you what your daddy has or what your husband could. Do you understand that?"

I gave up my old life the minute I packed my bags and shoved them in the closet of the house I shared with Robert. I did it again when I closed the car door, peering at

Daddy from inside the quiet cocoon. And again when I pulled away from the house without a last look over my shoulder. I knew what I was doing, and now that William was part of my new life, it all made perfect sense.

I nodded. "I understand."

He pulled me tightly to his chest, kissing my cheeks, my eyelids, my forehead. "Okay. We're in it. Let's show everyone how far we can go."

Later that day, I bumped into Mrs. DeBerry as she stood bent at the waist, rummaging around in the closet by the front door.

"Can I help you with anything?" I took her arm and helped her straighten up. Her face was red and beads of sweat had formed on her upper lip.

"I'm fine. Just cleaning out a little. I haven't looked in this closet in ages." Around her sat beautiful pieces of clothing I'd never seen her wear. Impractical things, like Chinese satin-soled shoes that would fill with water the first time they touched the dew-saturated grass and a chocolate-brown floor-length mink coat.

I ran my hands up and down the coat. Mother had a mink she only wore during Mardi Gras season. It could be sixty-five degrees on Fat Tuesday and she'd still pull it out. "Luxury is luxury, Margaret, regardless of something as temperamental as the weather," she'd say.

"You can have that old thing," Mrs. DeBerry said when she saw me touching the mink. "Henry brought it back from a trip to Russia ages ago. It's too warm to wear it in Alabama, but maybe you'll make a trip up north someday. I'm too old to be making trips anymore."

She stopped rummaging and glanced around the house, her gaze pausing on a pair of artists painting at easels in front of the large living room windows. She shook her head. "Henry would turn in his grave if he could see what our B and B has turned out to be."

"Maybe not. It still has a charm."

"It must. After all, you're still here. It's been a couple of months now. How long do you plan to stay, dear?" She tossed items into a box at her feet, but her gaze remained on me.

I picked up the red satin shoes from the floor. The fabric was worn away near the soles, but the embroidery on top was still perfect. I tossed them in her box. "I don't know. Can I let you know a little later?"

She exhaled. "Stay as long as you want. That's what everyone around here seems to do anyway, and it'll probably continue long after I'm gone."

"Are you going somewhere?"

She glanced around the room again. "I'm getting old. I'm probably not the best proprietor for a place full of young folks such as yourself, but here I am. Next to losing Henry, giving up this house would be the hardest thing I could ever do."

She hoisted her box and took a deep breath. She'd avoided my question, but her face was still flushed and damp, and I worried for her.

"Are you sure I can't help you with that? I could take it to your room for you."

"No, no, I'm fine." She turned toward the hallway but paused. "Mrs. Parker, you've been good for this house. You straighten up, clean what needs to be cleaned, help organize meals. You even shooed the artists out of the living room and outside into the fresh air. And you've done it all without being asked. You're taking care of this old place, and I want you to know I appreciate it."

The emotion on her face surprised me. As she eased her way down the hall toward her room in the back, her box tight in both hands, she called over her shoulder, "Are you ever going to tell me your real name?"

I smiled. She'd probably seen through me

that first night, but she chose to let me have my time of anonymity, even if I was only anonymous to her.

"It's Maggie. Maggie Van Buren," I said just before she turned into her room.

"Good night, Maggie."

12
SARA

APRIL

I spent most of the next morning calling contractors I was familiar with in New Orleans. It turned out not many were willing or able to work two states away. I found a couple with satellite offices in Alabama who said they'd look into it, but it didn't sound hopeful. Each one I talked to asked why I wasn't using a local contractor, but when I asked if they had any referrals for contractors in the area, they all asked some variation of "Now, where's Sweet Bay again?"

With reluctance I did what I never do when looking for help on a project. I opened the Yellow Pages. I'd thought the days of thumbing through the phone book looking for a particular business were long gone — who didn't just type it into Google? But after a lot of thumb-typing, it was clear Google's long arms hadn't reached Sweet Bay.

I flipped to the beginning and called the first entry listed under A: A1 Contractors. Clever. Twenty seconds on the phone with Earl Weathers told me all I needed to know about whether local people still talked about The Hideaway.

"You know that place used to scare all the kids around here," he said when I told him I was renovating the house. "Or maybe it was the lady inside who scared us. My buddies and I used to dare each other to go to the front door and ring the doorbell, then run away. We were just kids. Big imaginations." He laughed. "I wondered what would happen to the house now that the old lady's croaked. So they hired you to take care of it? What'd you say your name was, sweetheart?"

"I didn't," I said through my clenched jaw. "It's Sara Jenkins."

"Jenkins," he said, pondering. "Wait, you're not . . . ?"

"That's the one. Mrs. Van Buren was my grandmother."

"Oh, I . . . you — Lord'a mercy," he sputtered. "I guess I spoke too soon."

"Nope, just soon enough." I hung up, cutting off his apologies.

The next two calls were similar. Their eagerness to get inside the house and see

131

what it was like was unprofessional at best, offensive at worst. I thanked them all for their time — although I wished I hadn't given them a reason to think of Mags again — and ignored their protests as I hung up.

I finally found one that looked promising. Coastal Contractors. The logo had a silhouette of a heron standing in front of a sun setting over water. At least they had a logo. And a brick and mortar office. The other ones I called appeared to be working out of their homes. Nothing wrong with that, but I imagined Earl sitting on his back porch, picking his fingernails with a pocketknife, waiting for work to come calling. I couldn't stomach being the reason he folded the knife away, hitched up his pants, and climbed into his work truck.

No one answered at Coastal. Instead, I was greeted with a message on an actual answering machine. The mechanical click at the beginning of the message told me it wasn't a typical voice-mail recording. The message told me if no one answered, they were likely out on a job or working out back. *"Leave a message or feel free to stop by for a chat."* The voice was friendly, giving me hope that maybe this wouldn't turn out to be just another dead end.

■ ■ ■ ■

When lunchtime rolled around, I made a plate of chicken salad and coffee cake left over from the mountain of funeral food and headed out to the dock. Dot and Bert were in town for groceries, and the house was calm, a stark contrast to the previous day's whirl of activity. I sensed that this quiet peacefulness was how the house had been for much of the time since I'd left. From what Major said, they'd all settled into a tranquil existence here. I remembered the old magazine articles that featured the house as one of the top vacation destinations in the Southeast.

Taking in the house from the long grassy hill that sloped down to the water, I had trouble imagining The Hideaway as anything but a tired, sprawling old home. The house had been a much livelier place when I was a child, but nothing close to the resort featured in the magazines. Fireworks, boat tours, badminton on the lawn — it was more than hard to imagine. It was impossible.

I settled in a chair out on the dock and took my first bite when I heard a voice behind me.

"Well, if it isn't Sara Jenkins, back from the dead."

Clark Arrington. Perfect.

"That's probably not the most appropriate thing to say, considering my grandmother just died," I said in place of a greeting. Clark had always been just socially awkward enough to offend most people, even if he wasn't trying.

"I sure was sorry to hear about Mrs. Van Buren. How are you holding up?"

"I'm fine. I see you still live across the street."

"Yeah. I'm in the apartment above my parents' garage, but I'm moving out soon." I wondered how long he'd been telling people he'd soon be moving out of his parents' home. "You here for long or just for the funeral?"

"Looks like I'll be here for a little bit. I'll be doing some work on the house."

"I see." He walked to the edge of the dock and peered into the water below. "Tide's coming in." He straightened up and stared at me with an expression I couldn't decipher. "And the owner's okay with you doing the work?"

"The owner? That'd be me now. Mags left me the house in her will and asked me to fix the place up, so yes, I'd say the owner is fine with it." Why was I defending myself to him?

"I'd just be careful if I were you."

"What's that supposed to mean?"

"You haven't been here much lately. A lot has been going on."

I assumed he was messing with me, like he did when he used to taunt me in the yard on his bicycle. I once threw a Coke can at him as hard as I could because he had made fun of Mags. The can fell short, landing feebly in the water at his feet, adding embarrassment to my anger. I ran into the house, the sound of his laugher echoing in my head, and flung myself across my bed in tears. Part of me was mad at Mags for being so easy to make fun of, for having this grand old house but letting it be so shabby, for not caring about rules and the way things were supposed to be, but on the heels of that came guilt for being mad. Mags was my grandmother, kooky but loving.

This time, I didn't have a Coke can to throw at him, but I wouldn't have given him the satisfaction anyway. "Thanks for the heads-up, Clark. I have things to do, so if you'll excuse me." I picked up my plate and cup and headed toward the house.

"You remember Sammy Grosvenor?"

I stopped walking. Sammy was a well-known Baldwin County developer. He'd been sticking his nose into waterfront property owners' business for decades. He used to knock on Mags's door, reeking of body odor covered with strong cologne, mopping his forehead with a damp rag. Each time, he'd say he had been out walking around and admired the property. And each time, Mags told him to get lost.

"It's a lot of money, Mrs. Van Buren," he'd say. "You could turn in the keys and spend your golden years with your feet up and a drink in your hand."

"Do I look like someone who wants to snooze the rest of my life away, Mr. Grosvenor?" She'd spit his name out like it tasted bad. "This is my home, and I'm not selling it. If you were smart, you'd stop sniffing around here."

Sammy was the one thing on which Mags and many of the other townspeople agreed. No one liked the way he scoped out homes and businesses as if he imagined a theme park in their place. Dot always told Mags she should be careful with Sammy, but Mags was never too concerned. If she didn't let wind blowing through a broken glass pane in the kitchen bother her, she definitely wouldn't be bothered by a land developer who had so far been all talk.

Clark's name-dropping let me know Sammy was still on the prowl, still trying to get his hands on the property. I wasn't worried, though. Mags could be a bear when she wanted to, but I had more professional ways of making him get lost. Starting with a court order if necessary.

"Yeah, I ran into him a while back," Clark said. "He started babbling about this old house here. Something about his time finally coming. I don't know what he meant, but it smelled fishy to me. He was excited though. I'll tell you that much."

I kept walking toward the house. This was nothing more than Sammy attempting another dead-end scheme and Clark trying to get in the middle of it all. However, deep down, in some small, hidden part of me, something squeezed. Sammy could be ruthless if he wanted to be.

I walked up the porch steps and made sure the screen door slammed shut behind me.

13
SARA

The office of Coastal Contractors couldn't have looked more opposite than what I had imagined. The mental image of Earl sitting on the porch in his dirty overalls quickly dissipated as I turned off County Road 1 at the sign bearing the now-familiar heron and setting sun. The cottage overlooking the water was quaint, its cedar-shake siding weathered to a relaxed gray — the kind of gray that sent people back for paint chips again and again, trying to get the same shade on their walls.

I collided with a mess of black fur and a wet tongue as soon as I walked through the open door.

"Popcorn, down!" a male voice said. "Sorry, she just gets excited. It's been a quiet day, so you're the lucky recipient of her pent-up attention. Here, try this." A towel, dry and mostly clean, appeared in

138

my hand as I held my now-damp dress away from my legs. I wiped at my arms and right cheek, trying without success to remove all traces of the sticky slobber. I had never been much of a dog person. Too much wet, not enough manners.

Giving up the futile attempt, I looked up to see a man pushing the dog out the back door. "Crawford, she's headed your way," he yelled before closing the door on Popcorn's protests.

"Sorry about the commotion." He wiped his hands on his shorts. The room smelled strangely like raw fish. "I'm Charlie Mack. How can I help you? Or do you need directions somewhere?" His gaze drifted down to my dress and sandals, a few notches too dressy for an afternoon on the bay and the affections of an exuberant Labrador.

"Actually, I do need some help. I'm an interior designer in New Orleans, but I'm in Sweet Bay working on an old bed-and-breakfast."

"Is it a tear-down?"

"No. It's an old house and not in the best shape, but its bones are good. It's probably best to consider everything suspect — wiring, gas lines, the whole bit. It'll need a thorough inspection first. From there, I'm thinking about taking down a couple interior walls, updating the kitchen and baths, and a whole lot of painting."

He nodded and scratched out a few notes on a piece of paper he'd pulled out of his shirt pocket. When he finished, he sat back in his desk chair, his heft leaning the chair back almost horizontal. He was two-fifty easy, maybe more. Older than me, but not by much. Did the plural on *Contractors* mean Popcorn and him?

"I can tell you now, we're the right people for the job. We do everything from new construction of massive bay houses to little old ladies who want their bathrooms to look like the one they saw in last month's *Southern Living*. How did you find us, anyway?"

"Yellow Pages. I started with A."

He laughed. "So you called A1 first, got Earl on the phone, and quickly went on to the Bs, then found us. That's how it works sometimes. However clients come in, we'll take 'em."

"So you're a sort of one-man, one-dog operation?"

He laughed again. "No, it's my buddy Crawford Hayes and me. Popcorn's just around for laughs. She's the company dog. Crawford's outside, banging around on something, as he usually is when he's not on a job site."

"Banging around? Should I be concerned?" I peered around Charlie to look out the back window of the office.

"Crawford builds things, or attempts to. He's got a work space out back. He calls it his shop, though it's not much more than a messy hardware store. Right now, he's building me a boathouse. I just bought a twenty-five-foot Regulator," he said proudly. He stood and gestured for me to follow him to the back of the house. "Crawford's the best contractor in Baldwin County, so don't think you're getting a country carpenter."

We walked out onto a deck overlooking a tidy lawn. The scrubby grass mingled with sand at the edge, and calm water lapped the shoreline. He pointed to a shed off to the side.

"I'm lucky he let me join in this operation. It was one-man and one-dog, like you said, before I came on. Now we can take on more work together, although Crawford's probably the one for what you need. Point him to some old, falling-down house and he's a happy guy. I don't have the heart the historic places require, but he's a different story."

Popcorn nosed her way out of the shop just before the door opened wider and Crawford walked out. It was the second time Coastal Contractors had surprised me. I'd expected another big guy like Charlie — well past college years, but still retaining the good-natured frat boy look of too much beer and not enough exercise.

Instead, Crawford was slim, but not skinny, with thick brown hair sticking up in front like he'd pushed it off his forehead with the back of a sweaty wrist. He'd rolled up the sleeves of his checked button-down against the late-spring warmth. His khakis had a scuff of dirt at the bottom hem and a small hole near one pocket. A pencil stuck out of his hair, tucked behind one ear. He was a far cry from Mitch's sleek suits and power ties. He looked more like a mad scientist — albeit a cute one — than a contractor.

"Crawford, this is . . . I'm sorry. I didn't even get your name," Charlie said.

"I'm Sara Jenkins." I held out my hand and Crawford shook it firmly. Small calluses at the base of his fingers pressed into my hand. "I tried calling a few times before I drove over, but I kept getting the machine."

"Sorry about that," Crawford said. "I've been out here all day trying to finish up the framing on this boathouse, and Charlie — well, it looks like he's been out fishing."

Charlie grinned, unapologetic. If this was

how they spent their days, how did these guys make enough money to afford the nice office and shiny trucks parked out front? As if reading my mind, Crawford answered my question.

"This isn't a typical week for us. I just finished up two big jobs over in Point Clear on the boardwalk, and Charlie is wrapping up a house in Spanish Fort and starting another one next week. We decided to take a few days before jumping back in."

We went back into the tidy office and sat at the table in the middle. I explained again, this time in more detail, what I envisioned for the house.

"I thought we were dealing with just a big house," Crawford said when I finished. "I didn't realize it's a bed-and-breakfast. What'd you say the name is?"

"I didn't. It's The Hideaway. In Sweet Bay."

I waited, but Charlie just kept scratching Popcorn's ear and Crawford wrote the name down on his notepad and sat back in his chair. I couldn't believe I'd found the only two people in Baldwin County who'd never heard of the place.

Then Crawford smiled. "I've always wanted to see inside that house."

Here it comes.

143

"I saw it a year or so ago by accident. Turned down the wrong driveway looking for another job site. The house was obviously in disrepair, but I could tell it had been beautiful once. I'd seen the sign before but didn't know anything else about it. Then again, I'm not a local. How'd you get the job? Didn't you say you're from New Orleans?"

"I live in New Orleans now, but I'm actually from Sweet Bay. Born and raised."

"No way," Charlie said. "Don't see too many girls around here who look so classy. No offense," he said quickly. "But you kind of stick out like legs on a fish."

I smoothed my still-damp dress over my knees and ran my hand down my ponytail, making sure nothing was out of place.

Crawford's gaze on Charlie was a laser beam, then he shook his head and smiled. "Please excuse my partner. Sometimes he doesn't know when to stop. And he's used to the taste of foot in his mouth."

I smiled, grateful for his easy removal of awkwardness.

"The owner hired you to redo the place?" he asked.

He really doesn't know anything.

I took a deep breath. "It was my grandmother's house, and she just passed away.

In her will, she gave me the house and asked me to renovate it. It used to be very different from what it is now. It was written up in magazines and everything. But over the years, I guess the clientele changed. People who checked in usually ended up living there. I know it sounds strange," I said, seeing his eyebrows rise. "I have no idea how she ever had the money to keep the place going."

"Sounds like a beast of a project." Charlie grinned.

"I don't know about that, but I do need professionals to come in and tell me just how bad it is. The place has always been a little wild. Four of my grandmother's friends still live there, and I'm staying there for the time being, so the house will be occupied during renovations. We'll need to work on it in stages, I suppose, rather than ripping it all up at once."

"You're staying in town during the work?" Crawford asked. "I would have expected you to set the plans in motion, then hightail it back home."

I uncrossed then recrossed my legs, uncomfortable with his laser beam directed at me. I smoothed my hair down again.

"I considered it, but there's so much work to do. Rather than spend the next several weeks on the phone checking on things here, I'm treating it like a normal job. I'll see it through to the end, then hightail it back."

Crawford held my gaze for a moment, then looked at Charlie, who nodded.

"We'd love to take on the job," Crawford said. "I'm biased, but I think we're the best ones by far to do the work. As Charlie probably told you, old houses are my thing. I'd love to get in there and peel back the layers on this one. If you'll have us, of course."

Charlie leaned back in his chair, his arms crossed over his considerable girth. Crawford sat closer to the table, fingers twirling a pencil, eyes on me. Popcorn whined at the door, waiting to be let out.

"Sure. Of course. You're hired."

"Okay then," Crawford said, a smile lifting a corner of his mouth. "When can I see it?"

That evening, in the purple dusk after sunset, I strolled out into the backyard. An old streetlight attached to a wooden beam marked the path to Mags's vegetable garden. It wasn't what it used to be — rows of tilled earth straight as an arrow, little markers noting what each row contained, tall wooden spikes to stake the tomato plants —

but it was clear Mags had been doing her best to keep the garden up. The rows weren't as obvious and some of the markers were missing, but from what remained, it looked like there'd be a bounty of snap beans, purple-hull peas, and cucumbers later in the summer.

The garden sat adjacent to the house and overlooked the bay. Mags used to say that, sitting in the garden, she could see everything that was important to her — the house, her plants peeking their heads through the soil, the water making its unhurried way to the Gulf. She could listen to the voices of her friends and the laughter of seagulls.

Memories surfaced as I settled down on the worn bench. I used to run barefoot up and down the deliberate rows of fertile soil, flapping my arms to scare away the crows. I'd squat over delicate strawberry vines, the aroma of dirt and life permeating the air, and carefully choose the plump, red berries that Bert would later use in his not-yet-famous strawberry pie. Even as a teenager, I welcomed the chore, eating at least as many berries as would end up in my basket. Sitting there in the falling dark, I could imagine the furry skin on my tongue, the tiny seeds popping, a burst of summer sweetness in each bite.

I ran my hand over the surface of the bench next to me. It was a gnarled, weather-beaten thing, but beautiful in its own way. No frills, just cedar boards fastened with wooden nails and dovetail joints. It still bore remnants of an old coat of green paint.

As my fingers rounded the edge, they found an indentation in the wood on the underside of the bench. I took it for another mark from a carpenter bee, but as I rubbed it, a shape began to emerge. I got down on my knees and peered underneath. As I tipped the bench back, the glow from the light fell across the wood and revealed the engraving of an old skeleton key.

I recognized that key.

Mags's headstone had been simple — it bore her name and the dates of her birth and death. It wasn't until after the graveside service that I noticed the carving at the very bottom. It was a small key, just like this one, along with the words, "You hold the key to my heart."

I never knew my grandfather, though I'd always referred to him as Granddaddy. My mom was only a few years old when he died, so her memories of him were few. Anytime I asked Mags about him, she just repeated that it was a tragic, too-early heart attack but wouldn't offer any more information. She was single my whole life. No other romantic interests that I knew of. It seemed strange that she would have made such a public pronouncement of love for her long-gone husband when I'd never once heard her talk about him, other than the few times I'd asked. The sentiment seemed too romantic for my simple, often stoic grandmother.

But she chose to add a last whisper of love on her headstone. Could it have been for someone other than Granddaddy?

14
MAGS

Mrs. DeBerry didn't show up for her usual morning toast and pot of tea out in the yard. A few of us stood outside her bedroom door. I knocked but got no response.

"Maybe she died in her sleep," Starla whispered. "What? It happens," she said when we shushed her. "She was old. Maybe her ticker gave out."

I knocked again. "Y'all were up late last night. Did any of you notice anything? Maybe she fell."

"No, nothing," Gary said.

"You wouldn't have noticed a garbage truck if it had rumbled through the living room," Starla said, laughing.

"I can't help it if —"

I cut off their banter by pushing open the door. Inside, Mrs. DeBerry's small room was neat and clean. And empty. The furniture remained, but every personal item was gone. The dresser top was bare, and pale squares stood out on the walls where frames had hung for decades.

I backed out of the room and bumped into Daisy.

"Oh, Maggie, I was just looking for you. This was on the kitchen counter this morning." Daisy handed me a creamy envelope — heavy paper, fine stationery — with my name printed on it. "That's Mrs. DeBerry's handwriting," she said.

As Starla, Daisy, and the others talked over each other, trying to decide what exactly had happened, I retreated up to my room. On the way, I tore open the envelope and pulled out the card inside.

Maggie,
It just got to be too much. I hope you of all people will understand. I can tell you come from good people and you'll take care of the house as it deserves. The spare key is under the pansies on the back porch and six extra sets of sheets are in the closet in my bedroom. Call Ned Lemon if the pilot light goes out.

I sat on my bed and dropped the card on the quilt next to me. Mrs. DeBerry had said her good-bye to me the night she gave me the mink and I hadn't even realized it. She'd gone through the house, taking what was important to her, and left everything else for us to figure out.

"Who else would she have asked?" William said when I escaped to his workshop to give him the news. "No way would she trust the others around here who float in and out of the house all day and night."

"People don't just go leaving houses to strangers."

"She must have seen what I see in you. You're smart, hardworking, and determined. You do what needs to be done. Think of it this way — you want something different out of life, right?"

I nodded.

"This could turn out to be a very good thing for you. Maybe even for us."

I leaned into him and closed my eyes. "This is insane. What do I know about running a bed-and-breakfast?"

He wrapped his arms around my back. "We'll figure it out together. And anyway, what else do you have to do?"

I could have thrown out a dozen reasons why I wasn't a good candidate to take over the house, but as I stood there wrapped in William's arms, the idea began to take root in my mind. After all, with no husband to support me, no formal job training, and no money other than the check from Daddy, I didn't have much going for me.

But there was something else. This house had offered me a respite, a shelter from the storms in my life. And it had given me William. If taking over the house would allow us to stay safe and undisturbed in The Hideaway's cocoon, then that's what I would do.

That night around the dinner table, William and I told everyone about Mrs. DeBerry's departure and the note she left behind. A stunned silence met us, then everyone began to talk at once. A few were angry and some were distraught, thinking they'd lose what had essentially become the ideal artists' retreat. But most were satisfied and gave me their blessing, just as William had predicted.

"It's okay with me if you run the place," Starla said. "You've turned out to be all right. At least you're not wearing that pillbox hat anymore." She grinned at me and I returned the smile.

"I don't exactly have experience running a business."

"You'll be fine," Starla said. "How hard can it be?"

As the conversation around the table grew lively, I saw what The Hideaway could be under my care. Mrs. DeBerry likely hoped I'd be the one to turn it back into the pillar of Southern hospitality it used to be. True, it would be a place for hospitality, but not the kind she had in mind. No ladies in hats and gloves and no dashing men — not unless they bore wood dust on their legs or carried a paintbrush in their hands.

William carved a new sign for the house. He worked hard on it, making sure each letter was smooth and perfect.

"This could be your ticket to fame and fortune," he said once we pulled off the side of the road next to the old, faded sign. "People will come from all over just to see your Hideaway. You just wait."

I helped him heft the enormous wooden sign out of the back of his truck.

"I'm proud of you," he continued. "You can make something of yourself here — something that's just you."

I stayed silent as we leaned the new sign up against the post of the old one. His insinuation that I hadn't been my own person before didn't sit well. But hadn't I said it myself? Wasn't it true? I'd been fit into a mold before, and I was only now experiencing life with full breaths of air and space to move.

We stood back against the truck to admire the sign. It was perfect. It would guide just the right kind of traveler to The Hideaway. Not those looking for a resort or a game of badminton on the lawn, but those folks who needed a place to stay. A place to call home.

15
MAGS

APRIL 1960

The warmer spring temperatures allowed us to finally stow our blankets and heavy soup pots. When I wasn't working in the house or helping William with odd jobs in his wood shop, we made light meals of sandwiches or grilled fish, listened to music, and spent long afternoon hours in the cove, our pale limbs stretched out on a towel to soak up the spring sun.

One evening, I found a can of bright blue-green paint on a shelf in his workshop. On a whim I grabbed the can, a paintbrush, and a box of sandpapers and carried it all to the front porch. Using a firm hand and long strokes I'd learned from watching William, I sanded the peeling paint off the shutters and door, then covered them with fresh paint. Later, I blew my damp hair out of my eyes and stepped back into the driveway to examine my work.

A woman walking around the side of the house paused and backed up a few steps. She cocked her head and stared at the porch, then turned to me. "Did you do that?"

I nodded.

"Hmm. Not bad."

Over the span of a few weeks, William carved a house for me — intricately detailed, but small enough to fit in the palm of my hand. He presented it to me at the cove on a blessedly warm Saturday. He pulled me away from dinner preparations that afternoon, saying he needed to show me something. I'd been chopping peppers and onions for pasta. I wiped my hands on my apron and followed him, thinking we were headed to his workshop. Instead, he led me to his truck and opened the passenger door.

"I can't leave right now — the pasta . . ."

"Yes, you can. Starla can take care of it. This is important."

I shook my head, frustrated with his spontaneity, but good Lord, he was handsome and so earnest. I abandoned the dinner and climbed into his rusty old truck.

At the cove he took my hand and led me to the water's edge. "I'm going to build a house in this cove one day. Just for us." He held the delicate carving out to me. "Hold on to this for now, and our real house will come."

"Is this your way of proposing to me?" I turned the house over in my hands, trying to cover my smile with a frown.

"No, when I propose, you'll know. This is just my way of saying, hang on, there's more to me than what you see. I can give you more than sawdust-covered hands and an old truck that won't even play the radio for you. I can't build it right now — it might not even be soon — but one day, I will."

"Right now, you're enough for me. Just you."

His eyes searched me, as if trying to decipher something written on my face. Whatever he saw must have satisfied him, because he smiled and retrieved a camera from the bag he'd brought with him. I held my hand up, but he snapped a picture anyway.

"What was that?" I asked as he placed the camera back in his bag.

"Just want to remember this day. Come on," he said and began to remove his pants.

"What are you doing?" I laughed and turned away.

"What are *you* doing? I'm going swimming."

■ ■ ■ ■

William built other things for me — a sideboard buffet for the dining room, several small occasional tables, and a corner armoire with glass doors to hold dishes. On each of these pieces, just out of sight so no one noticed but me, he carved an old skeleton key. It became his trademark, and he carved it into each piece he made, even the ones he sold to other people.

My favorite piece was a simple cedar bench with practical, sturdy legs and a coat of moss-green paint. I'd started a vegetable garden in a sunny patch of grass next to the house, so he placed the bench there where I could keep an eye on things as they grew. We often went out to the garden together after dinner and sat on the bench while the sun went down, listening to the late-day sounds around the house. I imagined us sitting on that bench at the end of the day for the rest of our lives, listening, watching, loving.

As life with William was smooth and easy, the situation at the house was deteriorating. I didn't know just how poor The Hideaway's finances were until I spent some time in Mrs. DeBerry's account book. It was a mess, but even I could see that she'd fallen behind on house payments the last several months. The bank had sent two letters, the second less friendly than the first. The men in suits must have come after Mrs. DeBerry ignored the letters. With only a couple hundred dollars left in the account at First Coastal Bank and not much coming in from the "guests," it wouldn't be long before we had no money to keep the lights on, much less satisfy the bank.

I still had the check Daddy gave me the day I left home, but I hadn't even looked at it — it was buried in the pocket of my suitcase, along with my wedding ring and pearl necklace. In a way, that check was tied to Robert, and until now, I'd wanted nothing to do with it. I'd planned to save it until it was really needed. Now, it was. With the possibility of losing The Hideaway right in front of me, it made the most sense to use that money to pay down what Mrs. DeBerry owed to the bank. When I cashed the check at First Coastal and asked to deposit the money into the account to pay the house payments, the teller smiled.

"I don't know where you got the money, but I'm glad for it. I would have hated to see that lovely house shuttered. It seems like a nice place."

I smiled back. "It is."

I held a meeting one afternoon — a family gathering of those living in the house at the time. I stuck notes under everyone's doors, asking them to meet me in the parlor at 4:00 p.m. sharp. I wanted the note to express authority and the gravity of the situation.

"Thank you, everyone, for coming," I said, once they all settled down on chairs and couches. I willed my voice to be strong. "As you know, Mrs. DeBerry is gone and she has left The Hideaway with me. You all have an invitation to stay on as guests in the house as long as you like, but I need you to be able to pay somehow."

Most answered me with grumbles and whispers.

"We had an understanding," someone piped up. "With Mrs. D."

"It wasn't exactly an understanding from what she told me. She needed the money, but she didn't have the heart to ask. Now, I need your money, and I'm asking you to pay. Before you all get mad, I understand your professions as artists dictate that your financial . . . statuses may not be steady. I get that. But I need you to pay something. Get a part-time job, find new galleries to show your work, whatever. The bottom line is room and board can no longer be free. We'll all have to pull our weight here or we'll sink. As it is, we're behind on several bills, and sinking may not be far behind. This house is all we have right now. We need it to work."

I took a deep breath, expecting an onslaught of angry voices or overturned easels. Instead, there was silence.

"I just booked a show at Peterson's Gallery next month," said Daisy. "They asked for seven paintings — it'll be my biggest show yet."

"I've been hired to teach yoga at a studio in Fairhope twice a week," said Starla.

"I'm working on two armoires for Tom Grimmerson," came William's smooth voice. "He stopped by last week and asked to see what I was working on."

I scanned the room until my eyes found him leaning against the door frame in the entryway. He wore a red work shirt and scuffed boots. A thin coat of sawdust covered the front of his pants, and he smiled that familiar, slow smile I'd come to love. My body told me to cross the room in one stride and bury my face in his neck. I smiled my thanks.

"He has a friend who may be interested

in some of my work too," he said, as if just to me, although everyone in the room watched us. "Good things are coming."

I kept my gaze on him as the room buzzed with talk of upcoming shows and income possibilities.

This could work. But my thought wasn't just about the house. It was William, me, a new life. All of it. Good things were coming, indeed.

Then Daddy showed up.

16
SARA

The next morning, after breakfast and a quick shower, I pulled the string on the bare bulb hanging in the center of the attic ceiling. It didn't illuminate much, but sunlight trickled in from the eaves on each end of the house. It was a bright day, and the light caught the dust motes my feet stirred up.

I'd decided to start at the top and go down. I had no idea what mementos and clutter previous guests had stored in the attic over the years, but I suspected it would be full to overflowing, much like the rest of the house.

Taking my first look around, I wasn't far off. One end of the attic housed furniture jumbled together — it was dark under the low ceiling, but I could make out the shape of a few small tables and a bench that used to sit in the dining room along one wall. The back of a small chair caught my eye.

When I crept closer, I recognized the little red rocking chair I'd been so proud of as a child. I'd gone with Mags to a yard sale and begged her to buy me the broken-down chair — painted an ugly, faded yellow and missing one armrest. I knew I could make it look better.

We hauled it home, and I went after it with sandpaper, wood glue, and paint. I even fashioned a cushioned bottom out of some old batting I found in Glory's quilting box and a few squares of left-over fabric printed with smiling cats. I ran my hand over the dusty cotton and wood. My first restoration job. I couldn't believe Mags still had it.

Bags and boxes littered the rest of the attic, along with a few broken suitcases, an easy chair missing its bottom cushion, and an artificial Christmas tree.

I peered in a few of the boxes — musty clothes, discarded kitchen items, a few ratty teddy bears. Goodwill wouldn't even take this stuff. I opened the trash bag I'd brought with me and tossed in items no one would miss.

When the bag was bulging, I dragged it across the floor to the ladder. As I backed down the narrow steps, I noticed a box I hadn't seen earlier. It was pushed so far under the eaves, I could barely see it, but just enough light bounced off it that I could make out a keyhole at the top. I paused with my feet on the ladder, then climbed back up and pulled the box farther into the light.

Dull green metal, the box was unremarkable except for the keyhole. I remembered the envelope Mags left for me, the small key falling into my hand, weightless. I had yet to come across anything in the house with a hole small enough to fit it. I scrambled down the ladder to the blue room and retrieved it.

Back in the attic, I crouched down and slid the key into the hole and turned it. The lid popped open. Inside were several small photo books, a tiny house carved out of wood, yellowed newspaper clippings, and a few loose photographs. Wood chips, still smelling faintly of cedar, littered the bottom of the box.

I paused, hands on either side of the box. It was for me, right? Mags left me the key, and it fit into the lock perfectly. The lid had snapped open willingly. This had to be something she wanted me to see, to have.

I reached in and pulled out the black-and-white photo sitting on top. It was unmistakably Mags, but not the Mags I'd grown up with. Her tiny frame, light eyes, and sharp cheekbones were the same. And her hair — the humidity must have been high, because the edges were beginning to frizz. That was the Mags I knew, but the similarity ended there. This young, unfamiliar Mags wore a shimmery cocktail dress with a rounded neckline, narrow belted waist, and full skirt. A strand of pearls adorned her neck and she wore large pearls in her ears. Her hair, the part that hadn't frizzed, was rolled into gentle waves peeking out from under a white pillbox hat. Lacy white gloves covered her hands, and she carried a small purse with a silver clasp. On her face was just the barest hint of a prim smile, one that didn't reach her eyes.

The date stamped along the edge of the photo was 1957.

I'd been in Mags's closet before — nothing in there even came close to resembling this dress. A dainty and demure Mags? Not a chance. Who was this woman?

The carved house was the length of my hand. It had four rooms, a porch across the front, and a chimney on top. Whoever carved it had exceptional skill with a knife and an obvious love of such fine work. I turned it over in my hands, examining each side. The underside bore the rough engraving of a skeleton key.

The rest of the items in the box begged to be picked up and examined, but laughter from downstairs floated up into the attic. My watch showed it was after nine, and Crawford had said he'd be here at nine on the dot. I placed the wooden house carefully back in with everything else. That's when I saw the blue velvet box. I pulled it out and gently pried the box open.

Inside, nestled in soft white cotton, lay an exquisite diamond ring. Beautiful not for its cut or size, but in its simplicity. It was breathtaking, perhaps especially because it shone in such opposition to my grandmother's disdain for anything having to do with money or luxury.

Underneath the box was an envelope, the seal on the back jagged as if it had been ripped open. I worked my fingers inside. Instead of finding something whole, my fingers brushed small pieces of paper. I hesitated, then turned the envelope over and poured it all out into my hand.

The bits of paper were torn, with rough edges and angry rips. The pen had faded but words written in a steady, sure hand were still legible: *Maggie, discomfort, your finger, cove.* Seen together, maybe they would have meant something, but in my quick scan of the words in the dim light, they meant nothing. The last bit of paper stopped me though.

Love, William

My grandfather's name had been Robert.

The words from Mags's headstone floated back to me: *"You hold the key to my heart."*

William? Who are you?

My heart thumped and a bead of sweat trickled down the center of my chest. I carefully slid the bits back into the envelope, then pulled the ring from its home in the box and held it in my palm. I had no way of knowing how long it had been tucked away in the attic, but it sparkled as if it had been cleaned just yesterday.

After glancing at my watch again, I reluctantly put the ring back in its place. I closed the lid on the box and climbed down out of the attic. I'd come back as soon as I could to retrieve the treasures.

When I reached the first floor, I stopped to brush dust off my skirt and pull down my shirtsleeves I'd rolled up. I gathered my hair — still damp from the shower and starting to curl — into a neat bun, took a deep breath, then followed the voices into the dining room.

Crawford sat at the table with Bert, slices of chocolate pie in front of them despite the early hour. They were laughing like old friends. I hesitated at the doorway, not sure how to break up their camaraderie and still trying to slow my hammering heart. Bert noticed me first.

"There you are. Come on in and have some pie. My friend here says it's his favorite."

"It's true. Chocolate pie makes me lose all rational thought," Crawford said with a smile. He forked the last bite into his mouth and dropped his napkin on his plate. "Thanks for the treat. I'd love to talk some more, but I imagine Sara is ready for me to get to work."

"You two have fun." Bert's smile dimpled his cheeks. He picked up their plates and forks and moved toward the kitchen sink. "Let me know if you need anything while you're poking around."

"Looks like y'all hit it off," I said to Crawford once we were out of earshot.

"I can't turn down pie. And he was so eager for me to have some."

"It's the funeral food. He tries to force it on whoever happens to walk into the kitchen." My voice was casual, belying none of the butterflies fluttering in my stomach. Nervousness was rare for me in a professional situation, and I blamed it on my findings in the attic. Even still, something about being near Crawford made me feel flustered.

He laughed as he walked into the hallway, his hand barely brushing mine on his way past. "Why don't you show me around?"

We spent the next hour scrutinizing each room of the house. He made notes in a small notebook as I outlined my ideas. Since the funeral, I'd formed a clearer picture of the new Hideaway. Mags said I could do whatever I wanted with it, and after Allyn assured me everything at the shop would go on without a hitch, I'd begun to enjoy the feeling of freedom — both the time away from my hectic work schedule and the anticipation of diving into a new project.

The house had six rooms and a kitchen on the first floor, each room separated by walls to create choppy, awkward spaces. I wanted fewer walls, more open areas, and more light — both in color palette and in natural light flowing in from the tall windows on the south and east sides of the house.

Upstairs, the bedrooms were spacious but dated and plain — fine for Mags and her friends, but not for a more modern B and B. With only three bathrooms, guests — the few who ever came — had no privacy. I wanted the rooms to be luxurious, each with its own private bath and cozy dining space. A small table, a couple of chairs, a microwave, and a mini fridge would appeal to out-of-towners coming for a relaxing stay.

"How I'll get those out-of-towners to come, I have no idea," I said as we descended the stairs. "My first point of business is to get the house ready for them, then I'll figure out the rest. Or if I end up selling it, someone else can figure it out."

Crawford was quiet as we walked out onto the back porch. I opened the screen door to head into the yard, but he didn't follow. I turned and saw he was still standing in the doorway.

"You know, I see a lot of houses in the work I do," he said. "A lot of *old* houses. I'm not going to say I'm jaded, but I'm also not often blown away by what I see. This one is different though. For one thing, look at these floors." He gestured down the wide center hallway. "These are heart pine planks. They probably came from a single tree. Cut, planed, and sanded by hand. No one makes houses like this anymore."

Charlie was right. Old houses were Crawford's passion. I could see it in the way he stared down the hallway, the way he ran his hand up and down the time-smoothed door frame.

"Even if you do decide to sell, at least you're not tearing it down. A lot of people buy property down here on the water just for the sunset views. They tear down whatever house sits on the land, often before they've even walked through it, and then build an Italian villa in its place. I get it — modern conveniences and all that — but there's something to be said for the character a century of life can bring to a house."

"I'm not much for new." I sat on a wicker chair and tucked my legs under me.

"Right."

I knew what he was thinking. My trendy silk blouse, slim skirt, and J. Crew ballet flats hardly screamed vintage charm. "I'm serious. Most of what I work with every day is old."

"I thought you were an interior designer. Don't most people want new things when they redecorate their houses?"

"Not always. I am a designer, but I also sell vintage furniture in a shop on Magazine Street. I go to estate sales, yard sales, whatever I can find, and buy gorgeous old things for pennies. Usually the owners don't even know what they're selling. They're just trying to clean out Grandma's house after she died."

Crawford glanced down and my words hit

me. I rubbed my forehead with my fingertips. "Well, that wasn't very nice of me, was it?"

"I do a little of the same thing," he said, taking a seat in the chair next to me. "But I make the old furniture instead of looking for it. I pick up old wood — mostly scraps I find on job sites — and turn it into tables, chairs, that sort of thing. It's all pretty haphazard, to be honest, but my mom likes it." He smiled. "I've sold a few pieces here and there, and I'm working on a table for a client now. That is, when I can find time between work and this boathouse Charlie's talked me into building."

"I'd love to see your work sometime."

"I doubt it's anything you'd be interested in. To be honest, it looks like it was made in someone's woodshed in the backyard. And most of it was."

"Trust me, if it looks in any way like it's had a past life, I have customers who'll eat it up."

Glory stuck her head out the back door then. "Can I get y'all anything? Iced tea? More pie?"

Crawford stood. "No, ma'am. Thank you though."

"Don't leave on account of me, now," she said.

"It's time for me to head out anyway. I have a stop to make in Fairhope before I go back to the office."

I walked him back through the house to the front door. He said he'd be in contact soon about prices and materials.

"You really think you'll sell it once you finish all this work?" he asked at the top of the front porch steps.

I picked at a string on my skirt and shrugged. "I haven't decided. It seems like the smartest thing to do. I sure can't stay here and run a bed-and-breakfast."

"That's too bad. Once this house is fixed up, you'll be sad to let it go. Mark my words: it's going to be a showstopper."

Later that afternoon, I waited until the upstairs hall was quiet before I pulled down the creaky attic stairs and climbed up to retrieve the box. After Crawford left, I hadn't been able to focus on anything except the box and its mysterious contents. Part of me felt like I did when I scored a big find at a junk shop or estate sale — excited to dive in and see what I could make of something old — but another part was scared to wade any further into who Mags might have been.

I tiptoed back to my room with the box

and closed the door behind me. I reached into the box, gently pulling out the envelope, and emptied it onto the blue quilt, turning each piece over so the words were visible. They were still disjointed, but I moved them around until most of the torn edges lined up and it seemed maybe they were in the right places. There were gaps, sections of the note that had been lost to the years, but what was left was an even bigger mystery.

Dearest Maggie,
. . . leaving now to save . . . the discomfort . . . is the right choice . . . know our time . . . your finger . . . be mine and I . . . in the cove, just as we planned . . .
Love,
William

I stared at the broken note for several long moments trying to sort out the emotion behind the words. Anger? Frustration? Passion? With the missing pieces, it was so hard to tell.

I pulled the box back toward me and laid everything else on the bed — the ring box, stack of newspaper clippings, tiny wooden house, and handful of photographs, the one of Mags on top. But there was something else I hadn't seen earlier. Stuck down along the edge of the box was a yellowed postcard. It had a picture of Mobile's Bellingrath Gardens on the front. The postscript on the back was dated June 1960. There was no return address, just one line written in small, neat cursive.

Margaret,
You made the right choice.

Mother

I heard a faint knock at the door, and Dot poked her head in. I discreetly nudged a newspaper clipping over the ring box.

"We're headed out for dinner. You sure you don't want to come? We're going to our regular meat-and-three over in Daphne. Bert hates to miss the early bird specials, and the food is actually pretty good."

I smiled. "No thanks. I'll find something here."

She gestured toward the assortment on my bed. "What's all that?"

"Just some things I found up in the attic earlier." I almost said more, but something stopped me. I craved more time alone with all I'd found before I brought Dot into the mystery.

She nodded, her eyes scanning the items. "Okay then. See you when we get back. I'll try to bring you some leftovers."

She stepped away from the door but paused before closing it. "Secrets may come to light the deeper you dig in this old place. Feel free to ask me anything. I may not have all the answers, but I can probably come pretty close to the truth."

17
SARA

Crawford and his team worked fast. The electrician came during breakfast the next morning. Glory grabbed her coffee and hurried up the steps, her long nightgown billowing out behind her. Ten minutes later, we heard knocking at the door again. It was the foundation specialist. Back at the table, Dot was folding and refolding her napkin.

"It's okay," I said. "They're just here to see if the house has any major problems, which it probably does. It's better to find out quickly. Remember, this is a good thing."

Dot's eyes filled. "I trust you. It's just hard to see other people trampling around the place."

"But it's a bed-and-breakfast. That's kind of the idea, isn't it? Didn't it used to be this way?"

"That was a long time ago. And we made

friends with the guests quickly. Look at Major and Glory."

"You're welcome to make friends with Larry the electrician, although I doubt he'll be moving in. He'll be up in that hot attic checking the wiring, but I'm sure he'd love a piece of Bert's pie."

"I know you're poking fun at me, but maybe I'll do just that. At least let them know those of us who live here care about the house and are keeping a close eye on them."

"Just remember they're here doing a job I hired them to do, and I care about the house too."

Dot reached over and patted my hand. "Don't mind me. I'm old and set in my ways. I'm sure whatever you have in mind for this place will be just fine. I'm going to check on that pie."

I hadn't planned to say anything just yet about my findings in the attic, but since no one else was around, I took advantage of our privacy. "Dot, did you ever know Mags to be . . . well dressed?"

She paused in the hallway. "Well dressed?" She laughed a little with her back still turned. "Not unless you count those hideous hats as formal attire. What in the world makes you ask that?"

"It's probably nothing. I just found this old picture of her up in the attic yesterday. She was much younger and looked . . . well, different than I ever saw her."

"Mags was very pretty." Dot walked back to the table. "Even as she grew older, she still had that beauty, but when I first moved in here, she was a knockout."

I nodded. Mags had been pretty — the photo beside my bed in New Orleans showed that. But mentally peeling back the layers to the woman she might have once been and actually seeing that younger woman were two very different things.

I wanted to ask about William and the ring too — the words danced on the end of my tongue — but just then, the front door banged open, followed by the sound of work boots on the hardwood and a tinny radio belting out a Spanish love song. Dot pulled the belt on her robe tighter.

"It's okay," I said. "Go on and get changed."

"I'd love to talk more about this though. Could you show me the photo later?"

I nodded. "It may be nothing. I just thought I'd check."

"You never know. Mags wore some getups in her life, that's for sure." Dot glanced left and right in the hall before hurrying to the stairs, the pie for Larry the electrician long forgotten.

I sat there a minute longer. Dot's reaction seemed innocent enough, but that hesitant pause before she turned around spoke louder than her casual dismissal of the photo. I'd said it may be nothing, but Mags's neat hair and prim smile told a different story.

I spent the rest of the morning taking inventory of all the furniture in the house. So much of it had to go — La-Z-Boy recliners, a velour couch with cat scratches along both arms, at least fifteen water-stained occasional tables, even a strange orb-shaped plastic chair that shouldn't have been allowed out of 1972.

Hidden among the ugliness were a few pieces I could work with. Mags's chair for writing letters sat in a corner of the main living room. It was an old Chesterfield with nailhead trim, its leather in surprisingly good condition. Even after the invention of e-mail — not to mention texts — Mags kept in touch with former guests by writing letters to them. She always used thick, creamy Crane stationery embossed with a breezy, swirly *M* in the upper left corner.

Such traditional stationery always seemed

out of character for her, but she said it was a sacrilege to use anything else. Saturday was her day for writing, and this chair was the place. Her old cat, Stafford, would sit with her, his hind legs on the back of the chair and his front paws draped over Mags's shoulders.

I sat in the chair and ran my hands up and down the armrests. Under me, the cushion gave way just enough to create a scoop of soft leather. I picked at a stray cat hair stuck in the seam of the cushion.

A gorgeous old buffet table stood next to the chair under a bank of windows. It had slim drawers on the front and carvings of vines and leaves snaked up its curved legs. Sunlight glinted off the table's surface, despite the layer of dust. A closer inspection revealed a small key engraved along the edge of one of the drawers. I smiled — the key was becoming a familiar sight — and ran my fingers across the indentation.

Major stuck his head into the room. "What's the order of business today?"

I stared at him. We hadn't spoken more than a few polite words since the conversation at the dinner table my first night at the house.

"Put me to work," he said. "I don't like to see these other people working on the house while I just sit here. Makes me uncomfortable."

"Okay, I was about to move some of these older pieces of furniture outside to take to Goodwill. I won't do much before talking to Dot and Glory, but some of these things are useless." I gestured to an orange plastic love seat. I loved refinishing things, but I couldn't do much with spray-painted plastic.

"I'll give you permission myself. You can't imagine what it's like to have to look at some of this stuff every day. I'm no decorator, but even I know when something's ugly as a three-eyed cat. And I don't like cats."

Together, we moved the most offensive pieces outside. While carrying a bulky coffee table to the driveway, he cleared his throat. "Glory tells me I'm not good with apologies," he said. "The other night at dinner —"

"It's okay, I understand. If I were in your position, I'm sure I'd feel the same way."

"I was just caught off guard." He grunted as we backed down the front steps with the table. "The four of us wouldn't have been able to take care of this house for too many more years on our own, anyway."

"I don't know about that. Y'all have been here so long, the house is a part of you."

"It's a part of you too, even if you don't live here."

We set the table down and surveyed the furniture we'd amassed in the driveway.

"Who's going to want that old thing?" Major pointed to a side chair with springs exposed and fabric hanging off the back.

"We're keeping that one."

"You're getting rid of a perfectly good coffee table" — half upholstery, half glass, there was nothing good or perfect about it — "but you're keeping an old busted chair?"

I smiled. "It's ugly now, but just wait." Whenever I saw chairs like this at an estate sale or garage sale, I couldn't snatch them up fast enough. As long as the wood wasn't too banged up, it was the easiest thing to refinish and recover. I regularly picked up chairs like this one — stuffing pouring out, ugly fabric, scratched wood — for less than fifty dollars and sold them for a few hundred. I wasn't going to sell this one though. "It'll be your favorite chair when I'm done with it."

Major snorted. "Doubt that."

He continued shuffling things around outside while I sat in the gravel next to the frayed side chair. Using a pair of pliers I'd found in the kitchen, I ripped the staples out of the upholstery and carefully pulled off the tattered fabric, laying the strips down by my feet. I'd already decided to reupholster it in a cool graphic print to downplay the fussy Rococo design carved into the wood. After a while, Major paused in the shade, wiping his forehead with a handkerchief.

"You okay?" I asked.

"Of course. Just thinking of Mags. She talked about going down there to visit, you know. She even looked into buying an apartment so she'd have a place to stay."

"In New Orleans?" It wasn't difficult to imagine Mags meandering through the little streets and alleyways of the *Vieux Carré* with her flowered hats and ponchos. But still — Mags in New Orleans?

Major nodded. "Especially if bad weather was coming. If there was even a hint of a hurricane out in the Gulf, she'd keep that darn TV on the Weather Channel all day long." He turned a chair around so it faced me and sat down. "I don't know if she actually would have gone down there. I can't imagine her anywhere but here."

I smiled. She probably would have fit right in, making friends with George the jeweler, Allyn, and all the other misfits.

"She hated being so far from her only family," Major said. "She figured if you weren't coming this way very often, she could go to you. Then at least you couldn't blame your lack of visiting on distance anymore."

I sighed. "It wasn't the distance so much as —"

"I know, I know, your shop. I'm just calling it like I see it."

"Thanks. That hurts," I said. But he was right. Regardless of my reasons — the still-sore memories of my parents, my suffocation at the hands of small-town life, even my childish embarrassment of Mags and her friends — it had been a mistake to allow so much time to pass between visits. The phone calls hadn't been enough, even if they were as regular as clockwork.

"Just speaking the truth, young lady." He folded his handkerchief into a tight square and stuck it in his pocket. "But it's water under the bridge. You're here now, and wherever Mags is, I'm sure she's happy you've come."

He sounded confident, but I wasn't so sure. What kind of ungrateful granddaughter would I have been if I'd ignored Mr. Bains's summons to come to the reading of the will? If I'd stayed away from the funeral? If I'd come back to collect Mags's things long after Dot and the others had moved out?

187

It hurt to admit it, but those were my first thoughts on the streetcar after talking to Mr. Bains. Of course, they were fleeting — I knew I'd return to Sweet Bay, regardless of whatever memories waited for me. And now, back at the house I thought I'd left for good, I no longer yearned to leave. New Orleans still beckoned, but Mags — the one I never knew — beckoned too.

Later that day, I went into town to buy a few items for Bert.

"Teriyaki? What in the world for?" Major asked when Bert asked me to pick up a bottle for him. "You getting adventurous in your old age?"

"I don't want Sara to think all I can cook is chicken, butter beans, and cornbread," Bert said. "She's used to better things in New Orleans. I've never made an étouffée, but I can make a good roux. In fact, scratch the teriyaki and pick up some shrimp. We'll have gumbo instead." Bert was hunched over a battered church cookbook, thumbing through pages.

"Bert, I'd eat a wooden chair if you cooked it," I said. "I'm sure whatever you whip up will be delicious. Don't make something special just for me."

"Go ahead and pick up shrimp and teriyaki," he said. "Maybe I'll combine the two and come up with something new."

Major wrinkled his nose. "Just stick with chicken and butter beans. You're good with those."

I laughed and grabbed my keys. Outside, the air was light and breezy. I inhaled — cut grass, salty air, and the faint scent of coconut. I smiled. Close by, someone was sunbathing on a dock.

I picked up Bert's ingredients at Grimmerson's Grocery, then paused on the sidewalk. Paint chips hung in the window of Grant's Hardware across the street, practically begging me to dive right into my job at The Hideaway, but the diner next door advertised fresh-squeezed lemonade. The day had grown warm, and my thirst won.

I took a deep breath to steady my nerves before opening the door. The last time I stood outside the diner, Mags had bumped into me from behind.

"What are you standing out here for?" she'd asked. "The lemonade is inside, not out on the stoop. I'm sweating through my shirt. Let's go in."

But I couldn't make myself grab the door handle. My parents had been gone less than a year, and my nerves were still raw and exposed. The diner was *their* place. I'd been afraid to see someone other than my mom manning the register, someone other than my dad slinging plates of catfish and coleslaw across the counter.

In the end, I backed away from the door, bumping into Mags in the process. Red-faced and sweating, and not from the summertime heat, I escaped around the corner and found a bench outside Sandifer's Music Shop. A few minutes later, I felt Mags's small hand on my shoulder. I looked up and there she stood, holding a huge Styrofoam cup of lemonade. Her bird's-nest hat sat askew on her head, one of the birds dislodged from its nest and holding on by a string. With two fingers, she pulled her shirt away from her skin and flapped it back and forth in a lackluster attempt to create a breeze. She kept her other hand on my shoulder, the heat from it radiating into my bones. After a moment, she pointed the straw toward me and offered me a sip.

I didn't make it into the diner that day, but this time, a bell dangling off the doorknob announced my entrance. The cash register sat in the same place, although the counter now sported wood pallets and metal sheeting, giving it a modern, industrial look. It didn't fit with the country décor in the rest of the diner, but it was a step up from the old red laminate counter. The place was quiet with only a couple other customers. I found a booth by the door and scanned the menu sitting on the table. On the back of the menu was a note in memoriam:

DEDICATED TO ED AND JENNY JENKINS,
THE ORIGINAL OWNERS OF JENNY'S DINER.
WE LOVED THEM AND WILL KEEP THEIR
MEMORY ALIVE.

"Miss Jenkins?" The voice came from the other side of the diner. I scanned the room until I saw a vaguely familiar man holding a hand up in greeting. He heaved himself out of his booth and lumbered toward me. It wasn't until he stood by my table that I recognized him as Sammy Grosvenor. I smiled, but it was short and tight.

"Condolences for your loss, Miss Jenkins." He wiped his hands on a napkin. Cornbread crumbs dotted the front of his shirt just under the Middle Bay Land Development logo.

"Thank you."

"I remember your grandmother well. Was she still living in that delightful little bed-and-breakfast on the bay?"

"She was, and I'm the owner of the bed-and-breakfast now. Although I feel certain you already know that."

He nodded. "Ah yes, that's right. I do remember hearing that ownership had changed hands. Now would be a great time to sell, you know. Property values in Sweet Bay are on the rise. I'm sure you'd find a willing buyer if you were to ask around."

"Let me guess. You'd prefer if I started with you."

"Only if it strikes your fancy." He smiled sweetly.

"I'm not selling, Mr. Grosvenor."

"I don't give up easily, Miss Jenkins."

"Neither do I."

He balled up his napkin and tossed it in the trash can on his way out the door. I released my breath and sat back in my seat.

"Sara, is that you?" I turned to see Mrs. Busbee, the new owner of the diner, walking toward me, tucking a dish towel into the apron tied around her waist. She hugged me, her doughy arms smelling of fried chicken, and set a glass of lemonade on the table in front of me.

"It's good to see you," she said. "Don't you worry about ol' Sammy. He's always blabbering on about something or another. My opinion is it's always best to just ignore him."

"That's my plan."

"I was so sorry to hear about your grandmother. She was a big part of life around here."

"Thank you. We got your chocolate pie at the house."

"Good, good. Are you here for long, or will you be heading back to New Orleans? I'd sure love to get over there one day and see your shop. I bet I'd find a million things there I'd just have to have."

It was a funny thing about small towns. People knew too much about me when I lived in Sweet Bay, so I left. Years later, people still knew my business, but now I didn't mind as much. It was kind of nice to hear the pride in Mrs. Busbee's voice.

"I'm sticking around for a bit. I'm doing some renovations at The Hideaway that'll keep me in town for longer than I expected."

"That's wonderful. It'll be nice to see your face around here again. I wasn't sure if you'd ever want to come back in this diner. It must hold a lot of memories for you."

Another customer waved at Mrs. Busbee. She tapped my menu with her finger. "Let me know if you want to order anything else." She turned and, after grabbing a tea pitcher off the counter, made her way to the thirsty customer.

A small picture of my parents accompanied the memorial on the back of the menu. I'd never seen this particular photo before. They stood next to each other behind the counter, red aprons around their middles, my mom holding a metal spatula. Smiling, heads tilted toward each other, they looked satisfied with their life of running a small-town diner, living with a young child, and checking in on the family matriarch and her dusty old house.

They didn't need much extra money — which was good, because the diner didn't bring it in — or prestige, even though they had a lot of that. Everyone who came through Sweet Bay — especially tourists on their way to Gulf Shores — stopped at Jenny's for a bite to eat. Everyone knew them. Everyone loved them.

I was staring into nothing, thinking about my parents, when the bell rang and a group of boys rushed into the diner, all laughs and jeers. They pushed each other around, joking about a teacher. One of the boys came too close to my table and bumped it. My lemonade tipped, and before I could grab it, the sweet liquid spread over the table.

"Oh . . . sorry," the boy mumbled, before sprinting to his group at the counter.

I scooted to the side, but not before some of it dripped onto my lap. I moved farther over and tried to wipe the liquid from the seat.

"You don't seem too upset about it," said a voice from the edge of the table. I looked up. Crawford Hayes stood next to my table, eyes crinkled and smiling.

"Not much I can do about it now." I pulled at the napkin container to keep him from seeing the pink flush creeping up my cheeks, only to find one napkin left in the box.

"Here, let me help." He swiped a box from a neighboring table and dried the table, then grabbed a clean towel from Mrs. Busbee. "For your pants." He handed it to me.

"Thanks. I can't be too mad about it. Aren't kids always jumpy after being cramped in school desks all day?"

He smiled. "Yeah, I remember that. You probably do too."

"Not really." I glanced at the boys now congregated at a booth in the back. "I was more of a homebody. Even though my home was — well, you've seen it."

"You lived there? I didn't realize."

I nodded. "Not always, but I did for a while. My parents died when I was twelve, and I moved in with Mags. Living in a house like that with a bunch of old people is a great way to alienate yourself from people your own age."

He was still standing next to my table, so I gestured for him to sit. Under the table, his legs brushed against mine. I moved my legs out of the way, then slid them back an inch or two.

"Wow, both your parents died? I'm so sorry."

"It was a long time ago."

"So you left town the first chance you got?"

"Something like that. I moved away for college and kept the holiday visits short. I think in my mind, I'd already escaped, so I didn't want to stick around too long."

"Were you afraid you might stay? Because I have to tell you, as an outsider moving to Sweet Bay, this town seems perfect. It's something about being right on the water and . . . I don't know, maybe there's something in the air too. I'm not sure I could ever leave."

I must have sat on the end of Mags's dock as a kid a thousand times while the rest of the world floated away — pelicans gliding overhead, fish jumping, the tide creeping toward the Gulf. Even back then, I couldn't deny its allure.

"Sweet Bay is magical in its own way," I said. "But it wasn't for me — at least not when I was eighteen and ready for more than fish fries and pep rallies. I don't think I worried I'd get pulled back in. I think I felt guilty because I knew I didn't intend to move back."

"And yet here you are, back in Sweet Bay. And you're doing what your grandmother asked you to do. Not everyone would follow through with it."

I shrugged. "Maybe you're right."

I sat up straighter in my seat and smoothed my hand down my hair. "Enough about me. Charlie said you're the best contractor in Baldwin County, and you love old houses the best. Where'd that come from?"

He laughed again, the sound of it calming something inside me. "I told you he sticks his foot in his mouth."

"No, he just sounded proud."

"To answer your question, my parents used to live in a ninety-year-old house back in Tennessee. They worked on it for my entire childhood. That thing was never finished — they were always working on some project or another. Once I was old enough to hold a hammer or use a hand sander, they put me to work. I guess that's where I got my passion for old houses, for loving on them and giving them the attention they deserve. That probably sounds weird."

His eyes turned down a bit at the sides when he smiled, making him look younger than he probably was.

I shook my head. "It's not weird. Or if it is, it describes me too. I get it — it's a passion you either have or you don't."

"Exactly. I did something similar to my house here. It was built in the 1920s as an old fishing house, and it was a train wreck when I bought it. The real estate agent thought I was crazy, but I promised her a gourmet meal in my new kitchen when I finished. She never thought she'd actually get the dinner."

"Did she?"

"Sure did. I'm not much of a cook, so I overpromised. I ended up ordering from a restaurant and serving it on nice platters so she'd think I cooked it myself."

"That's terrible," I said, laughing.

"She wasn't there for the food anyway."

I smiled. "I see."

"No, I don't mean that. She's sixty years old and happily married. She only wanted to see what all I'd done to the house."

"Was she impressed?"

He nodded. "It's a fine house, I have to admit. Now it is, anyway. It took a long time and a lot of patience digging through years of ugly updates. I did most of the work myself, and I'm proud of it. It was a hard time in my life, and I was thankful for the distraction."

He grew quiet and looked away for a moment. The bell rang again and two old men entered. They lowered themselves into a corner booth and one pulled out a deck of cards.

"I need to get back to the house. Bert is waiting on this." I picked up the grocery sack I'd laid by my feet.

We walked out of the diner and I turned toward my car parked a few spaces up. The late-afternoon sun was warm on my face. The air was that perfect spring temperature when it's hard to tell where your skin stops and the air begins. A faint Southern breeze lifted wisps of my hair.

He moved toward his truck parked across the street, then stopped. "We'll probably be seeing a lot of each other at the house with everything that's going on, but . . ." He cleared his throat.

He's nervous. The thought caused a pleasant tightening in my stomach.

"I'd love to see you again like this. Separate from the house, I mean." He jangled his keys in his pocket.

Why not? My life in New Orleans was a flurry of phone calls, customers, and client meetings. I pored over cash register receipts until late at night, mulling over every dollar made and lost. I often ate takeout because I wasn't home enough to go to the grocery store. Mitch was the closest I'd come to having a boyfriend in a while, but my life was so taken up with the shop, I hadn't even stopped to consider whether I wanted him to be my boyfriend.

But here in Sweet Bay, I had nothing taking up my time except the house. No late nights, no early mornings. I had all the time in the world. Plus, Crawford seemed genuine. For one thing, he ate chocolate pie with Bert at nine in the morning because he didn't want to seem unappreciative. And I'd found that people who loved old houses tended to be trustworthy.

I nodded. "I'd like that."

He smiled and headed for the truck, turning once to look back at me over his shoulder.

18
SARA

MAY

Bert still couldn't decide what to make for dinner even after he spread all the possible ingredients on the kitchen counter. He waffled so long, Major put his foot down. "Gumbo, minus the teriyaki. There's your decision, old man. Oh, and use chicken. That shrimp was practically cooked by the time Sara got home with it. I don't want a late-night run to the ER with food poisoning."

"I can make it with chicken, but don't forget, the roux — it takes a while," Bert said, his hands already reaching for the peppers and onions.

"You mentioned gumbo, and now I've got a hankering for it," Major said.

Dot and I watched the exchange from the doorway. "Major's the only one who can get away with pushing Bert around in the kitchen," Dot whispered. "Bert usually

201

won't stand for it, but I think he secretly wanted to make the gumbo to impress you. He just needed a reason to do it."

I followed Dot out onto the porch. Glory was already there knitting and purling, a long strand of red yarn trailing from her fingers down into a basket on the floor next to her chair. Dot sat on the wicker love seat, but I was too jumpy to sit still. Both Crawford and Mags — the one from the old photo — danced through my mind. I stood by the screen door and surveyed the backyard.

After a few minutes of listening to Glory and Dot's conversation, I sat down. I pulled out the old photo of Mags that I'd stuck in my pocket earlier. During a lull in their chatting, I held the photo out to Dot. "This is the picture I mentioned this morning."

Dot pulled her glasses off the top of her head and settled them onto her nose.

Glory leaned over to take a peek. "Gracious. Is that Mags?"

I kept my eyes on Dot. I wanted to see her reaction. If she was as surprised as I was, she didn't show it. She just stared at the photo and gave a slow nod. Then she reached up and wiped the corner of her eye. Glory patted her knee.

"Did you ever know Mags to look like

this?" I asked.

Dot shook her head. "I moved in here in '61. By then, she was a little . . . freer. Granted, she was nine months pregnant when I got here, so that might have explained her not wearing nice dresses and expensive jewelry. Even after she had Jenny, though, she never dressed like this. Now, Robert . . ." Dot cleared her throat. "He always dressed as if he could be called away to an important board meeting at any moment — or maybe he just wanted to look that way." Dot rubbed her thumb over the date along the edge of the photo. "Nineteen fifty-seven," she murmured.

She handed the photo to me and leaned back in her chair. She seemed to choose her words carefully. "Mags didn't always dress and act like she did as we knew her. She had a different life before she arrived here — wealthy parents, high society, fancy parties."

She might as well have been talking about some woman I'd never known. Mags in high society? I would have laughed had I not been so surprised.

"She was mostly quiet about that part of her life — quiet about much of her life, mind you — but she let things slip from time to time." Dot smiled and tapped her finger on the arm of her chair. "I remember the first time she mentioned anything about her old life. It was my wedding day, about a month after Mags had Jenny. I'd picked out a beautiful orange taffeta number for her to wear as my one bridesmaid, and she was not happy about it. She had a hard time zipping up her dress in the back, so I helped her get it up the last couple of inches. She moved and twisted, trying to get comfortable in the dress. Finally, she flopped down on the bed and said, 'Lord, I've always hated tight dresses.'

"I laughed, thinking she was kidding. I'd never seen her wear anything other than baggy blue jeans, big tops, and wool socks. What in the world would she have to do with tight dresses? So I asked her.

" 'Oh, I used to wear them,' she said. 'Formal dresses, pearls, and an embarrassingly large diamond ring.' You can imagine my shock. Probably much like yours now," Dot said.

I nodded. I thought of the ring in the box in the attic. It was a diamond, but it wasn't large or embarrassing.

"She lay on the bed, fiddling with the boned bodice of that frilly orange dress. She said, 'I thought I was done with these things for good. No offense — it's a nice dress.'

Then she hopped up off the bed and pulled me out the door, saying I wouldn't be late to my own wedding on her watch."

"Did she say anything else?" I wanted to hear more.

"Later that night after everything had died down, she told me it had been a perfect wedding. Now, it wasn't much — just the other guests in the house, a few friends from the neighborhood, and Bert's brothers from Florida. I wore a dress from Irene's Dress Barn on Main Street, and Bert and I exchanged rings we bought at an estate sale. I didn't need any more than that, but I was a little embarrassed in light of what Mags had said about that large diamond ring of hers. I figured such a ring would have called for a rather large wedding, much fancier than the one we'd just had. I told her as much, but she laughed and said, 'Dot, you can't imagine the wedding I had.' I started to defend our little wedding, but I'll never forget what she said next. 'I never knew how much I wanted uncomplicated love and a simple wedding until the chance was gone.' I don't know what her wedding was like, but she was so wistful, it made me appreciate what I had with Bert even more."

I picked up the photo of Mags again. It was hard to imagine her life had ever included fancy parties and an elaborate wedding. The ring from the box would have fit in perfectly with a simple wedding and uncomplicated love. Why didn't she get what she wanted?

I pulled the postcard out of my pocket and handed it to Dot. "This was in the box too."

She read the words on the back, her lips barely moving.

"You made the right choice."

Dot cut her eyes over to Glory, who leaned forward to see. Dot handed the card back to me. "I don't know what that means," she said, but her eyes said something else.

Somehow, Mags had gone from wearing fancy dresses and pearls to a bird's-nest hat and rubber waders. Did it have something to do with her parents? Her mother? I wanted to ask, but Dot stood and called back into the house.

"Bert, I'm coming in and I want to taste a roux that will make Major's head spin!" She looked at me over her shoulder as she walked through the doorway and disappeared into the darkness of the hallway.

19
MAGS

MAY 1960

I was out on the dock, staring at the decrepit motorboat suspended by fraying ropes in the boathouse. The hand crank wouldn't budge, so I was trying to figure out how to lower the thing into the water to see if it would still float. There were no obvious holes in the hull, but I knew even pinpricks could sink it. Years before, Daddy gave me boating lessons on summer mornings. He spent a small fortune on a wooden Chris Craft and stored it in Point Clear. In the absence of a son to teach these things to, I was going to be his sportswoman — only I wasn't very good. The first time I took a turn at the wheel, I ran straight into a sandbar in Mobile Bay, damaging the motor so badly that Daddy had to jump in and pull the boat back to shore.

"I need rubber boots," I said under my breath. If I stood in the shallow water right under the boat, I'd get a better look at the bottom, as well as the motor, a rusty Evinrude.

"Don't tell me you're going to try your hand at boating again."

I spun around. Daddy stood on the grass at the edge of the dock, shielding his eyes from the sun. It was as if I had conjured him out of the still Sweet Bay air.

I waited for his image to float away, but he walked down the dock toward me, smiling. "I've missed you. Your mother made shrimp cocktail last night. Since you weren't there to share, I had to finish them off myself." He patted his round stomach. "I didn't mind so much."

"Daddy, I . . ."

"So, this is The Hideaway, huh?" He looked behind him at the house overlooking the bay. "I've read about it but never actually seen it. Looks like it could use a paint job — or two — but it's nice. Can I have a tour?"

He sounded friendly, but there was tension in his casual smile. I had no way to tell what he knew, and I didn't want to give too much away before I figured that out.

"Sure. Let's take a walk." I led him around the house to the front door. When we walked up the front steps, a group of three black-clad women passed through the door on their way out. Daddy turned to watch them climb into a waiting car, driven by yet another woman in black, this one sporting sunglasses and a black-and-white knit scarf. She waved at me and I waved back. Daddy raised his eyebrows but didn't comment.

Inside was surprisingly quiet, and I was thankful. Gary stood at an easel at the front window, his paintbrush suspended in air, apparently waiting for the muses to tell him what to paint. Starla was in the kitchen humming under her breath, preparing the evening meal.

I walked him around, showing him some of the artwork hanging on the walls and propped up against door frames. He nodded and smiled when appropriate and poked his head into each room.

"Oh, this is nice," he said when we got to the back porch. He sat in a glider facing the lawn. "I can see why you like it here. It's peaceful."

We sat silent a moment. Daddy settled into his seat, his arms stretched over the back, a picture of relaxation. I waited as long as I could.

"How did you know where to find me?"

"I didn't at first. When you left, I thought you'd bunk with a friend for a week or so, then get back home where you belonged. But when the weeks kept coming with no word from you, I grew concerned."

"I was going to call. I —"

"Then I remembered the check I gave you."

I inhaled sharply. *The check.*

"After a couple of weeks, I called my bank and asked them to alert me the minute you cashed it. I was relieved you were still close by. A simple call to First Coastal in Sweet Bay told me you were here. The teller I spoke to was terribly complimentary about this place. I wanted to wait for you to come home on your own, but it's tearing your mother apart not knowing what's going on with you."

I gave Daddy a look. "If it's tearing her apart, then why isn't she here with you?"

"Now, Margaret, that's just not fair. Your mother loves you. And so does your husband."

When I didn't respond, Daddy cleared his throat. "So this is a bed-and-breakfast, right? Did you check in for an extended stay?"

"You could say that."

"What have you been doing this whole time? I know you haven't just been working on that old boat out there."

"Actually, I'm managing the house now. The owner had to leave and she asked me to take over. I think the job suits me." I smoothed down my pants — wrinkled and linen, so different from the pressed pencil skirt I'd be wearing back home.

Just then, Daisy crossed the backyard in yoga attire, her mat slung over her shoulders. "Hi, Maggie," she called out.

I held up a hand in greeting.

"I just ran into William," she continued, unconcerned with the strange man sitting on the porch with me. "He said to tell you he'll be a little late for dinner tonight."

My breath caught in my throat and heat crawled up my cheeks. I kept my eyes on Daisy making her way around the side of the house, even though I could feel Daddy's stare.

Finally he broke his gaze and laughed to himself. "When you were born, I suggested we call you Maggie, but your mother refused. She said Maggie was the name of someone in pigtails and bobby socks. She said there was power in a name, and Margaret held the kind of power and influence she wanted you to have." He shook his head. "I still think Maggie's cute." He paused. "Is William a guest here?"

I closed my eyes. "Daddy —"

211

"You know what? Whoever he is doesn't matter. You've had your time away. I even gave you a little money to help you out, but you've made your point. It's time to come on back."

"What?"

"People are starting to talk, and you know how your mother feels about that. I don't particularly care for it either. I know you've had a hard time with Robert, but we've let you stay gone long enough."

"You *let* me stay gone?" I fought to keep my emotions under control. "You didn't let me do anything. It was my choice to come here, and it's been my choice to stay."

"Okay, fine." He held his hands up in surrender. "You've stayed gone as long as you needed to. But enough is enough. It's time to get home."

"Home? I don't even know where that is anymore."

"What are you talking about? Your home is with Robert, your husband. Where else would it be? Certainly not here." He gestured toward the house with his hand, casually dismissing the place that had become my entire world.

"I don't belong with Robert anymore — not in his life and definitely not in his bed." Daddy's mouth dropped open. I'd shocked him, but I didn't care.

"Margaret," he whispered. "Do not disgrace yourself by speaking of such matters."

"Oh, Daddy, you sound like Mother. We're both adults. Can't we speak that way?"

"You want to speak like adults? Okay, you're holed up here in this secluded hotel when all of Mobile is talking about how you packed your bags and left your war-hero husband. You may feel slighted by Robert's actions, but you're not coming out on the right side of this."

"If I cared what side I came out on, I wouldn't have left in the first place. And anyway, Robert left first, if you remember. Funny how no one mentions that. You knew it wasn't business — you said so yourself. His leaving just showed me it was my time to leave too. He opened the door and I walked through it."

"Tell me about this William, why don't you? You talk about the speck in Robert's eye, but what about you carrying on with another man?"

"What makes you think I'm carrying on with William?"

"Your red cheeks when that gal over there mentioned his name told me all I needed to know. If he's here in this hole-in-the-wall

213

hotel, he's no one you need to be associating with. Does he even have a job?"

"Of course he has a job."

"He does know you're married, right?"

I sighed while Daddy drummed his fingers on the seat next to him.

"Let's just forget about him for a minute. What about a job for you? A real one. You can work for me and I'll make sure you're paid double. Your own spending money in your pocket — that'll give you the freedom you want without having to make your point living and working at a place like this."

I shook my head slowly. "You don't get it, Daddy. I'm not here because I want a job. This job fell into my lap and I took it, simple as that. I'm here because I couldn't stay back home any longer. Not as the person I was. I've been forcing myself into molds for too long. I need to make my own life, and it's happening here."

"I don't understand what you mean by needing your own life. Your own life is all you've ever known." He threw his hands up. "I've worked hard to make sure you and your mother never have to go without a single thing. Do you mean to fling that in my face and tell me it was unnecessary?"

"No, I appreciate all you've done for me. It's just that what I want — what I need —

can't be bought and paid for. Not with money, anyway."

We both turned when we heard a noise coming from the doorway into the house, but no one was there. He took a deep breath before speaking again.

"Robert may have left, but he's back now." I raised my eyebrows and he nodded. "That's the real reason I came to get you. He's back in Mobile and he's sick. He needs his wife by his side. If he's a decent man, this William should understand."

"Sick? Robert doesn't get sick," I said with a laugh. "He's never even had a cold in the three years we've been married."

"I don't know why you're laughing. Death is not a laughing matter."

"Death? What are you talking about? Robert is not dead or about to be. He's been in the mountains with AnnaBelle. If folks are talking about anything, they should be talking about that."

"He may have started there, but he's been in a hospital these last few weeks. He had an episode — some sort of shock or mental break. From the war. He's home now and he needs you."

I shook my head. "This is crazy. If he's really sick, then all he needs is someone to nurse him back to health. That could be any woman with a cool washcloth as far as I'm concerned. He doesn't need me."

"Listen to yourself! You said 'in sickness and in health.' Yes, he did wrong, but Margaret, you have to understand that sometimes men do things to test those marriage vows. If you stand firm, he will see your strength and integrity and renew his commitment to you. It will happen. Believe me, I know."

I wanted to question him, but I was also afraid that would take us down a path I wasn't sure I wanted to go.

"This is one of those times when you need to put aside your differences and your . . . your stubbornness, and just be his wife. For the sake of your family. Your future family." He tilted his head, then looked down at his shoes and sighed. "I know nothing is perfect, but it's worth a shot. If something happens later and you still want . . ." He raised his hand and gestured to the house. "What comes is what comes. But right now, you need to stand behind the vows you took. I've talked to Robert and he sees the error of his ways. I believe him. He's ready to give you 100 percent."

I heard a rustle in the hallway again. I got up to look, but by the time I got there, the hall was empty and the front door to the

house was just closing. Probably just someone going out for the day. I took a deep
breath, my hand shaky on the smooth door
frame.

"This is a life-changing decision you're
asking me to make," I said. "I've already
changed my life once by coming here. Why
would I do it again when the end result isn't
a sure thing?"

"Is what you have now a sure thing? This
house? This William? You've only been here
a short time, and you've been married to
Robert for three years. Has your time here
had that much of an effect on you?"

I thought of William moving his hands
expertly across pieces of wood. Wiping the
dust from them before crossing the workshop to push my hair out of my face and
kiss my lips. I thought of the tiny house he
carved for me. Then I thought about Robert's and my house back in Mobile. The
gleaming countertops, the perfectly mani-
cured lawn, the cushioned window seat in
the living room that looked out over our
treelined street full of antebellum homes.

He stood and smoothed the creases out of
his pants. "I think you've already made your
decision. You need to get home to it." He
nodded, then walked down the hallway and
passed through the front door.

217

20
SARA

MAY

Over the next week, renovation work started in earnest, and stress levels in the house increased accordingly. When the team arrived to repair the cracked and water-stained ceiling in the parlors and dining room, Major and Bert were hard at work at the dining table, Bert looking up new recipes and Major balancing his checkbook. Bert hopped up and moved his cookbooks onto the back porch when the men brought out the plastic sheet to cover the dining room table. Major, in keeping with his nature, grumbled.

"This is my home, people. Why does no one understand this but me?"

"We all understand it," I said, trying to soothe his irritation. "I know it's inconvenient, but it won't last forever."

He slapped his checkbook closed and pocketed his calculator. "I don't know what

I'm even going to get out of all this." He trailed behind Bert toward the porch.

"You'll thank me for it later, Major," I called after him. I surprised myself by assuming Major would still be living in the house after renovations were over. In truth, I didn't know what would happen with the house when everything was finished, so I hoped I hadn't lied to him. If I had to ask him, and everyone else, to move out, no one would be thanking me.

On Friday evening of the first full week of work at the house, Crawford picked me up twenty minutes late for our first date. When I answered the door, he held out a creamy white rose as a peace offering.

"I'm sorry," he said. His still-damp brown hair curled around the bottom of his ears. He smelled faintly of cedar and fabric softener. Oddly, a splotch of mango-yellow paint stained the front of his khaki pants. The edges of the paint blurred, like he'd tried to wipe it off but only made it worse.

"Don't laugh. I had to go to a client's house in Daphne before I came this way. The woman said it was an emergency, so I dropped what I was doing, thinking my guys had taken out the wrong wall or something. Turns out, the painter used the wrong color on her dining room wall." He held his hands up. "She was mad."

"Looks like it," I said, biting back a laugh. I ducked inside and found a vase for the rose, then followed Crawford out to his truck. He opened my door for me, then closed it gently once I settled in.

My stomach had been bothering me for much of the day, and as I got dressed after my shower, it hit me that I was nervous. Had I crossed a line by accepting a date from a man I hired to work for me? I'd never done that with any of the contractors or builders I'd worked alongside back in New Orleans — it went against my nature to mix work with my personal life. But something about Crawford made me want to break the rules. As he pulled out of the driveway and onto Highway 55, the quivering nervousness in my stomach settled.

"I'm glad you said yes," he said.

I looked over at him. He'd left his window down a couple inches and the breeze ruffled his hair. I took a deep breath and exhaled. Tension slipped away and in its place was peaceful relaxation mixed with a surprising amount of anticipation.

"Me too."

We drove until we reached the mouth of Sweet Bay where it flowed into Mobile Bay. Turning south, we continued until Crawford pulled down a hidden driveway, much like the one at The Hideaway. At the foot of the drive, a tin-roofed, plank-walled restaurant appeared before us. Crawford pulled into a parking place up front just as a dog nosed its way out of the front porch screen door.

"Don't worry, it's better than it looks," Crawford said.

Inside, the hostess grabbed two menus and wound us through the tight quarters of the dining room and out onto the spacious deck in the back. Settled at our table, I leaned back in my chair. The bay was bathed in the bright pinks and deep purples of the late evening sunset.

"I've missed this," I said.

"Missed what?"

I looked out to the bay. "The water, the sunset, all of it."

"Correct me if I'm wrong, but there is water in New Orleans, right?"

I laughed. "Yes, of course there's water. The Mississippi River swims right through the city, but I spend most of my time at my shop or at home in the Quarter. I can easily go days, or even weeks, without seeing the water at all."

"That's a shame. Seems like a girl born near the water would want to stick close to it."

I smiled. "Sometimes on slow days at the shop, I'll close up for lunch and head for the levee near the park. I just sit and watch the barges go up and down the river."

"That's more like it."

"It sounds strange, but I usually end up closing my eyes and pretending I'm back on the dock at The Hideaway, the sun dancing on the water. No sound except the wind in the trees and the water lapping up against the dock. But then I'll hear a tugboat horn or smell someone's crawfish boil and I'm back in New Orleans."

I'd never told anyone about my Hideaway daydreams — especially not Allyn. He'd work his own brand of psychoanalysis on me, and I had no time for that.

It took me a second to realize Crawford was studying me, smiling.

"What?" I lifted my hand to check my face and hair.

"Nothing. You just look exceptionally relaxed. And beautiful. Like a picture in a magazine."

"Oh, come on now." I looked up at the waiter who appeared at just the right moment, providing distraction from Crawford's compliments.

We placed drink and appetizer orders and sat back to watch the sun dipping toward the horizon. On the other side of the deck, a man with a ponytail and dark sunglasses set up his guitar and a couple of speakers. Around us, couples and small groups filled the tables, as if everyone in Sweet Bay recognized the perfection of this South Alabama evening.

With fried crab claws and cocktail sauce on the table in front of us, we dug into both the food and typical first-date chitchat. Instead of boring, it was comfortable, fun even — a stark contrast to most of the first dates I'd been on with lawyers and businessmen in New Orleans. We talked about our childhoods and professional lives, dream vacations and things we'd do for a million dollars. I told him about Allyn and asked him about his partnership with Charlie.

"I knew Charlie in college. He was always the guy drinking too much at parties and ripping his shirt off at football games. You can see it, can't you?" Crawford said when I laughed. "We ran into each other down here a few years after we graduated. I had a lot of jobs going on at once, and I needed someone to man the office while I was out on-site. I hired him just hoping he wouldn't burn the place down, but he's been great."

He looked down at the table for a second. "He took over for me when I needed to bow out for a little bit. He's a true friend, and I don't take that lightly. He'd have to mess up pretty badly for me to let him go. Even then, I don't think I could do it."

"He must have really saved you."

He nodded but didn't offer any more, so I didn't ask.

"Tell me about your parents," I said. "You said they worked on your house a lot while you were growing up."

He smiled. "They were DIYers in the truest sense of the word. They never wanted to buy anything they could grow, build, or create on their own. It was annoying as a kid and embarrassing as a teenager, but now I appreciate it. They made me want to do things for myself rather than take the easy way out."

"I'm guessing it'd be easier to build something from scratch on an empty piece of property rather than take something crumbling to pieces and try to turn it into a gem."

"Exactly. And there's nothing wrong with building new houses. We do it all the time. But I'd much rather take a house that already has a life and turn it into something beautiful. You encounter all kinds of problems you don't have to deal with when you build new, but I get a lot more satisfaction at the end when I see something solid and real where before there had only been hope."

Just as the waiter asked if we wanted to try dessert, a couple came up to our table. The man put his hand on Crawford's shoulder. Crawford looked up.

"Peter, Janet," he said, standing up. "Good to see both of you."

"You are a lifesaver." Peter shook Crawford's hand. "In fact, it's possible your little redo of our kitchen saved our marriage."

"I wouldn't go that far," Crawford said.

"Oh yes," Peter said. "My wife is wonderful, but even she won't argue that she can be a handful at times."

"It's true," Janet said. "And he's right — our kitchen saved our marriage. Now I can fix my coffee and he can make his green-tofu-whatever smoothies, and we're not bumping into each other the whole time. Crisis averted, thanks to you."

While they caught up, I finished my wine and watched Crawford. He conversed easily with Peter and Janet as he reenacted having to calm their dog down when he arrived at their house early one morning. Peter clapped him on the shoulder and thanked him for not shooting the dog when it burst out of the gate. Crawford laughed.

Back in New Orleans, Mitch was always "on." He was loud and overconfident in front of other people and never wanted to miss an opportunity to impress. Crawford put everyone — even dogs — at ease. Being with him was as easy as the tide going out.

Crawford turned to me and introduced me to his friends. Peter shook my hand while Janet eyed me up and down. "You've done well for yourself, young man," Janet said to Crawford. "She's very pretty."

I swallowed and fumbled for a smile, but Crawford defused my embarrassment.

"She is — and she's also a great client. She told me exactly what she wanted on the redo of her house. She practically did all the work before she even hired me. All I had to do was get the guys in and follow her orders."

Peter laughed. "Sounds like she'd be a good one to keep around." He winked at Crawford.

Crawford laughed and kept his gaze on Peter, but he wrapped his warm hand around mine and squeezed it gently.

"Now if you'll excuse us" — Janet pulled on Peter's arm — "my husband promised his handful of a wife a dance before we leave. Crawford, the next one is yours." She winked at him as they wound through the tables to the open corner of the patio where others had gathered to dance. The man with the guitar had just started a slowed-down version of James Taylor's "Country Road."

"How about it?" Crawford held out his hand. He was confident in his own way, easy in his khakis and untucked button-down. I put my hand in his, and we found an open space away from the others. He put his other hand on my back and we began to move. The couples dancing, the waiters and tables, even the music all receded. It was only Crawford and me, the water behind us, and the sky, now dark except for a faint orange glow just over the horizon.

21
MAGS

MAY 1960

I didn't say anything to William that day about Daddy showing up. He knew me well enough to know something was wrong, but thankfully, he didn't press. The next day, I couldn't keep it from him any longer. I didn't like deceiving him, especially when it had the potential to destroy all the plans we'd made, however casual they may have been.

"William?" I sat in his workshop with him as he brushed long strokes of stain onto the armoire for Mr. Grimmerson. The earthy scent of newly cut boards tempered the sharp tang of turpentine in the air.

"Hmm?" He was concentrating on his work — eyebrows furrowed, brush moving evenly up and down the wood.

"I need to talk to you about something."

His hands went still, then he grabbed a ragged bandanna he used as a hand towel and wiped the stain off his fingers. He knelt on the floor in front of me where I sat. "Don't say it. I don't want to hear the words."

I couldn't move. I couldn't have spoken if he'd asked me to.

"Let's just discuss it later, okay?" He kissed me on the lips, then stood and went back to his work.

He didn't show up for dinner that night or later when everyone gathered for a game of backgammon in the living room. I kept an eye on the door all night, not wanting to miss his entrance, but he never showed up.

I awoke at some dark hour of the night to William slipping into my bed and tucking his arms around me. I repositioned, fitting my body snugly against his. He touched my hair, smoothed it, tucked it behind my ear. He raised up on one elbow and traced the side of my face with a finger, then my neck, then my collarbone. He leaned down, kissed me on the cheek, and lay back down behind me. A breeze kicked up the curtain at the window, and a touch of fresh air caressed my face.

The next morning, he was gone. In his place on the bed next to me was an envelope with a note inside.

My dearest Maggie. I'm leaving now to save you the discomfort of having to explain yourself to me. Or maybe it's to keep from hearing you say the words. But you are a good woman and this is the right choice for now. I'm not worried — I know our time will come. When it does, I hope you'll wear this proudly on your finger. For then, you will be mine and I will be yours. We'll spend our years in the cove, just as we planned.

Love,
William

Next to the note was a small blue box. I cracked it open. Inside was a perfect ring. A small, solitary, sparkling diamond on a simple gold band. I thought of the ring Robert had given me when he proposed: six diamonds clustered busily together on a gold filigree band. The comparison between the two, and the obvious perfection of the one that came from the man who understood the real me, would have been laughable had the moment not been so heartbreaking.

I threw the covers off and raced downstairs, still in my pajamas. Voices in the kitchen grew quiet as I hurried down the hall in my bare feet and slammed open the screen door on the porch. I crossed the grass to his workshop and found what I already suspected. All the wood was gone, all the tools. The only thing left in the room was an empty sandpaper box.

Back in the house, I bumped into Daisy. She'd been watching me from the back porch.

"I was up early this morning," she said. "He was packing his truck before the sun came up. I didn't ask where he was going. I assumed you'd know."

I shook my head and turned toward the stairs. Back in my room, I crawled under the covers, my feet still wet from the grass. I laid my head on his pillow with his note clutched in my hands, trying to detect any of his scent. I stayed there the rest of the day.

22
SARA

JUNE

Crawford stopped by frequently after that first date, adding a sense of humor and order to the blur of paint fumes, trash bags, and plastic sheeting in the house. One afternoon, he showed up with the plumber to check on the sewer line in the backyard. When he parked his truck in the driveway, I was on the front porch in a rocking chair going through some of Mags's mail, trying to decide what was junk and what was important.

"Do you have big plans for the morning?" Crawford asked, climbing the porch steps. When he got to the top, he walked over and squeezed my knee.

"Just deciding whether to go on a Caribbean Disney cruise or order this turbocharged commercial-grade juicer." I held up two brochures from the stack of mail on my lap.

He laughed. "Mickey Mouse or spinach juice. That's a tough call. Think I could pull you away from all this for a bit?"

"I think I could be convinced."

"I need to go over a couple of things inside, but my next appointment isn't until three. I could show you what I've been working on in my shop. If you're still interested."

"I'd love to."

"Great," he said, exhaling.

While he finished up in the house, I retreated to the blue room to find something to wear. When I'd left New Orleans two months before, I planned to spend a week in Sweet Bay and as such had packed mostly business casual clothes, appropriate for the funeral and meeting with the lawyer. I'd spent the last few weeks in running shorts and old fraternity T-shirts I'd found in the closet in my bedroom — not ideal attire for spending the day with someone I found increasingly charming.

I miraculously unearthed a clean pair of black capris and paired them with a thin sleeveless top. My only options for shoes were dressy sandals or heels. I opted for the black wedge flip-flops I found in the bottom of my closet. I twisted my curls up in a clip to ward off the humidity and hoped for the best.

Downstairs, Crawford was just finishing up. When I got to the bottom of the stairs, he looked up from the clipboard he and the electrician were poring over. He smiled and held up one finger. I nodded and slipped out to the front porch. He came out a few minutes later and gave a low whistle. "Quite a change from a few minutes ago."

"What? With the house?"

He laughed. "No, you. You look great. Way too nice for a ride in my work truck."

"Don't worry. I've seen worse."

He escorted me to the truck and opened my door. "After you."

"My workshop's not much," he said on the way. "It's really a glorified garage. And not that glorified, actually. But it gives me the space I need to work off some energy."

"When I started refinishing furniture, I did it on the sidewalk in front of my apartment with a stack of old newspapers and a can of spray paint."

"I bet your work space is a little more upscale now though."

"Well, I don't work on the sidewalk anymore, but it's still not fancy. I have a small space at the back of my shop, but I still pull pieces out into the courtyard sometimes when I need more room to work."

"I'd love to see your shop sometime," he said. "And have a guided tour of New Orleans."

He pulled off the highway at the sign for Coastal Contractors. The driveway was empty, and inside, the office was quiet. In the small kitchen area, Crawford pulled a small bone from a box under the sink. "For Popcorn."

Opening the back door, he whistled a quick tune and the same black fur and wet tongue flew at us from the left. Crawford got down on a knee and scratched under the dog's chin, then tossed the bone out into the yard. Popcorn leaped on it, wagging her tail. By the time we descended the creaky stairs leading down to the yard, Popcorn had settled in the grass, happily gnawing away. I leaned down and smoothed my hand down her soft head.

"Not much for dogs, right?" Crawford asked.

"They're fine as long as they're not directing their wet mouth at me." I massaged Popcorn's ears and snout, her fur soft as velvet. I stood and Crawford gestured to his shed. We crossed the small yard, and he pulled the door open for me.

Inside, the still air was laced with the scent

of turpentine and fresh wood. "This smell is so familiar. When I was younger, there was an old shed off to the side of The Hideaway. It always smelled like this."

I walked to the other side of the workshop, trailing my fingers across the top of his worktable. A couple of old doors were propped up along one wall and various electric saws and routers lined another. A bookshelf in the corner held how-to books mixed with well-worn paperbacks. He reached over and pulled a window open, allowing salt-scented air to trickle in.

He pointed out some of his unfinished work, then took me out to the dock and showed me the boathouse he was building for Charlie. The morning had been overcast, but the clouds were just beginning to part, letting bright sunshine peek through the haze. It was quiet on the dock, no sounds but the water lapping at the pilings and a sailboat at a neighboring dock creaking on its lines.

When his cell rang, it cut through the quiet and startled us both. He checked the screen and groaned. "I'm sorry, I've got to take this. I'll be quick."

I nodded and walked to the end of the dock where a hammock was strung up under a covered section. I kicked my shoes off and leaned back onto the thick strings, listening to Crawford's side of the conversation — something about not being able to move a garage to the other side of a house once it was already framed out. Before long, the gentle movement of the water against the pilings and the call of the gulls overhead lulled me.

I hadn't been able to stop thinking about the box in the attic and its treasures. Not to mention the key engraved on Mags's headstone and everywhere else. They remained at the edges of my mind, and I pondered the mysteries in every idle moment.

I was sure Dot knew something about the postcard from Mags's mother, but it was clear she hadn't wanted to say anything in front of Glory.

What choice had Mags made that so pleased her mother? And could it have anything to do with the words on the headstone?

It seemed the longer I stayed in Sweet Bay — and the more I uncovered of Mags's life before she came to The Hideaway — the more confused I was.

Soon I heard Crawford's footsteps approaching. "I'm so sorry. This client calls me every time she opens another issue of *Southern Living*. If she doesn't stop changing her mind, her house is going to be a mash-up of every house they've featured in the last year."

"Don't worry about it. This hammock was about to put me to sleep."

"Yeah, it'll do that to you. You look pretty relaxed."

I repositioned myself so I was sitting up, cradled by the strings under me, and he sat down on the bench opposite the hammock. He slung an arm up over the back of the bench and looked out at the water. "Coming from my landlocked hometown, I still get a kick out of living here. I don't think I'll ever be able to live anywhere I can't see the bay from my back door."

I breathed in. "It is special. I'm glad to be back, for however long I'm here." I surprised myself, but it was true. I was very glad to be right where I was.

We were both quiet a moment before he spoke.

"Tell me more about your grandmother. What was she like?"

I smiled. "She was a character. She was her own woman and didn't care a thing about what other people thought of her."

"That must be one of the perks of getting old. Just not caring what people think."

"I guess so." I laughed. "Mags had the

craziest collection of clothes — things like huge embroidered caftans and floppy hats embellished with flowers she'd picked up at the craft store. But she also had this gorgeous, long mink coat. I never knew where she got it, but it always seemed a little magical to me, like it came from another era. As you know, it rarely gets cold enough in Sweet Bay to actually need something like that, so she'd wear it as a bathrobe instead."

"She sounds like someone I'd liked to have met," Crawford said.

I nodded. "People who knew her well — her friends, folks in town — really thought a lot of her, but back when I was young, I just saw her as my strange little grandmother. There was this one . . . incident — it probably won't sound like much, but at seventeen, it felt like the end of my world."

"What happened?" Crawford leaned forward, resting his elbows on his knees.

"I was at a party the summer after I graduated from high school. It was in an empty barn on this guy's family property outside Sweet Bay. I'd missed my curfew by a mile, but I wasn't driving and I didn't want to ask someone to drive me home. It must have been one or two o'clock in the morning, tailgates down, music blaring from every truck, a huge bonfire. I was talking to this guy I'd had a crush on for all of high school when here comes Major's rusty orange van rumbling down the driveway."

"No way," Crawford said.

"It gets better. The van stopped before it got to the barn, but then it pulled right up next to where I was sitting. Mags hopped out of the van and walked over to me. I remember being so glad she'd skipped her bird's-nest hat and boots, but the four gray heads peering out the windows of the van was spectacle enough."

Crawford buried his face in his hands. "Stop," he said, laughing. "That's terrible."

"If you've never been the one whose grandmother and her friends shut down your party, it's a special feeling."

"I can only imagine." His laughter died down. "So, were you and Mags close? Or did you just bide your time until you could move out?"

"We weren't on bad terms by any means. She was my grandmother, and I loved her. But . . . it was complicated. It was hard to be really close to someone who seemed to try to be as eccentric as possible. I just didn't understand her."

"Is that why you left?"

I stood and walked to the edge of the dock. Out in the distance, a dolphin fin

240

sliced through the calm water. "It was a lot of things. My parents' accident, then living with Mags and her friends. The barn party was just the last straw. Plus, I knew if I did stay in Sweet Bay, the only designing I'd be doing would be helping Staci at Tips and Tans decide the best layout for her tanning beds and foot baths, or maybe decorating the principal's new office at Baldwin County High if I was lucky. I wanted to design houses and beautiful spaces, and I didn't feel I could do that in Sweet Bay where everyone saw me as just Mags's granddaughter.

"After college, I moved on to New Orleans and started working two jobs to save money to open my own shop. I came back often at first — at least every couple of months. But as I got busier, the amount of time between visits got longer. Once I opened Bits and Pieces, all my time went into the shop. I always came back around the holidays, and maybe once in the summer, but that's all I've been able to manage. But you have a business — you know how busy it is. How often do you get up to Tennessee to visit?"

He shrugged and gave a half smile. "Honestly? As often as I can. It's a long drive but my mom's alone, and I don't like to go too long without checking on her."

I looked out at the water and sighed.

"I'm sorry," he said. "That's probably not what you wanted to hear."

"No, there's no reason for you to hide that. You're a good son, and you take care of your mom. I should have done the same thing with Mags. It hurts to think . . ." I turned my head when my eyes started to fill.

He stood and crossed the wood planks toward me. When he put his hand on my shoulder, I leaned into him, and he wrapped his arms around me.

After that day, Crawford always came bearing gifts, climbing the front porch steps with a half grin on his face. He'd offer up a box of cinnamon rolls from the diner or a bag of cleaning supplies once I started tackling the years of grime on the porches and dock. Dot and the others loved it. Whenever he'd stop by, especially if it was after work hours, they'd make a big show of leaving the room. "We'll give you two some privacy," they'd say, tripping over each other to get out of the way.

One night when Crawford had a late meeting in Mobile, Bert requested we all gather around the coffee table after dinner for a game of Monopoly.

"You only like that game because you cheat," Major said as Bert set up the board and divvied up the silver game pieces.

"I don't cheat," Bert said, aghast. "Is it even possible to cheat at Monopoly?"

"If there's a way, you'll find it, I'm sure."

"Major," Glory said. "That's enough. No one cheats. You're just not very good. But that doesn't mean you can't close your mouth and indulge the rest of us."

We were an hour into the game when a car pulled up out front. Dot lifted a corner of the window curtain and peered into the dark night. "It's a truck. Let's see, it's black . . . the door is opening now. It looks like a man . . ."

"Thanks for the play by play," I said, hiding a smile. "I think it's Crawford."

"Oh heavens. My hair's a mess." Glory shot like a dart toward the stairs.

"Wait, Glory, you don't have to go," I said. "Crawford probably won't even notice your hair."

"Well, why not?" she asked from the bottom stair. "It's a new color and I think it's quite lovely." Dot joined her on the stairs.

I opened the door so Crawford could see their frantic exits.

"Where's everyone going?" he asked.

"I have no idea."

"We're old and in the way," Bert said. "You two don't need us cluttering up your evening." He stood from his place on the couch next to Major. "Come on, Major."

Major didn't budge. "I don't see why I have to get up and ruin a perfectly good lead in Monopoly just because this young fella decides to show up."

"Don't quit on my account," Crawford said. "I'll just join in."

Major narrowed his eyes.

"Or sit and watch," Crawford said.

"Don't you worry a thing about it," Bert said. "We'll continue our game another time. Major, you're coming with me." Bert bumped Major's outstretched legs with his knee, urging him to get a move on.

Major grumbled and stood. "All right, all right, I'll go, but I don't like it."

We watched helplessly from the front door until the room was empty and quiet. Crawford started laughing, then I did too, relieved that everyone's swift escape hadn't rendered the evening too awkward.

"What do you say?" He gestured to the game still spread out on the coffee table. "I've been known to win a game of Monopoly."

"You're on."

He settled down on one side of the table

and waited for me.

Getting involved with a man in Sweet Bay was the last thing on my mind when I left New Orleans. In fact, I was almost embarrassed at the thought of telling Allyn about Crawford — not because anything about him was even remotely embarrassing, but because I'd been so focused on doing what needed to be done in Sweet Bay, then getting back to New Orleans.

Now not only had I met someone, but I actually craved his company. More than that, I missed him every time he closed the door and walked away from me.

"Well?" He patted the floor next to him.

We picked up the game where the rest of us had left off. Crawford took over Major's spot in the lead. Amid conversation, walking through the house to look at odd mementos and souvenirs, and occasional game playing, I beat him by five thousand dollars and three hotels.

23
MAGS

MAY 1960

I let Robert move into The Hideaway.
Maybe it was the shock of William leaving. I
actually preferred to think that was it and
not that I was still able to be swayed by my
parents' wishes for my life. Whatever it was,
I agreed to my father's plan to keep us
together — although I knew it would only
be an illusion. I did put my foot down at
the idea of returning to our home in Mobile.
It was out of the question. If they wanted
us to have the look of a happy marriage, he
had to come here, because I wasn't leaving.

The day he moved in, I sat him down in
the living room when everyone else was out.

"Margaret —"

"It's Mags." I hadn't planned that, but it
worked. I was no longer Margaret, but I also
couldn't bear to hear William's nickname
for me coming from Robert's mouth. I
shortened it to the least proper thing I could

come up with on the spot.

"Mags?" He laughed, then went silent when he saw my face.

"Don't speak. If you're going to live here, we will have rules."

He nodded and waited, a grin still struggling to escape his lips.

"First, you are never to mention Anna-Belle's name. Or any other woman you may have . . . met . . . since we married. I won't have the guests in this house thinking I am a ridiculous woman for taking you in. They know nothing about you or where you've been. They'll believe me when I tell them you've been away on business. Because that is where you've been, right?"

He rubbed a hand over his face. "Marg—"

I held a hand up.

"Two, you are not to ask any questions about how I've spent my time since I've been gone. Not a word of it. It is mine and mine alone. Three, you'll have your own bedroom and I'll have mine."

"Wait a minute, you mean to say I'm sleeping alone every night? When my wife is in the same house?"

"I'm your wife in name only. I know how this works — it benefits both our families for this marriage to work out. Or at least look that way. I'll hold up my end of the bargain, but don't expect me to forget everything that's happened. And not just AnnaBelle. All of them. For all three years."

He drummed his fingers on the armrest.

Suddenly exhausted, I sat in the chair behind me. I sighed and rubbed my temples with my fingers. "Also, I'm pregnant," I said with my eyes closed. "If this is a problem, you can go ahead and leave."

I'd known for a few weeks — ever since I vomited in the kitchen sink one morning not long after William left. I'd just reached for my usual cup of coffee, but the smell left me reeling and retching into the sink.

Starla's eyes had widened as she handed me a dish towel. "Gary had it last week." She backed away from me. "I can't get sick — I have yoga to teach. Sorry. Let me know if you need anything." She hurried for the door of the kitchen.

"I don't think —" I began.

"Oh, you have the bug, all right. Either that, or you're pregnant."

I was carrying William's child. It was both perfect and absurd. Laughable and heart-breaking.

Robert fired back at me. "So you skewer me for my indiscretions when —"

I shook my head. "You have the option to leave. Believe me, the door is wide open."

He stared at me, his jaw clenching. "Okay, I won't ask. You're right — I have no right to do that. You're my wife. I'll help take care of you while you're . . . sick . . . unwell. Whatever happens when you're carrying a baby."

I smiled in spite of myself. "You don't have the first clue what to do around a pregnant woman."

"I've taken care of wounded soldiers on the battlefield with bullets whizzing two feet past my head. I think I can handle a vomiting housewife."

"We'll see about that. And just so we're clear, you are the convalescing housewife in this situation. I have a house to run."

Robert was true to his word over the next nine months. For the first time, he did exactly what I asked him to do. He brought me saltines and ginger ale when I needed them, answered the telephone when I couldn't get to it fast enough, and mopped the floors to a shine. He learned to peel shrimp when the sight and smell of the slippery little things sent me running to the toilet. He grew handy with a vacuum and even got the motorboat up and running again.

Dot and Bert checked into The Hideaway

when I was a few weeks away from giving birth. They had no reason to think the baby's father was anyone but Robert. That is, until the night Dot found me in the garden. I'd been going out there most evenings. Sitting on William's bench made me feel closer to him — thinking of his hands on the wood and on me, smoothing us and turning us both into something sturdy and beautiful. The fact that I was about to have his baby without him in my life made me feel like I was carrying much more than an extra thirty pounds.

In the garden, with the dark covering me like a cloak, I let myself cry. Since William's departure, I'd been able to hold back the threatening tears, resolutely going about the business of keeping the house in order and finding new ways for guests to pay for their stay. This time, with no one around to watch, I stopped holding back.

I didn't know how long Dot had been standing there, but by the time I looked up, I knew my face was a wreck. She sat beside me, took my hand, and rubbed circles onto my palm with her thumb. The gesture — and the lack of questions — not only calmed me, it solidified our friendship. I knew I could trust her.

She sat with me as my tears came and

went. When I was done, spent from the energy of letting out all my closed-up emotions, she handed me a tissue.

"I could have used this about an hour ago," I said, wiping my damp face and hands.

She laughed.

"You're not going to ask what that was all about?"

She shook her head. "Don't need to. That baby isn't your husband's, is it?"

My mouth dropped open, but I quickly closed it, then shook my head. "How'd you know?"

"Just a hunch. You and Robert don't seem exactly friendly toward each other. Is the father here?"

"He left. But I think it was partly my fault."

"You're pregnant, he left, and you think it's your fault?"

I sighed. "I — my father came and . . ." I didn't even know how to explain. "Anyway, he didn't know I was pregnant. I didn't know it then either."

"I see."

But I knew she didn't. She couldn't have. It sounded like any other misdirected love story — two people in love, someone gets hurt, and one leaves, never to be seen again.

Love stories end like that every day, but ours was different.

"It's just temporary. He's coming back." I willed my voice to sound sure, but to me, it just sounded tired.

"What about Robert?"

I shrugged. Was it wrong to wish for him just to disappear? He'd done it before — with AnnaBelle and others before her — maybe he'd do it again.

"What are you going to do?" Dot asked.

"I guess I'm going to keep waiting."

I still loved William, and he had to love me too. What we'd started here hadn't been a dream, that much I knew. We would be together again. Those truths were the only things that kept me going and allowed me to go through the motions of my life.

One day, I told myself again and again, *he'll come back.*

24
MAGS

OCTOBER 1960–OCTOBER 1962

As my body grew larger to accommodate William's baby, my heart grew as well. I cried over everything. Everyone attributed my weepiness and mood swings to the pregnancy. Only Dot and I knew the real reason for my tears. I assumed she told Bert what was going on, although he never let on that he knew. Bert was a loyal friend and a wonderful partner to Dot, but "women problems" weren't high on his list of topics to discuss.

My water broke early one foggy morning as I stomped around in the vegetable garden, trying to remember where I had planted the carrots. All the little rows of upturned earth looked the same. For some reason, it became important that I knew exactly where they would grow that fall. Okay, perhaps I was also letting off a little steam — mild contractions had rolled through my body all night, and anger was hot on their heels. I was furious with Robert for being in the house, with William for not, with my parents for conspiring to keep me from the man and the life I so desperately wanted. To be honest, I was mad at myself too. After all this time, I still couldn't stand up to Mother and Daddy.

At the hospital, Dot waited in the room with me while Robert stood with a handful of other husbands in the waiting room. He was likely the only man in the room about to greet a child who wasn't his.

Everyone assumed Robert was the father of the baby struggling to free itself from my body. A nurse by the name of Yolanda was the only one who found out the truth. Dot had left the room between contractions to find me some ice chips, leaving me alone with Yolanda.

In a burst of pain, I cursed Robert with all the strength I had in me.

Yolanda murmured and patted my hand. "Baby, I know it hurts, but you can't lay all that blame at your husband's feet. Sure, he put that baby in there, but this little one will make it all worth it. You'll be kissing Robert's face in no time."

"Robert may be my husband, but he did not put this baby in me," I spat out between clenched teeth. Finally, the contraction released its grip on me and I exhaled. "I should be raising this baby with William in our little house in the cove." I turned my head toward her. "But we're not, are we?"

Lord have mercy, Yolanda had no idea what hit her.

"That man out there didn't father this baby?" Yolanda's eyes grew wide.

I shook my head and wiped sweat off my face, waiting for the next contraction.

"Where's the baby's daddy?"

"I don't know." I didn't have the energy to explain.

Jenny was a sweet, beautiful baby, and I took easily to mothering. Perhaps it was because so many people had warned me of colic, diaper rash, and every other potential pitfall of a new mother's life. Jenny had none of that — she offered only gummy smiles, infectious laughter, and plump cheeks and fingers.

It was hard at first — having Robert around without William — but there were good times too. We had a picnic in the backyard for Jenny's second birthday. It was a sparkling fall day, brisk and sunny. Starla and I set up the long picnic table next to the house, and we scattered various toddler toys on the grass for Jenny to play with. The adults sipped apple cider and laughed at Jenny's antics with a two-foot-tall plastic Mickey Mouse. Bert found it on the side of the road "in perfect condition," he said. Dot disagreed, but Jenny loved her new Mickey.

After gifts and cake, everyone went back inside except the three of us. I sat at the wrought-iron table — one of Mrs. DeBerry's leftovers — to rest my feet in the shade while Robert picked up wrapping paper and empty cups. Jenny sat in the grass and dumped blocks from one box into another. When Robert finished cleaning, he picked Jenny up in the air and swung her around and around.

She squealed and laughed, her voice carrying through the quiet air. As soon as he put her down, she ran to me and threw her arms around my neck with the force of a tiny hurricane. I hugged her little body, and she ran happily back to her blocks.

Robert sat beside me and said, "What a great day. Jenny's happy, you seem to be happy — at least you have a smile on your face. I'm happy as a lark. See, we can make this work."

I looked over at Jenny. With her blonde hair and small round nose, she looked so much like William. I closed my eyes and pretended he was there.

25
Mags

I reread William's letter trying to find
something I'd missed. He said he'd come
back for me, but I didn't know how to reach
him to tell him I was ready. Lord, I'd been
ready since the day Robert arrived, since I
discovered just how wrong it felt to share a
house with a man I didn't love, regardless
of any sense of duty or obligation. But life
didn't slow down for my wounded heart,
and our big, strange family at The Hideaway
— cobbled together by circumstances, ac-
cidents, and varying degrees of luck —
charged ahead.

Robert needed care, as Daddy had said,
but not all the time. I didn't know exactly
what was wrong with him, but he'd have
these nightmares. I never knew when they
would strike. He'd wake up screaming,
sweating, and rolling in his bed, but I was
never able to calm him down. It'd take a

while before he was fully awake enough to hear me telling him it was just a dream. When the nightmares came, he usually spent the next day in bed. He wouldn't eat, wouldn't shower, and definitely wouldn't talk about it.

The following day, he'd hop out of bed as if nothing out of the ordinary had happened. If I asked about it, he'd respond with "What do you mean?" or "I just didn't feel well. No big deal." Bert, who'd fought in France, said it was common to most soldiers who'd seen time in battle.

The episodes were scary but infrequent, and I soon realized Daddy had exaggerated Robert's sickness. Sure, it helped to have someone around to look after him when the nightmares came, but he was far from death's door. When I mentioned to Robert what Daddy had said about the severity of his illness, he laughed.

"He did what was necessary to make sure you stuck around. I can't say I blame him. If Jenny ever ran off with some kid who wouldn't amount to anything, I'd do whatever it took to set her on the right path too."

It was the first time Robert had referred to William. A kid who wouldn't amount to anything? I stood up so fast the chair behind me fell back with a clatter, and I left the room.

Around the others Robert and I were mostly amicable, but I was simmering on the inside. I resented the way Daddy had manipulated me into taking Robert back, and I resented Robert's presence in my life when I thought I was done with him for good. All this had pulled me from William, so I fought back in whatever ways I could.

The house had never been perfect — not even when Mrs. DeBerry was in charge — but now I saw the imperfections as badges of honor instead of problems to fix. I was done with trying to make everything look flawless just for the sake of appearances. The house was warm and comfortable, if not magazine-ready, but no one living there really cared about that anyway. I loved that the place was a little off-kilter, and the quirkiness only solidified its charm.

I hoped the same was true for me when I spied a bird's-nest hat in the front window of Irene's Dress Barn on Main Street while shopping with Dot. I bought it and it became my favorite accessory.

My new eccentricities bothered Robert, especially since I'd been neat and organized before, but he knew better than to speak of me or the house like he owned either of us. He wisely took it as a trade for me allowing him to live in the house. This allowed him to keep up appearances to his friends, who thought it terribly romantic that he and his wife ran a bed-and-breakfast in Sweet Bay. He never bothered to give them the correct facts, and for some reason, I let him keep that bit of his pride intact. Anyway, I didn't care what his friends thought of him, or us.

26
SARA

JUNE

I was taking framed photos and prints off the walls and stacking them in a back bedroom for safekeeping when Allyn called. I'd been meaning to call him for days, but something — or someone — interrupted me every time I sat down to do it.

"I see how it is," he said when I picked up the phone. "You get back to your roots and forget all about me."

"That's not it, and you know it."

I was out of breath from carrying too large a load with the phone sandwiched between my shoulder and my ear, so I paused and sat on an ancient couch. This one had escaped a fatal trip to Goodwill because of its clean lines and still-firm cushions.

"So what's going on?" he asked as I stretched my sore neck muscles. "Are you becoming a permanent Sweet Bay-ite?"

I laughed. "That's not how you say it."

"Well, what is it then?"

"I don't know, but it doesn't matter. I'm not becoming a permanent Sweet Bay anything. It's just a big job and it's taking a while. You were the one who said I needed to relax and dive in."

"I know, and I'm glad you are. Things are just fine here, thanks for asking."

I smiled. "Tell me — how are things going with you and the shop?"

"Everything is still in one piece, if that's what you mean."

"It's not."

"I know, I'm just kidding. Everything is good. We had a busy weekend — oh, we sold the grandfather clock."

"Really? I wasn't sure that thing would ever find a home."

"Whatever. You find perfect homes for even the strangest little trinkets. Anyway, a man came in Saturday looking for something for his study. I showed him the clock and told him it would make him look professorial."

"Professorial?" I asked.

"I don't know where it came from, but apparently it was the right thing to say. He took it home that afternoon."

I laughed. Allyn could sell the shirt off

someone's back and make him glad to see it go.

"Now tell me what's going on with you," he said. "I know something's up. The last time we talked, you drilled me with questions about every item in the shop, and now you've hardly asked a thing. Spill it."

"It's funny you should ask. I've . . . well, I've sort of met someone." I held my breath, waiting for his reaction.

"I knew it!"

"You — what?"

"I just had a feeling you'd get down there and meet someone. You're away from your rigid schedule and routines, you have time on your hands — it's the perfect situation. And it's the only reason I can think of that would make you loosen up and actually trust me with your shop. Now you just have to convince him to come back to New Orleans with you."

"Hold on, we're not that far along. We've only been out a few times."

"I'm glad for you," he said. "You need something like this. What's his name?"

"Crawford."

"Hmm. Sounds sexy."

"I'd hit you if you were sitting here next to me."

"I know. That's why I said it — because

264

I'm over here and you can't do one thing about it."

The bell on the doorknob in Bits and Pieces jangled in the background.

"I need to run. Gotta go make some money for my absent boss."

"You sure do," I said, ignoring the drop in my stomach at the thought of life at Bits and Pieces carrying on without me. "Thanks for calling. I'm glad to hear your voice."

"Have fun with Crawford. Call me soon and give me more details. Or better yet, maybe I'll pop over there for a visit soon."

We hung up and I stared at the dark screen before dropping the phone on the couch. I tried to keep my mind from drifting to all I was missing at the shop as I scanned the wall across from me. Several small prints still hung on the wall along with a huge map framed in wood trim with no glass. I stood and walked over to take them down and place them with the others, but the map was too big for me to carry. Closer up, I could see it showed the Eastern Shore of Mobile Bay from Fort Morgan all the way up to the Tensaw River Delta. I scanned the shoreline, taking in the familiar towns, rivers, and bays. My eye stopped at a tiny hole pricked into the map, just south of Sweet Bay. Probably from a thumbtack.

But something else was there. A small hand-drawn arrow pointed at the little hole. I quickly scanned the rest of the map for other holes or marks, but it was clear.

The map showed no specific town or park at the marked spot, just a stretch of green along the shore where Sweet Bay met Mobile Bay. I tried to visualize that area but came up blank. The restaurant where Crawford had taken me on our first date was near there — we must have passed right by that point, but nothing stuck out in my mind as particularly noteworthy.

But it must have been important to someone.

It could be nothing — just a piece of real estate someone was interested in at one time or maybe a prime fishing location.

I chewed on the end of a fingernail and stared at the map.

Since finding the box in the attic and learning about Mags's previous life of privilege, I was curious about her in a way I had never been before. It seemed like everything I found in the house was part of the mystery of Mags. I'd always taken for granted that she was exactly who she appeared to be and nothing more, but I was beginning to see there had been much more to her beneath the surface.

I headed toward the kitchen to find someone who might be able to help. Dot and
Glory were out for the afternoon, but I
thought Bert or Major might be around
somewhere. A quick trip through the first
floor and a call up the stairs from the landing proved me wrong. The only other person
in the house was a man kneeling on the
floor in the upstairs hallway, patching a spot
on the wall with Spackle and singing along
with the radio.

Then the front door opened and Crawford
breezed in, a binder of paint chips under
his arm and his cell pressed to his ear. I
hadn't realized how dusty and quiet the air
in the house was until the open door ush-
ered in a wave of fresh air tinged with the
smell of new blossoms and freshly cut wood.

I stopped where I was on the bottom step
and smiled. He finished his phone call and
looked up at me, returning my smile.

"You look happy," he said.

"It's a good day." I motioned for him to
follow me, then showed him into the room
where I'd found the map. "What do you
make of this?"

He stepped closer and squinted. "It's a
map of Mobile Bay and Baldwin County.
Why?"

"No, not the map itself. Look at this little

hole." I pointed to the spot marked by the arrow. "What do you think that is?"

"Hmm. Sure looks like someone wanted to remember this place." He scratched at the faint stubble on his chin. "I think I may know where this is. I could take you there sometime if you want."

I looked at my wrist, but I hadn't worn my watch in weeks. "You couldn't — you don't have time to take a drive now, do you?"

"With you? Absolutely. Let me just drop this stuff off in the kitchen."

A few minutes later, I walked with him toward his truck, then stopped. "Wait, don't we need to bring the map? I may be able to get it out of the frame."

He chuckled. "Don't worry about the map. I can find my way there."

All I knew was the spot was just south of where the two bays met, but Crawford seemed to know exactly where to go.

"I know most of the landowners around the mouth of Sweet Bay, but I've always wondered about this one stretch of empty land. It's not marked from the road, just a long, twisting driveway like all the others." He peered through the trees on either side of the road as we drove.

He'd taken my hand as we pulled away from the house, and it was still wrapped in his. His hand was sturdy and warm, and I liked the sensation that our hands fit together like two paired objects that had found their way back together again.

"It's hard to believe there's still undeveloped land around here," he said. "Most people wouldn't dream of letting a coveted piece of property by the bay sit empty, you know?" He slowed as he approached a dirt road leading toward the water. "I think this is it."

We went around one bend, then another. Finally, the tree-covered dirt path, just wide enough to accommodate Crawford's truck, opened up into an inlet of some sort, protected on three sides by craggy old oak trees. Spanish moss draped across low-hanging limbs.

The place was more than undeveloped — nothing marred the mix of sand and grass except a pair of seagulls picking through a clump of wet seagrass next to the shoreline. The sun shone overhead and reflected off the water, a brilliant prism. I pulled my sunglasses down from the top of my head.

Crawford parked the truck along the path and we stepped out into the soft sand. I tossed my sandals on the floorboard before

I closed the door.

"I can't believe no one has built here," he said as we picked our way through the prickly grass and then sand to the water's edge. "It's gorgeous. I don't know anywhere else around here that's so private and tucked away like this. The owners probably field offers left and right from people wanting to buy."

"If they haven't wanted to build, I wonder why they haven't given in and sold it. They'd make a fortune."

"Who knows? Maybe some things are still more important than money." He turned and walked back toward his truck. "Maybe they're hanging on to it for a reason," he called over his shoulder.

He opened the passenger side door and pulled out a drop cloth from behind the seat. Back on the sand, he spread it out next to me as a makeshift blanket.

"So what's the deal with the map?" he asked. "Was this the first time you'd seen it?"

I shook my head. "I vaguely remember seeing it on the wall when I lived at the house, but I never paid much attention. I was taking pictures down earlier today when I noticed the little hole and the arrow."

"If this is the right place, it makes sense

someone would want to remember it. It could be a great private retreat. And it's off the main roads — you have to know where you're going to get here."

I ran my fingers through the sand next to me. If this even was the right place, had Mags been the one to mark the location on the map? So many other people had come through The Hideaway's doors over the years, that map could have belonged to anyone. But the place where it hung — centered on the wall and directly across the room from the couch — made me think she put it there so she could keep an eye on it, like a tiny speck on a map could get up and walk out of her life.

As if reading my mind, Crawford asked, "Do you think this has anything to do with your grandmother?"

I inhaled and blew the air out slowly. Maybe I was reminiscing about things so long forgotten they didn't even matter anymore. Mags was gone, and whoever else knew anything about this stretch along the bay was probably long gone too.

"I don't know. I'm wondering if this place played a role in her life before I was born. Maybe even before my mom was born. I feel like I'm trying to put a puzzle together without all the pieces."

"Isn't that always the case? Especially with grandparents," he said.

"Maybe so."

"We tend to know a lot about our parents' lives, but our grandparents? The big events of their lives happened long before we were born. By the time we're old enough to be curious about what made them who they are, they're old and forgetful. Or not even around anymore."

"Sounds like you're speaking from experience."

"My grandfather died when I was ten. I was sad when he died, but the sadness passed, as everything does when you're that young. It wasn't until much later, after college even, that I began to wonder more about his early life. But by then, I'd long missed any chance to ask questions."

"That sounds about right." I thought of the ring and jumbled note from the mystery William. One part of it stuck out to me more than the rest — something about a choice. And that it was the right one. It was similar to the postcard from Mags's mother, which I still knew nothing about. I wanted to know what the stakes had been. What effect did this choice have on Mags's life? Her mother and William were of the opinion that it was the right choice. Did Mags think so?

And why couldn't I have found these bits of information while Mags was still alive? But I knew the answer. Everything I needed to know — including Mags — had been right in front of me my whole life. I just never chose to look.

"I think Mags may have dealt with a lot more in her life than I ever gave her credit for. I always knew she was self-sufficient and determined, but I never gave much thought to what made her that way. The kicker is I had almost thirty years to ask questions, and now, like you said, I've missed my chance."

"Maybe just the fact that you're here matters, that you're even trying to figure some things out. Not everyone would care. Most people would sell the big house they'd just inherited, make some money, and get back to real life."

I shifted my legs. My "real" life in New Orleans had beckoned so loudly when I first arrived in Sweet Bay. It had been a siren call until I met Crawford. And Mags.

"But you're still here," he continued. "I bet that wouldn't be a small thing to your grandmother. It's definitely not a small thing to me." He tucked my hair behind my ear and traced my cheek and jaw with the back of his fingers. "This thing with us has . . . well, it's caught me by surprise." He laughed a little. "I wasn't expecting someone like you to show up in my life."

"Someone like me?" I smiled. "I can't tell if that's good or bad."

"It's good. I know you have a life — not to mention a business — to get back to, but for some reason, I'm not worried about that. Am I crazy, or do you feel the same way?"

"You're not crazy." We sat near enough that his leg pressed against mine. His warm breath was so close and the wall around me was falling down, brick by brick.

He traced long strokes down my arms with his fingers, and my skin prickled in response. When his lips met mine, something inside me landed. I hadn't been aware that part of me hung loose and disconnected, but now it slipped into place, anchored and safe. The heat that started in my belly flooded my brain and escaped into the air, becoming part of the water, the sky, and the sunshine.

Crawford forgot about any work he had to do at The Hideaway, or anywhere else for that matter. We stayed on the beach all afternoon, our only company the occasional skittering sand crab or stilt-legged heron. Only when the sun began to descend did

we shake the sand off the drop cloth and
make our way back.

27
SARA

JUNE

The workers were packing up for the day when we arrived back at the house from our trip to the mystery beach. Crawford stayed a bit, going over checklists with the workers and double-checking the position of recessed can lights planned for the kitchen ceiling. After he left, I took a glass of wine out to the garden and sat on Mags's bench. The evening air felt cool on my skin, which was still a little pink from our afternoon in the sun.

I'd been there a few minutes when the screen door slammed on the back porch. I turned to see Dot strolling across the yard toward me.

"Good heavens, from behind you look just like a young Mags sitting out here on this bench."

"I do?"

She nodded. "You sure do. Except that

smile on your face is brighter than a light-bulb." She sat next to me. "I could see it even with your back turned."

I bit my lips, trying to wipe away the smile.

"It's okay," she said. "You have permission to be happy with that boy. He seems like a good one."

I nodded. "I think he is."

"Did the two of you have a nice afternoon? You were gone when Glory and I got home."

"We took a drive. Have you ever noticed that big map on the wall in the front parlor?"

"Of course. It's been there for decades. Why do you ask?"

"I noticed a hole in it today — a place near Sweet Bay that someone had marked with a thumbtack or something. And there was a little arrow drawn on it, pointing toward the hole."

"What in the world? I've never noticed that."

"I saw it when I was taking the pictures off the wall. Crawford and I drove out to the spot to see what was there. Or at least, I think we were in the right place."

"What was there?" she asked.

"Nothing more than sand, grass, and water. It's beautiful though. I'd love to know what was so important about that little cove."

Cove. The word triggered a memory. Someone else had used that term, but I couldn't remember who it was.

"You think it was Mags who marked it?" Dot asked.

"Maybe," I said, my mind in high gear. All afternoon, I hadn't been able to shake the feeling that the stretch of beach was more than just empty sand. Something about the seclusion and the barrenness of it felt significant.

We sat in silence a few moments. I was about to ask Dot again about the postcard I'd found, but she spoke first. Her voice trembled in a way I'd never heard from her.

"Now that we're alone, I have something I need to tell you." She paused before continuing. "I've held it in a long time out of respect for Mags, but with her gone, I think I'm the last person around who can tell you the truth."

I exhaled. "I have some questions too, but you go first."

She smiled. "I told you earlier you reminded me of Mags sitting here on this bench. I came out here one day, a long, long time ago, and found her crying. She wasn't making a big deal about it, no drama, just big tears making tracks down her face and dripping onto her shirt."

"What was she crying about?"

"Did Mags ever say anything to you about a man named William?"

My heart started to pound. "No, she didn't, but there was a note . . ."

That was it. William was the one who mentioned the cove. It was in the note he wrote to Mags: *"in the cove, just as we planned."* I still didn't know what it meant, but at least it validated my feelings about the place.

"A note from William?" Dot prompted.

I nodded. "Pieces of it, at least. It was in a box up in the attic. I found it when I was cleaning. The box was full of all these little mementos. That's where the postcard from Mags's mother came from. The note was in pieces, like someone had torn it up, but I put it together as best as I could. There was . . ." I couldn't bring myself to mention the ring. It felt too sacred. "It was signed, 'Love, William.' "

She nodded. "Yes, I do think a lot of love was involved."

"Who was he?"

Dot put her hand on top of mine. Her skin was thin, the back of her hand and her wrist speckled with brown age spots.

"William was your mother's father."

"No, my grandfather's name was Robert.

You know that. Wasn't he here when you moved in?"

"That's true, Robert was here. But he was not the father of Mags's baby — of your mom. That was William."

I swallowed hard, then shot to my feet. Dot pulled her hand back to her lap, her eyes patient. I walked a few paces away, then turned around. "That's not possible. I don't even know this man. Do you? He can't be Mom's — my grandfather. It's impossible."

"I know it sounds that way, but it's true. William and Mags met here after she left Mobile. Things between them escalated quickly, and she got pregnant."

"Did Mom know about this?"

"I don't think so. I know it sounds bad. I think it was hard for Mags to talk about."

"What about Granddaddy? Was she married to him at this point?"

"Yes, she was. But before you jump to conclusions, you need to know a little about Robert. He was not a faithful husband. Mags didn't tell me much, but she told me that. He had other women over the years, one in particular. When he went away with this woman and left Mags in Mobile, she decided to leave too. She started a new life here, and William was a big part of it."

"So Robert was just her first husband?

Did Mags and William ever marry?"

My head was exploding, but I tried to ask rational questions.

"No, they didn't. I was never sure exactly what happened. I moved in after William left and Robert was back. Mags was weeks away from giving birth to your mom. She told me William was the father and he had left. She was heartbroken. At first, she said it was her fault, but I found out her parents had something to do with it. The way they saw it, Robert was a more appropriate husband for a woman of means, like Mags had been."

Dot snorted. "Appropriate in the wallet, maybe, but money doesn't guarantee happiness or loyalty. To my knowledge, Mags and Robert slept in different bedrooms every night he lived here. Robert thought it was a big secret, but we all knew. She may have been willing to allow him back into the house, but not into her bed."

"William left even though Mags was pregnant?"

"He didn't know. Apparently, he was supposed to come back. Maybe they had some plans that never worked out."

"That postcard from Mags's mother . . . ," I said.

"Right. I didn't want to say too much on

281

the porch with Glory. She and Major moved in well after your mom was born. They don't know anything about William. I'd never seen that postcard before, but her mother must have been talking about Mags choosing Robert over William. Although I'm not sure it was exactly a choice — her mother was likely the one pulling the strings. It was very important to her that her daughter marry the right last name."

Pictures flew through my head like an old movie reel. The photo of Mags at the funeral, her smile blazing, so unlike the photo from the box in the attic with her hat, pearls, and forced smile. The unspoiled sand and beauty of the cove, hidden among the trees and moss, safe from a world of rules and propriety. The little hand-carved house, complete with a porch, fireplace, and bedrooms for children.

Mags had ended up with a cheating husband over what sounded like an uncomplicated love that had produced my mother and, in a way, me. Why?

28
SARA

Once Crawford began making frequent visits after work, I found myself listening for the crunch of gravel signaling his arrival, his footsteps on the porch, his quiet knock. Each time he came, he stayed a little longer, leaving the house late, the dark night alive with a cacophony of cicadas and crickets.

He came by one evening with a box of fried chicken in one hand, a six-pack in the other, and a bottle of 409 cleaner tucked under an arm. "I'm here to work. But first, you have to eat dinner with me."

I smiled. "Let me run upstairs and get cleaned up first."

"Don't do a thing."

I looked down at the dirt-smeared T-shirt and blue jeans I'd found in an upstairs closet. My usual neat ponytail was now a messy bun at the back of my head, curls escaping everywhere.

He reached over and rubbed a smudge of dirt from my cheek. "You're kind of sexy right now."

I laughed. "And you're kind of crazy."

He took my hand and led me to the kitchen. I put the chicken on paper plates while he searched for a bottle opener.

"So have you discovered any more mysteries we need to decipher?" He rummaged in a drawer of kitchen utensils. "Another old map, maybe a hidden door?"

I poked him with a plastic fork. "Very funny."

Balancing our plates and beer bottles, we walked down the back steps toward the dock.

"Actually I have found out a little more about Mags," I said, unable to keep quiet about it.

"Really? Fill me in."

We settled on the dock with our makeshift picnic. Crawford took a sip of his beer and looked at me expectantly.

How much should I tell him? Would he be interested in the life of my eccentric grandmother? What I'd found out had the potential to change the foundation of my entire world, but to anyone else, it would probably just be stories of an old lady's life.

I hesitated. "We can talk about it later.

Let's enjoy our dinner first."

"No, tell me." He leaned toward me. "I want to know."

Back in New Orleans, Mitch's eyes would glaze over anytime I tried to talk about something deeper than city politics or the New Orleans Saints. His hands would fumble in his pockets until he found his phone and pulled it out, at which point he'd relax. "Go on," he'd say, his fingers busy tapping on the screen. "I'm listening."

But Crawford kept his eyes on me. He seemed sturdy enough to take on the murky waters of my life without buckling, and I wanted to let him in, to push open that iron door in my heart that Allyn always bugged me about. So I told him everything I knew — about the Mags I'd known my whole life and how I'd gotten her wrong all those years.

He shook his head when I finished. "That's a lot to take in."

I picked at the cold chicken on my plate. "I know. All I ever knew about the man I thought was my grandfather was that he died of a heart attack. I wish I could ask her about everything. She was a lot tougher than I ever knew."

"Do you think things would have been different if you'd known this part of her life all along?"

I'd already asked myself the same thing. If I'd known the Mags who had the courage to leave her home and a bad husband to search for something better, who had such a deep capacity for love and heartache, would my life have been different? Would I have still left? Or would I have stuck close by her side to absorb that rebellious iron will and courageous strength?

When we finished our chicken, Crawford ran back up to the house to see if Bert had left any pie on the counter. He returned a few minutes later with half a cheesecake on a silver pie plate. "It's not chocolate, but it'll do."

While we finished the cheesecake, I told him about Clark and the Coke can incident in the backyard and the short period in middle school when I wanted to be a rock-and-roll singer.

"You can sing?" he asked.

"Not a bit. I just thought Eddie Vedder was sexy. I figured if I wanted to snag a guy like that, I needed to sing in a band."

"Did you wear plaid and stop washing your hair?"

I laughed. "Well, I didn't go that far. I had

too much polite Southern girl in me to go full-grunge. Plaid didn't look good on me anyway."

"While you were singing to Pearl Jam, I was the biggest Garth Brooks fan in Tennessee."

"No!" I laughed.

"Oh yes. I was proud of my 'Thunder Rolls' concert shirt. I wore it until it fell apart and my mom threw it away."

"Probably best that we didn't meet back then."

"We would have been oil and water." He sat back in his seat and propped his long legs on the railing at the edge of the dock.

"So you have a hidden love for Garth Brooks and your business partners include a slobbery dog and a fisherman."

"And a bad fisherman at that."

"Tell me something else," I said. "You mentioned that Charlie took over for you at work for a little while. What happened back then?"

I couldn't help myself. I wanted to know.

He sat up and rested his elbows on his knees. I worried I'd pressed too much, but when he turned to look at me, his face was calm.

"My dad died, for one. He'd been sick for a while, so it wasn't a surprise, although

287

that didn't make it much easier. Soon after, my girlfriend left me. That one was a surprise. We'd been serious, but she found some other guy — actually found him before she left me. Those two events back-to-back were hard to handle. Charlie stepped in while I pulled myself back together."

He balled up his napkin and pushed it down into the neck of his empty beer bottle. "That was two years ago, and I haven't dated anyone since. I've kept myself busy with clients and making some furniture here and there. Things have been good. But the day you came into my office, you sort of kicked things into gear for me. I couldn't get you off my mind. I realized I hadn't thought about that old girlfriend in ages, and the old wound doesn't hurt anymore." He let out a small laugh. "Something about you makes me want to spill my secrets." He leaned back in his chair and turned to me. "What about you though?"

"Me?"

"Look at you. You must have a trail of broken hearts in your wake."

"Nah. I'm too busy to break hearts."

"Sure," he said.

"I'm at the shop all day and usually don't leave until at least eight. If I have a client appointment at the end of the day, that pushes me getting home even later." I wasn't giving the best impression of myself: a workaholic with no time for anything but battered furniture and wealthy patrons. Crawford owned his own business too, so I couldn't use that as an excuse.

"What about now? Am I taking you away from anyone?"

I shook my head. Mitch and all his inconsistencies and indifference didn't count next to Crawford, the first man who'd made me *feel* anything in so long.

"I would have figured you'd have all the single men in New Orleans lined up at your door."

"Allyn would love that. If it were up to him, I'd go on dates every night of the week. But the last thing I want to do at the end of a long day is go to some noisy bar for a first date with someone I'll probably never see again."

"Good thing this isn't some noisy first date," he said.

"Yes, very good thing." I leaned over and rested my cheek against his shoulder. I breathed in. The scent of the water was always the same. I imagined Mags and William on this same dock, planning for a future that never came to be.

"You know, you're different from the girl who walked into our office and wiped dog slobber off her fancy clothes."

I picked at a string on my cutoffs and shrugged.

"Now look at you. You're covered in dust and dirt, and you have fried chicken grease on your fingers."

I looked down at my hands, my last manicure a distant memory. "I bet Mags would be proud."

Crawford was right. I was a different person here. I liked having bare feet most of the time. I didn't mind wearing clothes I'd picked up from the five-and-ten store in town. I had no use for my suitcase of silk tops and skinny pants, and I hadn't pulled out my flat iron in weeks. I missed the shop and Allyn, but I was getting used to being back in Sweet Bay.

When we thought we saw a dolphin fin cut through the water, we moved to the end of the dock and sat on the edge to get a closer look. The wooden boards were still warm from the day's heat. After a moment, I looked over at the man sitting next to me. Moonlight trickled across the water and grazed his cheek. His shoulder rubbed against mine as we dangled our legs over the edge of the dock. When I arrived in

Sweet Bay, I was counting the minutes until I could leave. Now, the leaving part wouldn't be so easy. We'd both avoided talking about what would happen when the house was complete and I had to get back to my real life in New Orleans. Maybe now it was time.

"As fast as your workers are going, the house will be finished soon," I said.

"And . . ." He waited for me to continue.

"If we try to pursue this, we'll be stuck with a long-distance thing we haven't even figured out and too many hours spent on I-10 wading through coastal Mississippi." I hated the words even as they left my mouth.

Crawford raised his eyebrows and pushed my hair back from my face.

I looked down. "I could just save you the trouble now."

"Trouble of what?"

"Of leaving later. Of finding out that the driving back and forth isn't worth it. That I'm too busy, too remote, too attached to my work." I'd heard all the lines before.

"That won't happen."

"Why not?"

He took my chin and turned my face toward him. "It won't happen because you won't be too busy. Not for this. And I won't be either. If making the drive is the way I get to see you, I'll do it. I spend a lot of time in the truck anyway. Might as well make it worth my while. And as for pursuing this 'thing,' we've passed the point of choosing not to pursue it, don't you think?"

I nodded and he kissed me. It was soft but urgent, all traces of hesitation gone.

"I thought I'd be in and out of Sweet Bay in a week. And now here you are. And the house, and Mags . . . I thought I was done with this place."

"Mags and I were conspiring all along. We wanted to mess up your plans so you'd come back where you belong." He kissed me again. "We'll figure it out," he whispered.

We stayed on the dock long after the last lights had gone off inside The Hideaway and on down the bay. We finally picked up the remains of our picnic and walked around the house to his truck parked in the driveway.

"I would've made time for you," I said, pushing that heavy door in my heart open even farther. "If I'd met you in New Orleans, I mean. Even if you'd stumbled into Bits and Pieces on a day with clients swarming all over the place and deadlines staring me in the face, I wouldn't have been able to say no to you."

"That's good to hear. Because I sure don't

want to hear you say it now." He stood with his back against the truck and took my hand to pull me toward him. "I'm all in, and I want to see where this can take us."

I nodded. "Me too."

"Okay then." He put his forehead to mine and kissed me, then climbed into the truck and rolled the window down. "We're not going to talk again about what happens down the road. Let's get the house finished, then we'll discuss the impossibility of you leaving."

"Deal."

"And anyway, these guys work for me. I can slow them down as much as necessary to get you to stick around here longer." He winked and pulled away.

29
MAGS

Jenny turned three in October, and we were cruising toward Thanksgiving when the brakes hit. Everyone in the house gathered around the television to watch the newscasts about President Kennedy's assassination. Even the men were emotional. The women cried in clusters, but I tiptoed around the sobbing as much as I could.

Robert found me standing in front of the kitchen sink one night after dinner. The only light in the room came from a small lamp sitting on the telephone table. I didn't realize I was crying until he walked over and brushed the tears away from my cheeks. At the rare physical touch, I leaned my cheek into his hand, then remembered. I shrugged his hand away and turned off the faucet.

"I was just . . . I just wanted to help," he said.

"Thanks, but I'm okay." I busied myself

by drying a few cups sitting by the sink.

"I'm sorry. I just thought after all this time . . . Do you think we'll ever be able to go back to how it used to be? We have Jenny now, we —"

"How it used to be?" I said softly. "You must remember that time more fondly than I do."

"I don't mean all that. I know I made mistakes. But you've stayed with me. It must mean something that you haven't kicked me out." He chuckled as if he'd lightened the mood.

"Maybe I should have done that a long time ago," I said, my back still turned.

"What's that?"

I turned around to face him. "You're right. I haven't kicked you out, although sometimes I wonder why. You've been great with Jenny and with the house, but I still can't forget everything that happened before. Everything that drove me here in the first place."

"But I still love you. I wouldn't be here if I didn't." He said it so simply, as if the fact that he loved me — or thought he did — erased everything else.

It had been almost seven years since Robert got down on one knee and proposed to me, promised me it would never happen again, that he wanted me and me only. He was still as sharp and handsome as he was back then, only now he had some gray at his temples and a track record of breaking promises.

"You only think you love me," I said. "I understand it — being married to me makes sense. Our families together makes sense. But I could never trust you again. Don't you see that?"

"I've been here three years now and I'm still trying to make it up to you. You can't see that? We can make this work. I'll never want anyone else, I promise."

My composure burst like a delicate bubble on a sharp blade of grass. "You promise? Your promise to love and cherish me was still rattling around the church the first time you decided to sneak off with God knows who. I'm not the same woman who sat at home waiting for you to walk back in the door."

"Good," he said, surprising me. "I don't want you to be her anymore. You're different now, and I like it. You're strong and focused. You have opinions and you're not afraid to let people hear them."

"Do you know what made me this way — this strong, opinionated woman you like so much? This house. And William." Neither of us had spoken his name — at least not around each other — since Robert moved in. "If I'd stayed with you, I'd still be that sad, passive woman standing in the kitchen, waiting on her husband to come home and eat her chicken dinner."

"Margaret, I will never cheat on you again. There will never be any other women. How many ways can I say it?" His voice rose along with the color in his cheeks. "I don't see why you won't just forgive me."

"Because you're not him!" I yelled, fresh tears spilling over.

"And how is that my fault?" he yelled back.

And with that one question, everything that was boiling inside me stilled, like a pot pulled off a hot burner. Years of pent-up anger and resentment flooded out, loosening the tight heat in my chest. It wasn't his fault. Yes, he cheated — that was on him. But our marriage, the culture that pushed me toward a certain type of husband and away from another — Robert had nothing to do with it.

I leaned back against the counter and pressed the heels of my hands into my eyes. "You're right. It's not your fault."

He moved toward me, but stopped before coming too close. "I'm sorry," he said, his voice brimming with emotion.

Robert cheated, I cheated, William left — all of this was true and couldn't be erased. But even still, the three of us had been mostly innocent bystanders, caught up in a society that dictated the who, what, and when of young people's lives.

He took a step closer and I leaned my forehead on his chest.

"I wish it had all gone differently," he said. "If I could go back . . ."

"I know." I straightened up and looked at him full in the face. "And my forgiveness — you have it."

On his way out of the kitchen, he paused with his hand on the door frame. "For what it's worth, I'm glad you came here. This house, this mysterious place — it turned you into a different woman, and we're all the better for it. I'm just sorry I don't get to be the man who . . ." He looked out the window, then back at me. "Well. Anyway, good night."

He let his arm drop and left the room. I remained in the kitchen with my arms hanging loosely at my sides. Then I folded the dish towel I'd used to dry the dishes and turned the lamp off.

The soft glow from the light in the garden filtered through the windows and made everything look watery. We were all floating in the semidarkness — me, Robert, maybe even William, wherever he was.

30
MAGS

Significant exits in my life were always preceded by me finding a note. A small, handwritten piece of paper, either hurriedly scrawled or carefully written. Either way, a note was a note, and it meant someone was leaving.

This time, the departure was inevitable.

Four long years after moving into The Hideaway, Robert left a note saying he couldn't stay. He gave some details, but I didn't pay much attention. Deep down, I knew the day would come. He'd spent all that time promising he'd never leave again, but in the end, he was never a man of his word.

After Robert's exit from my life, joy came a little more frequently. William was still a barren place in my heart, but I had Jenny, I had my own slice of waterfront paradise, and I lived with my best friends. Things could have been worse. While part of me still longed for William to come back, another part of me — the part I showed to everyone else — was willing to move forward into whatever my life would hold.

I heard on the six o'clock news one evening that a vet in Daphne had rescued a flock of Canada geese from a pond between two busy highways, and I knew they were meant to live at The Hideaway. For some reason, the vet let me take them home in Major's orange van. I expected him to put his foot down and demand that I find a more suitable vehicle, but I think my yellow rain slicker and captain's hat threw him for enough of a loop that he just watched me waddle the geese out of his office and into the van.

He held his hand up for a moment like he was going to wave me down before I pulled away, but he let it drop, so I tooted the horn and drove off. Those geese saved me from irritating solicitors and salesmen peddling everything from penlights to kitchen knives. They'd take one look at those birds walking around, unchecked by gate or fence, and take off in the other direction. Lord, it was funny to see them run.

Eugene Norman, a self-taught potter, moved in not long after the geese arrived.

His only request was that he be able to practice his trade while living in the house. He pulled his potter's wheel out into the backyard and made all sorts of odds and ends while staring at the water. He probably should have kept a closer eye on what he was making. After presenting me with several sets of misshapen and unusable dinner plates and coffee cups, he hung up his potter's apron.

Next, he tried glassblowing. He and Bert constructed a furnace on the empty lot next door, where he built fires so hot the flames turned blue. He'd found his niche though — he made green-glass paperweights by the dozen and actually sold some at a gallery in Fairhope.

Less than a year after Robert left, I got another note, this time from AnnaBelle. I wondered if she still fit into that tight Mardi Gras dress. She wrote to tell me Robert had died at her house in Tennessee. She heard him yell out in his dreams, which wasn't unusual, so she shushed him and went back to sleep. In the morning, he was dead.

As his wife I was asked to write his obituary. His parents tried to change my words, but I'd already sent it to the newspaper to be printed by the time they read the proof.

MR. VAN BUREN DIED IN THE ARMS OF HIS
LOVER, ANNABELLE WHITAKER, IN TENNES-
SEE. HIS WIFE, MAGS, CAN NOW REST IN
PEACE.

31
SARA

As the days went on, I dug through drawers and closets, cleaning out forgotten cardboard boxes, duffel bags, and file folders. Drywall dust, paint thinner, and wood polish swirled around me to create a headache-inducing fog, but I kept searching for anything that held meaning. Someone had saved stacks of newspapers and crates of plastic egg cartons, but I didn't care about those — I wanted to find things that would show me more of who Mags had been.

While sorting through the drawers of an old rolltop desk in the parlor, I found a thin photo book in the back of the bottom drawer. When I pulled it out, a portion of the back page disintegrated in my hands.

The swirly, vintage script on the front read "Picturewise Vantone Prints Are Better!" A sticker on the back said "Mann's Photo Supply — The Gulf Coast's Top Photo

Finishers." The photos showed random people in various states of work and relaxation. Each black-and-white photo bore a date stamped along the white edge — June 1960 — and a handwritten name.

There was a young and handsome Mr. Norman standing next to a rock-faced furnace built into the grassy slope next to the house. He held a long tube into the fire with a clear bulb of glass attached to the end, the flames just reaching the bottom of the bulb. "Nella" sat in what appeared to be her bra and sturdy underwear out on the dock, a bottle of Johnson's Baby Oil next to her on the chaise. "Daisy" stood before an easel in what I recognized to be the front parlor, her paintbrush poised over the canvas. Several pages of the book had been torn out, leaving just jagged edges behind. Who had filled those pages? And what moments from The Hideaway's past were captured in those photos, now forgotten forever?

As I stood to place the book into my shoe box of items to keep, two photos fell to the ground. I leaned down to retrieve them and crouched back on my heels to look closer. The first one showed a man standing on a beach, the shoreline just visible at the edge of the frame. I'd seen one photo of Robert in my life, and this was not him. Robert had been young in the photo, clean-cut, dressed in a serious suit, and carrying a briefcase.

This man had shoulder-length light hair that looked damp at the ends. He wore blue jeans and an unbuttoned plaid shirt. I felt sure I was looking at the face of William, my real grandfather. With his eyes closed and his mouth just barely open, he seemed to be caught in that moment just before laughter takes over. I brushed my fingers over the photo, trying to find bits of me in his face. A wave of longing pulsed through my chest.

The second photo was similar to the funeral photo of Mags that Dot had placed next to the casket. It had the same huge, moss-draped oaks in the background, and she wore the same button-down shirt, one tail hanging free. Her eyes still crinkled in happiness, but her angle was different. In this photo, she didn't hold her hand up toward the camera, as she had in the photo at the funeral. She'd crossed her arms lazily in front of her body, and her stance was confident, flirtatious even.

I held the two photos next to each other. Even though the images were gray and blurred with age, their faces spoke of love and desire.

The front door opened and Dot and Glory's animated conversation filled the house. Glory walked past the living room toward the kitchen without seeing me, but Dot paused in the doorway.

"Finding anything interesting in here?"

I held up the two photos.

She walked closer and peered over my shoulder at them, then fumbled a hand on top of her head searching for her glasses. "Never have 'em when I need 'em," she said under her breath. She took the photo of Mags and held it out at arm's length.

"This one, I've seen — or at least one like it." She tilted the photo to look at the date. "A little three-by-five of Mags smiling this same unbelievable smile was in the junk drawer in the kitchen for as long as I can remember. Whenever I'd ask Mags about it, she'd just say it was a long-ago happy day. That's why I wanted to use it at the funeral. I didn't know there was another photo from that same day. Now this." She took the second photo. "I'm guessing this is William. I've never seen a picture of him." She rubbed her thumb over William's face. "I can see why she was so smitten."

I stood and stretched my sore legs. Dot patted my shoulder and moved back toward the hallway, then stopped.

"I know I told you a lot the other day — William and Robert and all. Are you disappointed? Do you wish I hadn't told you?"

"No, I'm glad you told me. It was shocking, and still is, but I'm glad I know the truth — or at least parts of it."

"Good. I was so worried I'd ruined the picture you had in your mind of who Mags was."

"Well, you did, but the picture I had in mind wasn't the right one. I'd rather know the truth than forever think she was just a woman who liked to wear caftans and weird hats and poke fun at the neighbors."

"She was all those things," Dot said, "but it was just her armor. Underneath, she was tender. Not as unbreakable as everyone thought."

"But why did she keep it all such a secret?"

"You know how most women tend to talk a lot about feelings and emotions?"

I nodded.

"Mags wasn't that kind of woman. I was her best friend and she didn't even give me all the details. She told me a little, but I had to string most of it together as best as I could. I think it was too hard for her to talk much about William."

She paused for a minute. "William's shadow followed her all those years. She never fully admitted it, but I could see it. Even as an older woman, his presence was still very much a part of her."

"Those nights she'd sit in the garden . . ."

"Oh yes. William made her that bench. He made a lot of the pieces in this house. I'm not exactly sure which pieces, but I know he made some of them." She squeezed my hand. "I'm not sure I answered any of your questions."

"You did. Thank you."

She padded away to the kitchen, leaving me in the parlor with the photos in my hand. I placed the photo book in the shoe box but stuck the two loose photos in my back pocket. Those were staying with me.

I continued my rummaging that afternoon. In the downstairs coat closet, I found a black leather jacket with laces on the arms and braided tassels hanging off the bottom. It had been pushed all the way to the back for who knows how long, hidden by more useful raincoats and light winter jackets. Allyn would snag something like this from a cluttered vintage shop and wear it until it fell apart.

I laid the jacket across the back of the couch and picked up my phone. He answered on the first ring. "Bits and Pieces, how may I help you?"

"It's me."

"Hello, you." I could hear the smile in his voice. "Checking up on me?"

"Nope, just calling to check in. I'm following your orders."

"We're doing fine. I got that order of linen pillows we ordered months ago. They got a piece of my mind, and we got a 10 percent discount on our next order."

"Good for you. Go ahead and call —"

"I'm all over it. Mrs. McMurphy has already picked them up. I can't talk long, but fill me in. How's it going with Mr. Sexy?"

"It's Crawford. And he's wonderful." I couldn't say it without smiling.

"Mm-hmm. I know that voice. You're happy."

"So what? I'm always happy."

"Not like this, you're not. So you two have been out again?"

"We're not exactly going out. He's just spending a lot of time at the house. After work."

"You scandalous woman! Sneaking around with the boss after hours."

"He's not my boss. I hired him."

"Even better. Sneaking around with a hired hand. I love it."

"Allyn, I love you, but you're making this sound dirty."

"Of course I am. I'm happy you've found someone. Now don't screw it up. And before you get all testy, I just mean don't let your head into the game too much. That's when you start to back off. Let it go and see what happens."

"That's my plan." I could hear commotion in the background, so I hurried. "I've found some of Mags's things in the house as I've been cleaning out."

"What kind — ? Oh, hang on a sec."

I waited while Allyn answered a customer's question. I could hear the soft hum of voices in the shop, the tinkling of Allyn's music of the day coming from the speakers. Things were just fine, as he'd said.

"I need to run," he said when he picked up the phone. "Barb here is interested in the sofa."

"*The* sofa?" I asked. Over the winter, I'd refinished a Victorian-style sofa from the 1800s with curved walnut arms and a tufted back. It was in mint condition and the most expensive item in the shop.

"That's the one. I'll let you know how it goes. But I do want to hear about Mags. We'll talk soon."

With a click, he was gone. I put the phone

down on the desk and sighed. My presence at Bits and Pieces wasn't as necessary as I'd thought. Everything was running like clockwork even in my absence.

32
SARA

I'd just sat down on the front porch after dragging a trash can to the road when a car approached. The small blue sedan came to a stop in the middle of the driveway. I couldn't see the driver's face through the shadows of the trees overhead.

The man who eased out of the car had a full head of thick white hair under a plaid cap, and he stretched each leg out in front of him as if relieving them of stiffness. I'd seen that same white hair and plaid cap in my rearview mirror when I drove away from Mags's grave. When the man stepped away from his car and turned toward me, I knew. This was William.

He shuffled to the bottom of the porch steps. I would have spoken first had my mouth — my brain — not been so empty of words. My heart thudded when he finally spoke.

"My name is William Cartright. I'm looking for — well, I'm not sure what. Is this . . . are you . . . ?"

"I'm Sara Jenkins. This is The Hideaway."

He nodded and looked up at the house. "I couldn't forget this place," he said, before turning to me again. "I was . . . I knew Mag — Margaret — Van Buren. It was a long time ago. I read her obituary in the newspaper. It took me a while to get up the nerve to come back here." He ran a hand across his stubbly cheek.

It was hard to speak over the lump in my throat, full of both affection and sadness. "I'm her granddaughter." My voice broke, but he was so caught in his memory I wasn't sure if he noticed. I swiped my finger under my eyes.

He offered a small smile. "I thought you might be. You look a lot like she did. The paper said her one survivor was a granddaughter, but I didn't think I'd have the luck to run into you. I don't mean to be presumptuous, but would you have a few minutes to talk to me?"

I gestured to the rocking chair next to me, and William began the climb up the steps. When he settled into the chair, he took a breath and seemed to relax a little. I couldn't take my eyes off him.

314

Even in his old age, it was obvious he had been handsome once. He had an angular jaw and chocolate-brown eyes framed by still-full lashes. I tried to imagine him with hair to his shoulders, as it had been in the photo of him at the cove. His hands — large, dotted in age spots, and mottled with purple veins — pulled at the zipper of his jacket. They were strong, useful hands.

"Thank you for talking to me. You probably haven't even heard my name." William ran his hand over a small Band-Aid on his chin. A dot of blood showed through the bandage right in the center, as if he'd nicked himself shaving.

"I have," I said quietly. I didn't know how much to tell, so I went with the truth. "I found a note you wrote to Mags."

He raised his eyebrows and gave a slow nod but didn't speak.

"It was in pieces in a box with some old photos and a few other things. I didn't understand what it meant — I still don't, really — but I've been piecing bits together. Mags's best friend Dot still lives here. She's told me what she knows."

I wasn't ready to mention the biggest fact I'd discovered — that William was my grandfather. It was still outlandish to me, and I suspected it would be even more so to him if he didn't know, and according to Dot, he didn't.

"Then maybe you can tell me a little of what I missed," he said. "Again, if I'm not asking too much. I know she must have had a full life after I left — she has a grand-daughter, after all." He smiled. "So life must have treated her well. I don't want to pry, but I've always been so curious . . ."

"It's okay. She lived here until the very end. She was always surrounded by friends. The ones who live here now lived with her for years. The house made her happy. I think she had a good life."

Despite the fact that you left her heartbroken and pregnant.

I couldn't argue the facts, but this gentle man didn't seem like the kind of person who would have done that. I wanted answers but I didn't know how to venture into those waters. Turns out I didn't have to. William dove right in.

"I came back a year or two after I moved out." He took his cap off and placed it in his lap. "I saw her sitting at the table where I first spoke to her — a fussy little wrought-iron table Mrs. DeBerry left behind — and she was laughing. A man was swinging a little girl around in a circle in the grass. When he put her down, she ran and threw her arms around Maggie's neck."

William paused. "I knew it had to be her husband, and the little girl was theirs. I couldn't bring myself to barge in. Especially not when I saw the girl. I suppose that was your mom?"

I nodded even though he didn't have the story right. "Why did you leave?" The question tumbled out before I had a chance to censor myself. "The first time, I mean. Where did you go?"

He shifted in his chair and recrossed his legs.

"I'm sorry. Maybe I shouldn't have asked that."

"Yes, you should have. I knew coming here that if I wanted answers about Maggie, I'd likely have to answer for what I did." He slid his hands up and down the arms of the rocking chair. "Maggie's father showed up at The Hideaway soon after she took over the house. I was looking for her when I overheard them on the back porch. Her dad was scolding her about staying here instead of being back home with her husband." He stopped and looked at me. "Forgive me. I don't know how much you know, and I don't want to be the one to — Well, I don't want to change your view of your grandmother."

"It's all right. I know about you and Mags. Some of it, at least. I need to know the rest."

He nodded. "We fell for each other quickly. I knew what we were doing — all I had planned for us — was wrong, but I couldn't help myself. That is, until I heard her talking to her father. I realized then that he was right."

"And you just gave up? If you really loved each other, couldn't you have made it work somehow?"

"Not then, we couldn't. I saw exactly what I was up against. Who was I to be carrying on with another man's wife and trying to plan a future with her? Aside from the fact that what we were doing was wrong, I was nobody — I couldn't pay to put gas in my truck half the time, and her husband was a wealthy socialite with a steady job. Maggie was used to nice things, even if she had turned her back on her old life. I wasn't sure she'd really thought of what it would mean to stick with me and turn down a life of money and ease. I knew I had to get myself together and make a real plan before expecting her to stick with me."

I thought of Mags sitting on her bench crying to Dot, missing William. I shook my head. "Knowing Mags and who she turned out to be, she probably wouldn't have cared about the money."

"You have no idea how many nights I've laid awake thinking that same thing. I made a mistake leaving like I did, but I always planned to come back for her. I thought I'd spend some time away, make a decent amount of money, and then return to whisk her away like a knight in shining armor." He chuckled.

"What happened?"

"I came back a few weeks after I left. I'd wanted to give her time to settle things with her parents and her husband, but it was so hard for me to stay away. I stopped at Grimmerson's first to pick up some flowers. I'd made some furniture for Tom, and he knew Maggie and I were — well, together. He sold me the flowers but advised against taking them to her. He told me her husband had moved in. I didn't go see her that day, but I was just young and headstrong enough not to give up." He shook his head.

"I did stay away for a while then. I worked hard, made some money, and I came back again, but I guess I waited too long. When I saw them in the backyard, I didn't have the nerve to wreck what she'd built with Robert and their little girl."

My heart caved inside of me. I closed my eyes and worked the tension out of my forehead with my fingers. I wanted to tell him the truth about that little girl, my mother, but I couldn't. Not yet.

"I didn't see any mention of Robert in her obituary," he continued. "Did he . . . did they stay together?"

"He died of a heart attack when Mom was just a few years old. But I don't think . . ." I paused, unsure of how much to explain. "I think their situation was complicated."

"I see," he said quietly.

"You don't seem surprised."

He shrugged. "I just worried about her, is all. He'd already left her once."

"Seems a lot of people left her. The only ones who stuck by her are the ones who still live here."

"So she never remarried?"

"There was never anyone else."

We rocked in silence for a few moments. "What about you?" I asked. "Did you ever get married?"

He nodded. "Twice."

I raised my eyebrows.

"I tried to forget her, but no one could ever measure up. In their defense, they were good women. Both times, it was my fault it didn't work out. I compared everyone to Maggie. I was twenty-eight when she arrived here with a red coat draped over her arm. She was stunning. I've been in love with her ever since."

In the photo of Mags at the funeral, and the other one I'd found in the desk, she'd had such a radiant smile. Her hair was messy and free, and even the sand and sky around her seemed ripe with life. William had been the man to make her so happy. He'd been her heart and soul. Regardless of how he and Mags had ended, I felt a sudden closeness to him, an appreciation that he'd drawn so much life and joy out of her, even if I never got to see that side of her.

"I've taken up enough of your time." He straightened in his chair. "I appreciate you talking to me."

"I'm glad you came." I wanted to say more, but it was still a little strange to be sitting next to my grandfather — one, he wasn't named Robert, and two, he wasn't dead. But despite the oddity of the situation, we had an undeniable connection and I wanted to know more about him.

He rose from his chair and began the walk back to his car.

I stood and walked to the top of the steps. "Would you mind if I called you? Maybe we could meet again."

He smiled. "I'd like that."

I put a hand on the door behind me. "I'm

going to get some paper and a pen. Don't go anywhere."

He chuckled and stopped on the bottom porch step. "Don't worry. I'll stick around this time."

I sat in the rocker watching the taillights on William's car disappear in the trees. Not a minute later, the front door opened and Dot's gray head popped out. "Is your friend gone?"

"He is. Although he wasn't a friend."

"Well, I wondered." She sat in the chair William had just vacated. "I didn't take you for a woman with gentleman callers as old as Bert."

"Aren't you and Bert the same age?"

She waved the thought away. "Don't tell him that. So who was the visitor?"

"It was William."

Her rocking chair creaked to a stop. "William?"

I nodded. "He saw the obituary in the paper. Remember me telling you I saw a man at the cemetery after everyone else left? That was him."

"The thought crossed my mind, but it seemed unlikely. It's been so many years."

We rocked in our chairs, each lost in our own thoughts. Around us, crickets practiced for their evening serenade, stretching their legs and testing instruments.

"What was he like?" she asked.

"Amazingly, still lovestruck. He's been married twice, but he's still in love with her — or at least, who she used to be. It was sad to hear him talk that way about her, especially since she's not here to see him again. Do you think she still loved him at the end?"

She shrugged. "On the one hand, Mags was a smart woman — I'd like to think she wouldn't have let her heart stay tied to a man she met in her early twenties, but the head and the heart rarely agree. A woman never fully forgets her first love. And I'd imagine that's especially true if she never finds love again — not to mention if she carried his child. I know she loved him, but I always had a hard time swallowing the fact that he left and never came back."

I told her about William overhearing Mags's conversation with her father and how he planned to come back with the means to compete against Robert's wealth and status.

"Then why didn't he? Mags would have gone back to him in a heartbeat — especially after Robert died."

"That's the thing — he did come back,

but he saw Mags and Robert in the backyard with a little girl — Mom — and he assumed it was Robert's and her child. He didn't want to disrupt their life or hurt the child."

"My goodness."

"It's terrible, isn't it? It would have been so easy for them to be together again, but neither of them knew." I sighed. "I wish Mags hadn't held on to her secrets for so long. I wish I had known all of this." I cradled my chin in my hand. "I wish I had known her."

33
SARA

JULY

At the house, the construction team took out the wall dividing the kitchen and dining room and the one between the foyer and the main parlor. Even with everything covered in dust and plastic tarps, I could tell the decision to remove the walls was a good one. Despite the noise and dust, it was easier to breathe in the house with the rooms opened up.

The new bathrooms upstairs were framed out, and the old ones were updated to include spa baths and separate showers. Major was the biggest fan of the new bathrooms.

"Have you seen those bathtubs?" he asked Bert one morning over cowboy coffee on the back porch when the electricity had been temporarily turned off. "They're huge. I'm not too keen on men soaking in tubs, but these may change my mind."

Downstairs, the kitchen floors went from yellowed tile to hardwood and the counters from ugly linoleum to butcher block. I walked in the kitchen one day to find Bert leaning over the new counter, his ear an inch from the wood and his eyes closed. Major stood in the corner of the kitchen, just out of Bert's line of sight, doubled over in quiet laughter. I gave Major a stern look and walked over to Bert.

"Bert?" I whispered. "Are you okay?"

He straightened up and smoothed his hand across the surface. "I'm just fine. And Major, I see you over there laughing. I read that some butcher block comes from ancient trees, and if you listen hard enough, you can hear the sound of wind in the branches."

Major couldn't contain himself any longer. "Ancient trees? Wind in the branches? Did you forget to take your pills this morning?" He laughed and grabbed a dish towel off the counter to wipe his eyes under his glasses.

"I'm not crazy," Bert said. "You know how you can hear the ocean in a seashell? It's the same thing."

"I do know about the seashells," I said, hiding my own laughter. "And you may be right about some butcher-block wood, but I ordered these from Ikea, so I don't think they're ancient. More like Swedish."

"Sweden? I bet they have ancient trees there."

I chose creamy white paint for the cabinets and a soothing pale gray for the walls throughout the rest of the house. It would make the spaces feel even larger and pop against the new white crown moldings. Everything was coming together just as I'd imagined. My favorite change was in the center hallway, which had previously been lined with built-in bookshelves, making it seem slimmer than it was. I asked Crawford to rip them out, and what a change it made. The hallway was now ten feet across, and when I opened the front and back porch doors, the breeze floated through the house like a cool whisper.

I ended each day a hot, sweaty mess, but I was satisfied. Exhausted and bleary, but satisfied. It was early evening on such a day when a car pulled up in the driveway. I smiled. Crawford was coming over for dinner, and he must have decided to come early. The last of the workers would be out of the house soon, and he'd said we needed to celebrate my victory.

"Victory?" I said when he asked me about dinner.

"The house is incredible. I may have co-ordinated the actual work, but it's all your plans. You made this house what it's becoming. Your phone is going to be ringing off the hook with people wanting to book their vacations when it's finished."

"What vacations?" I asked. "No one even knows about this place anymore, other than the neighbors who probably don't care."

"You know how word spreads. Once it gets out that there's a fancy new bed-and-breakfast in Sweet Bay, they'll start coming. You haven't said it, but I think this is what you want. Otherwise, why go through with the renovations?"

Is that what I want?

"It's settled," he continued. "I'm bringing dinner and wine, and you don't need to do a thing. I'll be there by seven."

"Okay then. As long as you don't mind hanging out with a girl who's spent all day cleaning the bathroom floors."

"There's no one I'd rather spend my evening with. As long as you keep your hands to yourself."

I laughed. "Thanks."

"On second thought, forget I said that. I'll just need to check them for germs first."

I was still smiling when I heard the crunch of gravel in the driveway. I welcomed the pleasant clench in my chest as I thought about Crawford — his warm eyes, his slow grin, his rumpled clothes and hair. How was it possible that in this small space of time in Sweet Bay, my life had changed so remarkably?

Every time my mind crept back to New Orleans, I forced myself to focus on what was in front of me rather than what waited for me in my real life. It was a trick I'd learned since I'd been back at The Hideaway — pretend to be the spontaneous, go-with-the-flow person I wished I was and I could almost forget that I was going against the grain of my cautious, orderly life.

He knocked and I jumped up off the couch. When I got to the front door, I pulled it open and held my hands out. "They're so clean, you could eat off them."

But it wasn't Crawford.

"Miss Jenkins. I hoped I'd find you here."

Sammy Grosvenor. Middle Bay Land Development. My stomach dropped.

"I haven't seen you around the diner again, so I thought I'd come by for a little chat. Do you mind?" He put his hand on the door and pushed.

"I do mind." I held on to the door firmly. "If you need to talk to me about anything, we can do it out here. Although I can't imagine that we have anything to say to each other."

"Oh, there's plenty." He peered around me into the house. "Clark was right. He said a lot's been going on around here and I can see it. Looks good, Miss Jenkins. I hate to tell you it's all about to change."

I crossed my arms over my chest.

He raised an eyebrow. "Allow me to explain. You're the owner of one of the choicest plots of waterfront property in Sweet Bay. I tried to tell you this when we spoke at the diner a couple months ago. Only one other piece of property rivals yours in terms of desirability, but the owner has proven to be quite stubborn. With the unfortunate death of your grandmother and your refusal to sell, I've informed Mayor McClain that it's high time we get ourselves in gear and make some necessary changes."

He trained his eyes on me, his round face red with heat and exertion, his hair matted down on top. My stomach tightened into a ball of knots waiting for him to explain, but I wouldn't give him the satisfaction of appearing interested.

"I'll cut to the chase. My case to the mayor shows that this stretch of property serves no one but The Hideaway's cornucopia of senior citizens. The area will better

330

serve Sweet Bay, and the entire county, if it is developed into something a little more upstanding. I've always liked the idea of some fancy loft apartments. You know the kind — industrial look, exposed pipes, metal railings. Maybe some shops and restaurants underneath and a nice boardwalk along the water to connect it all.

"With my plan in the works, Sweet Bay could rival other tourist destinations along the Gulf Coast. I've assured the mayor's staff that these changes would move us up substantially in the eyes of folks looking to spend vacation dollars. The mayor couldn't say yes fast enough."

"Mr. Grosvenor —"

"Please, call me Sammy."

"*Mr. Grosvenor,* you've been trying to get your hands on this house for years, and my answer is the same as it was at the diner. You're not getting the house. Now if you'll excuse me, a friend is coming over soon and I'd prefer it if you didn't ruin our dinner."

I tried to close the door, but he stuck a foot in the doorway. I opened it back up and sighed. He was a bothersome bug, a pest that wouldn't go away.

"You misunderstand me, Miss Jenkins. I don't want the house. I have no use for it. I want the house gone."

"Gone?" I laughed. "You can't do that. It's not your house to take."

My voice sounded light, but inside, bells were going off. Sammy had come around many times, but he'd never had a real plan, just a desire to take land out from under an old lady's nose. This time, it sounded like he'd done his homework.

"The mayor agrees with me that eminent domain is the right road to take. It's the first step in paving the way for our new Sweet Bay. I'll allow time for the residents to collect their things and make some plans, but do inform them that they should be quick. I don't have time for the Ingrams and Greggs to sit around and bemoan their misfortune. We're all adults here and this is how the world works. I'll stop by again with the necessary papers, but I wanted to let you know what's going on."

"That's — this is impossible."

"I'm afraid it is very possible," he said with less bravado. "You know, Miss Jenkins, many of the residents in this town think I'm slimy. They think I do nothing but twiddle my thumbs and wait for someone to die or run out of money so I can swing in and take the house."

I raised an eyebrow.

"It's true, I do work that way sometimes.

332

But this time it's different. This is all in the name of bettering our town of Sweet Bay."

It was a lie and we both knew it. He didn't care about Sweet Bay — all he cared about was the money a hot new development would put in his pocket. Inside, I was seething, but I couldn't let him see it. I had to talk to Mags's lawyer first.

"Are you finished?"

"Yes, I . . ." He cleared his throat. "I'm finished. Do you have anything to add?"

"Not a thing. I'll have my lawyer contact you in the morning."

With the door closed, I let out a shaky breath. I pressed the heels of my hands over my eyes, then grabbed my phone off the dining table and walked to the back porch to call Crawford. The night couldn't have felt less like a victory if I'd walked off the end of the dock and fallen into the water.

"I'll have to take a rain check for tonight," I said when he answered.

"Why? What's wrong?" I heard the concern in his voice. Mitch — or any of the men I'd dated in New Orleans — would have been on his phone the minute I bailed, looking for other friends to meet up with. Instead, Crawford gave me a chance to lighten the load Sammy had just dumped on my shoulders.

I took a deep breath. "What do you know about eminent domain?"

In the backyard, the sky was solid lilac, the sun long gone below the trees. The sun-warmed grass poked the bottoms of my bare feet. Without thinking, I did something I hadn't done since I was a young girl. I stretched out on the grass on my back — toes pointed, arms stretched over my head — and stared up at the sky.

After my parents died, I often came out into Mags's backyard just to lie down and think. As the stars popped out, I'd imagine they were holes, and my parents were up there peeking through the sky at me. I thought if I only stayed still long enough, I could catch all the love they dropped down.

As Crawford had told me on the phone, there was no reason to jump to conclusions. "Wait until you talk to Mr. Bains. See if Sammy's plan even holds water, then we'll figure it out, whatever it is."

"But what about all your work on the house? The painters are coming tomorrow, and the electrician is coming back in the afternoon to —"

"Let me take care of the house. We can pause the work if necessary until we figure out what's going on. Most of the heavy lifting has already been done. The rest can wait."

I hoped it would just be a simple wait and not a permanent ending.

I rolled onto my side and looked up at the house. The lights inside gave the rooms a welcome glow. It sure didn't look like the neglected relic it had been when I first arrived.

Was it possible Sammy could take it all away from me?

34
SARA

I walked into Mr. Bains's office in Mobile the next day to find him swimming in paperwork. File folders and papers covered his desk and the floor surrounding it. His face, mottled and damp, showed the day had been a rough one. When he saw me in the doorway, he gestured to the paper-covered chair across from his desk.

"I wondered when I'd hear from you."

I sat down, desperate for him to tell me Sammy had it all wrong.

"My buddy over at the courthouse called me late yesterday and told me the news," he said before I could speak. "He knew I'd been Mrs. Van Buren's lawyer and thought I'd want to know. It's harsh, but this type of thing does happen. Granted, usually it's to make way for a road expansion or railroad tracks, not something as trivial as condos and a boardwalk. But Sammy has the may-

336

or's ear on this one. When he started chirping about tax dollars coming into the county and how that could change the face of Sweet Bay, the mayor turned to mush."

"So he can do this? It's really going to happen?"

"Looks that way. Unless of course . . ."

"Unless what?"

Mr. Bains sat back in his chair and clicked the end of his pen. "You can try to challenge Sammy's right to take the property. We can go to trial, show them that The Hideaway can be more than just a home for five — now four — people that doesn't do much for the town."

"Would it do any good?"

He shook his head. "I doubt it. It sounds like Sammy's nailed down all the loose ends. He's acting on the mayor's behalf, so it's legal for him to do it. His plan is to use the property for the good of the public, which always sounds good to a judge."

"Is making Sweet Bay a tourist destination a good thing for the public? Is that what the people want?" I couldn't imagine Sweet Bay becoming glitzy and high class any more than I could imagine Mr. Bains sprouting horns on his head.

He shrugged. "People in small towns like to talk about keeping things the way they've always been, but when you start talking about what the influx of money could mean — better schools and parks, a beefed-up police department, things like that — you'd be surprised how quickly some people can give up that idea of small-town charm.

"Now if you're up to it," he continued, "you could try to convince them that the work you're doing on the house could better the town in similar ways — attracting vacationers from around the South or what have you. That doesn't have quite the same punch as multiunit condos and high-end boutiques, but it's something, and it would appeal to the residents who will stand against anything Sammy tries to do just on principle alone. I must say, though, I was under the impression at the will reading that you were less than thrilled at being named the beneficiary of that place. I would think this might be a good thing for you — Sammy coming in and giving you a reason to let the house go."

"I wasn't thrilled at first, but . . . things are a little different now."

He nodded. "I can see that."

I closed my eyes and took a deep breath. Despite how I felt about the house now, was this a sign that Mags's death — and Sammy's timely plan for the area — was supposed to usher in the closing of The Hideaway?

"Could anything make Sammy change his mind?"

"It would have to be out of the goodness of his heart. And Sara — I'm not sure there's much good in there. I wish I had something different to tell you. I'd advise you to begin making your exit plans."

On the drive back to Sweet Bay, my phone buzzed in my purse. I pulled it out with one hand and saw Crawford's name. Blood pumped in my ears as I pressed End and dropped the phone on the passenger seat.

Don't push him away now, Sara.

But I didn't know what else to do. It felt like The Hideaway was slipping through my fingers, the path in front of me leading back to my real life.

At the house, so many trucks filled the driveway that I almost missed the motorcycle parked to the side under the oak. Two men with *Sears* stamped on the backs of their sweat-stained shirts struggled to fit the new stainless-steel refrigerator through the front doorway. They'd taken the door off the hinges, but it still wouldn't fit. I avoided the commotion and walked around the side of the house.

I found Allyn reclining in a wooden Adirondack chair on the dock, a drink in his hand, his black boots and socks in a pile next to him. He'd propped his pale, skinny feet up on the railing. Glory sat next to him, laughing.

Allyn turned when the boards on the dock squeaked under my feet.

"Remind me why you ever left this place. It's so relaxing. I think I might move in. If that's okay with you, of course," he said to Glory.

"Of course it is. You can stay as long as you like." She patted his hand.

I tried to smile, but my throat was tight.

"Oh dear," Glory said, noticing.

Allyn stood to get a better look at me, and I hugged him hard. "I'm so glad you're here," I whispered.

He took a step back, then tightened his arms around me. "Whoa, what's wrong with you?"

I let him go and wiped the corner of my eye. "Nothing, I'm fine. I'm just happy to see you. What are you doing here?"

"At the moment, Glory and I are getting acquainted. She told me a fascinating story about cutting Dolly Parton's hair back in Georgia."

Glory held her hands up. "I'll let you two

340

kids talk. Let me know if you need anything, Allyn. I'll be right inside."

She walked back to the house and held the screen door so it wouldn't slam behind her. I turned back to Allyn. "I can't believe you. You've already got her eating out of your hand."

"It's the hairdressing bond. We're two of a kind." He sat back down in his chair and picked up his glass. "Tell me what's going on."

"You tell me what's going on. If you're here, who's manning my shop? You didn't just close up, did you?"

"I wouldn't do that to you. Don't worry, it's all taken care of. Rick was more than happy to hold the fort down until I get back tomorrow. Now, spill it. You're not a hugger, so something's up. Plus, you're about to cry and you don't do that either."

I sighed and sat down in Glory's chair.

"I just left the lawyer's office. It appears the VIPs of Sweet Bay feel that some fancy condominiums and a shiny new boardwalk would serve the people of Baldwin County better than The Hideaway. So much better that they actually want to take the land and the house from me."

"VIPs of Sweet Bay?" He shook his head. "Who are they and how can they make that

341

kind of decision?"

"It's called eminent domain. The government — in this case, acting under the urging of a land developer — can take this property, no questions asked, and turn it into something else 'for the good of the public.' "

Allyn waved his hand around until I stopped talking. "Way over my head. I'll ask Jaxon about it."

"Jaxon? Who's that?"

"He's a new friend."

I raised an eyebrow.

"He's a lawyer. Very smart. Maybe he can help."

I pinched the bridge of my nose with my fingers. "Unfortunately, I think it's a slam dunk for the developer. Legally, he can do this, although ethically, it's pretty dirty. Plus, Mr. Bains has already looked into it. I don't need another lawyer. What I need is something to make this guy go away."

"He's actually taking the house from you? And what — tearing it down?"

I nodded.

"How long do you have before all this happens?"

"I don't know yet."

We sat in silence. Allyn handed me his glass of tea and I took a sip.

"Everything was going so well." I laughed, but it was only to keep the tears at bay. "The house is coming along and it's going to be gorgeous. The thought had even crossed my mind that I might be able to run this place as a B and B. I'd keep Bits and Pieces, obviously. And I couldn't move here — not fully anyway — but maybe I could do both. Crawford and I . . . well, like you said, Sweet Bay and New Orleans aren't that far apart."

I leaned back in the chair and tilted my face toward the sun. "So much has happened here, I just can't imagine it all ending now — and at the hands of Sammy, which makes it even worse."

I closed my eyes and forced my thoughts of William, the house, and all those pieces of furniture engraved with a skeleton key into a deep pocket in the back of my mind.

"It's probably a good thing this happened now," I said, willing my voice not to shake, "before I make any big changes in my life to accommodate this house. Sammy will raze it, throw up some atrocious condo building, and that'll be that. I'll head back to New Orleans and do what I'm supposed to be doing, and things will go on in Sweet Bay like they have been for years — except now it'll be filled with snowbirds and spring breakers."

Even with my eyes closed, I could feel Allyn staring at me. I sat up and took another sip of tea, forcing myself to look calm.

"What about Crawford?" he asked.

"He said we'd figure it out."

Allyn waited, but he dropped the subject when I didn't offer any more.

"It's beautiful here. A little . . . quaint" — he glanced around — "but I could sit on this dock all day. It's so quiet I think I can hear the fish breathing."

"That's just because the construction guys are wrapping up for the day."

"Construction guys?" He grinned. "Maybe you need to show me around."

After a ten-cent tour, during which Allyn was disappointed to discover that most of the workers had indeed left for the day, we ended up in the driveway next to his Harley. He handed me a helmet.

"I brought an extra in case I needed to rescue you."

"Rescue me from what?"

"Doesn't matter. You don't need to be rescued. You're doing just fine, and we'll figure out what to do about the house — and your man. I just need to do it over something stronger than sweet tea. Hop on."

With no energy to argue, I did as he asked. I directed him to the Outrigger Lounge, the only white-tablecloth place in Sweet Bay. The tablecloths were white vinyl, but in Sweet Bay, that counted. We sat at a table on the patio overlooking the bay. Allyn ordered white wine for both of us, along with fried pickles and a plate of Oysters Bienville.

"What?" he asked when I looked at him over the top of my menu. "If you're going to stay here, I need to make sure the food is up to par."

"Stay here? Did you not hear me tell you everything about Sammy?"

"I heard you. Tell me about Crawford."

"Crawford is wonderful. Almost too wonderful, considering."

"Considering what?"

"Even if I had considered staying in Sweet Bay — which I haven't — I might not even be able to. If the house falls through, I wouldn't have the option of staying."

"Of course you have the option. You're a big girl — you can do whatever you want. More than that, I'd say he gives you a pretty good reason to stay."

A reason to stay — was that what I was looking for?

"But what am I supposed to do — go buy

345

a house? I have the shop and clients and the Broussards' house coming up. It's not like I could just forget all that and move to Sweet Bay."

"You're overthinking this. We don't know how it all will play out."

I dipped a fried pickle in ranch dressing, then dropped it and leaned back in my chair.

"What?" he asked.

"I haven't been back home that long, but Sweet Bay was starting to feel — I don't know what it was feeling like, just something different than it did when I was younger. I think I was starting to like it."

"Did you hear what you said? You just called Sweet Bay home."

"I did?"

Allyn nodded.

"Hmm. Maybe it's that it feels like life here could be different a second time around. But you know how much I love the shop. And you. And New Orleans."

"Of course I do. But you've opened the door to a whole other part of your life. The house, your memories of Mags, those crazy old people living in the house now. Crawford," he said, tilting his head. "This isn't small stuff. And it's okay to feel pulled in two different directions."

"Sounds like my therapist just jumped in the conversation."

He waved the thought away. "That's why you pay me the big bucks. But you never finished telling me about Mags's things you found in the house."

I pieced everything together as best I could — Mags's privileged life and marriage to Robert, Robert leaving to be with another woman, and Mags moving to The Hideaway and meeting William.

"For reasons that made sense to him at the time, and I think due in part to Mags's parents, William left. He planned to come back for her, but it never happened. And he never knew she was pregnant."

"So little Mags had some secrets."

"Yes, but it's more than that," I said. "By the time she was my age, she was a widow and in love with a man she'd never see again. But despite all that, she was content. Or she seemed so. She loved her friends and her old house, gave the neighbors something to talk about, and never cared about how 'a woman of her age' should live her life. She was brave."

"Sounds like it," Allyn said.

"Maybe she worried I would have thought badly of her if I'd known all this."

"Would you have?"

"No, just the opposite. It would have shown me there was a reason for her oddness, that she was more than just the strange old lady I always thought."

"You think she was strange because of what happened with William? I don't get it."

"Not William, but Robert. And maybe even her parents too. From what I'm gathering, Mags was raised to be proper and ladylike, to always do the right thing, even to marry the right man. I'm thinking maybe she got to Sweet Bay and ditched all that. Maybe she went in the total opposite direction from what her parents and Robert represented."

I thought of her crazy hats and bright yellow ponchos that made me want to crawl under the nearest rock when I was a teenager. What if all that quirkiness had just been her way of pushing back against a lifestyle and culture that had crushed her dreams? "It all makes perfect sense now."

I flagged the waitress and ordered another glass of wine. The sun was setting. Long, thin clouds, now dark purple against the orange sky, draped across the sky like streamers.

"I drove by my old house last week," I said. "My parents' old house." We'd started on our entrées — blackened Gulf snapper for Allyn, grilled mahi wrap for me.

"How did that feel?" Allyn asked.

"Strange, I guess. I hadn't seen it in a really long time. Ten years, at least. It's white now — it used to be light blue. But my old wooden swing was still hanging from the oak in the front yard. Two kids were playing on it. My mom always hated that swing. I busted my forehead on it when I was little." I pointed to a spot above my right eyebrow. "Had to get four stitches right here."

Allyn smiled. "You've never told me much about your parents. Your mom. What was she like?"

I sat back and readjusted the clip in my hair. "She was kind. Soft-spoken. It was like she was put on earth to do exactly what she was doing — being my mom, Ed Jenkins's wife, owner of the side-of-the-road diner. And she was always good at accepting people and situations for who and what they were. Like with Mags. She had to have known her own mother led an unconventional life, but she took her for who she was without being bothered by any of it."

"Or maybe she was bothered and you just never knew. You were still young when she died, right?"

I nodded.

"Maybe she kept that part from you."

"Maybe." I remembered Mom's calm demeanor, her contentment with her life and everything around her. With me beating a trail out of Sweet Bay as soon as I could, maybe I was as unlike Mom as I was Mags.

"You're the same way, you know," Allyn said after a pause. "Or at least you were with me. I walked into your shop with green hair and a ring in my nose and you didn't even flinch."

I squinted an eye and held up my thumb and forefinger a centimeter apart. "Maybe just a little."

He laughed and nudged my chair with his foot. For a moment, we ate in comfortable silence. From a table across the deck, laughter came in bursts. A flock of pelicans coasted overhead.

"You're not really going to leave, are you?" Allyn asked. We'd finished our meal and were waiting to pay our bill. I traced my finger along the top of my empty wineglass — my third, two more than I usually drank. "It seems like you have a lot of unfinished business here," he continued. "You've only just met William, you have a hot romance of your own to deal with, and you need to look further into this emergent domain thing."

"Eminent domain."

"Whatever. See if it's a done deal."

I sighed. "I told you, Mr. Bains has already figured it out. It would take a change of heart for Sammy to give up the property, and that's not going to happen."

"Maybe. It's just a shame to lose such a fabulous house. I wish we could relocate it to New Orleans. It could be our hideaway when we need to escape annoying customers."

It was an attempt to lighten the mood, but I didn't feel light. My head throbbed and I was exhausted. He looked across the table and saw it.

"Let's get you home." He pulled me to my feet.

At the house, Allyn dropped our helmets in the yellow room, the one he had picked out during our earlier tour of the house. The painters hadn't yet reached the bedrooms, so they still boasted those original lovely color schemes.

He helped me to the blue room, and I curled up on the bed while he tugged off my shoes. Just before he turned the light off, my cell phone rang. He fished it out of my purse and looked at the screen.

"Crawford," he said.

"Not now. I'll call him in the morning."

He sighed. "Does he know about the house?"

I nodded, my eyes already closing. "I told him last night."

"You're going to involve him in all this, right? If this thing between the two of you is as meaningful as you say it is, you can't just ditch him and slip out of Sweet Bay. That would be the easy road, and you can't take the easy one this time."

"This time?" I opened my eyes. My brain was foggy, but his words cut through the muck.

"Something has changed in you since you've been here, and it's more than just Mags. I think Crawford is part of it. Don't cut him out yet."

"But what did you mean about 'this time'?"

He shook his head and stood up from the bed. "Look, you left Sweet Bay a long time ago when things were hard. Believe me, I'm glad you did, but you do have a tendency to skip out on the rough parts. It'll be messy if Sammy goes through with his plan and you have to figure out what to do with everything you've started here. But don't cut and run."

I pulled the sheets up tighter under my chin, fending off his words. It annoyed me to admit it, but he was right, as usual.

"One more thing," he said from the end of the bed. "You shut your heart down too much, which is infuriating, but when you do open up, all of us — me, Crawford, Glory, and her gang downstairs — we can't help but love you. You're magnetic in your own twisted little way, and I think you got that from Mags. These people attached themselves to her and her house, and all these years later, they're still here because they still love her. Listen to Mags — to who she really was — before you make any decisions about the house. And about your life."

He patted my feet under the blankets, then clicked the light off and closed the door behind him.

35
Mags

AUGUST 1970
We rented cabins at the state park in Gulf
Shores after Hurricane Lorraine blew
through. Lorraine didn't hit us dead-on;
she rolled ashore in Biloxi — close enough
to call for evacuation notices in our area
(which we ignored, as usual) and to take
down much of the electricity in Sweet Bay,
but far enough away that the beaches were
back to normal after a few weeks. We were
all exhausted after the cleanup efforts in
Sweet Bay, what with all the downed trees
and closed businesses. When we got our
heads above water, I suggested the vacation.

There were seven of us — Jenny and me;
Dot and Bert; Major and Glory Gregg, who
checked in for an extended stay not long
after Robert died; and Eugene Norman, the
potter-turned-glassblower. Starla, Gary, and
Daisy had long since moved on. After a
quick call to secure the cabins, we packed a

few things and piled into the Greggs' orange van to drive the half hour it took to get to the sugar-white sand of Gulf Shores. It was late August, the last weekend before Jenny started third grade.

Jenny and I sat in the back row of the van with Glory. Dot and Eugene sat in the row in front of us, with Bert and Major in charge of getting us to the beach in one piece. Jenny had just finished telling us a long story of how she and her friend from school, Doreen, had slipped an earthworm into the school bully's desk during recess. Jenny laughed out loud and looked back and forth at Glory and me until we laughed too. It was hard to be around Jenny and not feel lighter.

Glory took Jenny's soft face in her hands and smoothed her hair back. "Child, you are a beautiful creature, but I must say, you look nothing like your mother." Glory looked at me. "She must have her father's look. Was he as blond and fair as this?"

Dot turned sideways in her seat so she could make eye contact with me. She raised an eyebrow and waited for my answer.

"Mama? Was he?" Jenny asked.

The first time Jenny asked about her father, I couldn't have forced the right words out even if I'd wanted to — which I didn't, because she was too young. I gave her the same easy answer I gave everyone — that he died from a heart attack when Jenny was only three. I'd tell her the truth one day, when she could handle it. Or maybe when I could handle speaking of it.

What Glory said was true — my child looked nothing like me. She was the spitting image of her father. She had William's fair coloring, wheat-colored hair, and full eyelashes. She also had my daddy's tall forehead and Mother's strong nose. She deserved to know the truth about her father and her family, but not at the tender age of nine.

"He sure was, sugar." I patted Jenny's hand, my eyes turned out the window, looking at nothing in particular.

We arrived at the park to discover there had been a mix-up, and only one cabin was available for rent. Several had been damaged in the storm, and it seemed lots of other people had the same idea we did — it was the weekend before Labor Day, after all.

"It's a fine cabin," the woman at the front desk told me. "It's one of our larger units, so you won't feel too cramped." She eyed our ragtag group as if she didn't believe the words she was saying.

"Cramped? Seven people in a two-room cabin will be more than cramped."

"Major, don't make a scene," Eugene said. "We drove all the way here. We can't turn around and go home now."

"Home is thirty minutes away. We'd be back before *Columbo* starts."

Before Major and Eugene could continue arguing — or worse, compare the merits of *Columbo* with those of *Hawaii Five-O,* a favorite pastime at The Hideaway — I spoke up.

"Enough. We already live together, so what's the problem with sharing tighter quarters for a few days? We won't be in the cabin much anyway. Mark it down," I said to the clerk. "We're staying."

Once the decision was made, everyone got into the spirit of the vacation. Bert emptied the coolers of food supplies he'd brought for the weekend and set out ingredients for a feast, Glory retrieved her suitcase of board games and beach toys, and everyone relaxed enough to enjoy the last real weekend of summer.

At some point during our stay, I took a notebook and a plastic lounge chair to the edge of the shoreline. I nestled the chair down in the sand, pushed my toes under the thin layer of seashells, and started to write. A little later — fifteen minutes or an hour, I couldn't be sure — Dot appeared and sat in a chair next to me. Baby oil glistened on her shins and she smelled like a coconut. She'd bought her bathing suit — a perfect yellow polka-dot bikini — especially for this trip, and she'd hardly taken it off since we'd arrived. She felt good in it, and it showed.

"Does that have anything to do with Jenny?" she asked.

I looked at her. "It's a letter. How'd you know?"

"I knew that conversation in the van got to you. Then here you are writing away in your little notebook — I just put two and two together. When are you going to give it to her?"

I shrugged. "One day. When the time is right." I could feel her stare, but I kept my eyes on the water. "She's the best part of us. He would have loved her so much."

"You sure about that? Why hasn't he come back?"

"I don't know, but he must have a good reason." Dot didn't believe me — I could see the pity in her eyes despite the oversize sunglasses. I knew what she was going to say before she said it.

"What if he met — ?"

I cut her off quick. "Don't say it. You didn't know him. You didn't know us."

"Okay, fair enough." She took a breath as if to speak but paused. "What if he's dead?"

"He can't be. I'd feel it."

Dot held her hands up in surrender. "I'm just trying to help you figure this out. You say the two of you were in love, but I still see a man who abandoned you for no good reason."

I sighed. "And I still say it wasn't totally his fault."

"Right, your parents and all that. Then where is he?"

Who knows? I shrugged again.

"Do you regret loving him?"

"No." My voice was firm. "The only thing I regret is that I never actually told him I loved him. I never said those words. If I had, maybe he would have stayed and fought for me."

That was the truest thing I'd said about William since he left, and the admission left me sore in my chest and a little angry.

"Regardless, it's been more than ten years." I slapped my notebook closed. "Whatever the reason, he hasn't come back and I have no way of knowing if or when he'll return. I have to make sure Jenny doesn't go through her whole life thinking her dad was a fine chap who just happened to die of a heart attack."

"Are you going to tell her about Anna-Belle?"

"No, there's no reason. Robert's actions don't affect her — he wasn't her dad, and at this point, she hardly remembers anything about him. Her real father was — is — kind and good. That's what she needs to know. He never would've wanted to do anything to hurt his family."

But he did. He hurt me.

I pushed that thought away, just out of arm's reach.

The water lapped farther and farther up our ankles each time it rolled in. To our left, a cluster of gray-and-white sandpipers nibbled at tiny clams as they burrowed into the soft, wet sand. The sun had inched down in the sky while I'd been writing, and only a few brightly colored umbrellas dotted the beach. Dot leaned her head back on the chair and stretched out her legs. She was long and lean and brown as a berry.

"So when are you going to let Bert get you pregnant?"

Dot let out a half laugh, half snort. "You don't beat around the bush, do you?"

"Sounds like someone else I know." I

flicked a few grains of sand at her with my fingers. "Anyway, it's about time. You've been married a while, and we could use some more little ones running around the house again."

"What? And ruin my figure?" Dot wiggled her hips. Grains of sand stuck to the baby oil shimmering on her skin. I laughed and handed her a towel.

"What about you?" She brushed sand off her legs and repositioned herself on the chair. "You could quit with those crazy hats and outfits and men would line up out the door for you. You know they would."

"Yes, those Sweet Bay men really ring my bell."

"It's a big world out there, that's all I'm saying."

"If there's more outside Sweet Bay, I don't need it. And I'm done with men. I gave it a go twice, and you see how far that got me. At thirty-three, I'm long past the age of letting myself get swept up by a man, no matter how handsome or charming he may be."

The words sounded believable — even to me — but I knew my heart. If William had walked onto that beach right then and there, I would have run to him and thrown my arms around him, no questions asked. I probably would have hit him too, but where

361

my heart was concerned, it would always belong to him.

I leaned my head back on the chair. The sun, still strong even in the late afternoon, baked my legs. The searing heat felt good and cleansing. I gave in to the pull of sleep until the rising tide skimmed the backs of my legs. At the same time, Bert's voice drifted to us from farther up the beach.

"We're going to have to toss out life preservers if y'all don't move back," he called. Jenny trailed behind him, a sand bucket in one hand and a stringy clump of seaweed in the other.

"Come on back to the cabin," he said. "I have grilled shrimp and West Indies salad waiting on the deck."

He turned to Jenny and said something we couldn't hear, then the two of them took off, running back the other way. My sweet girl ran as fast as her legs would carry her, beating Bert to the cabin by a nose. She gave him a high five and climbed the steps to the cabin.

Lord, I love that girl. I tightened my grip on the letter in my hands, the letter that would one day tell Jenny everything she needed to know about her father — nothing more and nothing less.

36
SARA

JULY

I didn't roll over until ten the next morning. As soon as I did, the pounding started, reminding me why I always stopped with one drink. With the shop to run and clients to please, I didn't have time to sleep in and nurse hangovers.

My phone was on top of the blanket next to me. I took a deep breath and called Crawford.

"Are you okay?" he asked in place of a greeting.

"I'm fine. I'm sorry for not calling earlier. Allyn came to town, and . . ." It was a limp excuse, but it was all I had. I hadn't deciphered anything else going on in my head yet.

"I'm glad you got to see him. I'll back off now that I know you're okay. I was just worried."

"Thanks. What do you mean 'back off'?"

"Look, I know you've got a lot going on and you have decisions to make. I want to help you with this, but I understand if you need to do it alone."

Whether I did it alone or had help, deciding what to do would not be easy. The situation had already tied my stomach in knots.

"And this should go without saying," he continued, "but if you have second thoughts about us — about me — just be honest."

"No, I'm not . . ." But was I? Thoughts swirled through my head like a tornado, but I couldn't put my finger on which ones were about the house and which were about Crawford.

"Come on, Sara. It's the first time you haven't taken my calls. This big thing happens — Sammy and his news about the house — and all of a sudden you pull away."

He'd been nothing but caring and concerned about me, and here I was trying to avoid the hard part, just like Allyn said. What kind of person did that?

"I'm sorry. I'm not having second thoughts about you, or about us. I just feel like the rug was pulled out from under me. Before, everything felt so . . . possible. Now, I don't know. If I'm not here in Sweet Bay, how would we . . . ?"

He exhaled. "We'll figure it out, just like

we said. Sammy may have pulled the rug out from under you, but I'm still here and I'm not going anywhere. And that will stay the same whether or not Sammy goes through with his plan. Okay?"

I couldn't speak over the lump in my throat, so I just nodded, even though he couldn't see me.

"Can I come see you?" he asked.

"Yes, please. I don't want to do this alone."

After we hung up I turned over to find a glass of water and two Tylenol on the nightstand. As I swallowed them down, the sound of laughter found its way up the stairs and into my room.

Downstairs, Allyn was holding court in the kitchen while Dot, Bert, Major, and Glory all drowned in laughter. Major laughed so hard he spilled his coffee. Allyn grabbed a dish towel and helped him clean up. Bert clapped him on the back. Not the sight I expected to see.

"Good morning," Dot said to me quietly when I entered. She put her arm around me and I patted her hand.

"Your friend fits right in. Mags would have loved him."

"You're right. She never would have let him leave. Can I talk to you for a minute?" I gestured into the adjacent dining room.

"Sure, hon."

We sat down at the table. In the middle was an arrangement of small vases. I reached over and ran my finger across the thin porcelain lip of a vase with tiny painted flowers.

"Mags loved having fresh flowers in the house." Dot picked up one of the vases and turned it over in her hand. "I found a box full of these in the mudroom the other day. I was going to add them to our Goodwill pile, but I thought better of it. These happy things deserve to be displayed." She wiped the dust off the vase with the hem of her shirt. "You wanted to talk to me about something?"

"Yes." I took a deep breath, then let it out slowly. "I have some bad news."

She waited, all the lightheartedness from the kitchen gone from her face.

"Sammy Grosvenor visited me a couple of days ago."

"Good grief, what does he want now?"

I didn't want to overwhelm her with details, so I just gave her a brief rundown of Sammy's plan.

"But I don't understand," she said. "He can't just swoop in and take the house, can he?"

I shrugged. "I've already talked to Mr.

Bains, and it sounds like my options are slim."

Dot stared absently out the bay window, her chin propped in her hand. Her bottom lip trembled and I had to look away. Finally, she reached over and took my hand. "What are you going to do?"

"I don't know. I'm not sure there's much I can do. I keep asking myself what Mags would do if she were here. How would she deal with Sammy?"

Dot smiled. "Mags always knew just what to do in difficult situations. When it seemed there was no way out, she'd always find one little sliver of daylight and scratch herself out. But I'm not sure even Mags could get out of this one."

"All this work," I said, looking around. The room smelled like fresh paint and wood polish, and through the hall I could see a worker in the parlor coiling an extension cord around his arm. The renovations were turning The Hideaway into a pearl instead of a crusty shell.

"Well," Dot said. "If nothing can be done, this may force Bert and me to grow up after all." She chuckled. "It's probably time, anyway. We've been talking for ages about needing to make the move down to Florida where his kids are. I know Major and Glory have family back in Georgia. Maybe it's time for us all to move on." Her words were confident, but her eyes were sad. She patted my hand again, then rose and walked back to the kitchen. I followed her.

From the doorway, we watched the scene before us. Bert mimed Major struggling to reel in a fish, while Glory narrated for Allyn an episode that included Major falling in the water only to discover it was an alligator on the end of the line. No one had ever seen him swim so fast.

"Y'all go on and laugh," he said. "But let's see how fast you swim when a six-footer is snapping at your legs. Ah, there's Sara, thank the Lord. A diversion."

"Feeling okay?" Allyn asked with a grin.

"Fine. Thanks for the Tylenol."

"I'm glad you two had a chance to catch up last night," Glory said. "You must have missed him. He's a hoot."

"Come on." Allyn linked his arm through mine. "Help me pack up. I need to get back to New Orleans and run your shop."

I trudged back up the front porch steps after seeing Allyn off, but the approach of another vehicle stopped me before I made it to the top. I turned as Crawford's truck rumbled down the driveway toward me. Tension slipped off my shoulders like silk. He parked, crossed the gravel to the steps, and folded me into his arms. I pressed my cheek into the soft space under his ear and tightened my arms around him. When we pulled away, he smiled. "Better?"

I took a deep, cleansing breath. "Yes. Thanks for coming."

"I want to be here. We have work to do. I can make some phone calls and see if we can dig up anything that would make Sammy rethink his decision. There has to be something."

I nodded. Tears threatened to fall, so I turned away.

Crawford tipped my face back toward him. "It's all going to be okay, whatever happens."

"It almost feels like everything would have been better if I hadn't come here. I fixed up the house and got everyone's hopes up for a great future for the house. Now I'm letting them down."

"You're not the one letting them down. It all would've happened the same way whether you were here or not. But by coming back, you got to know your grandmother — the real one. And you've reconnected with the folks here in the house who love you like you're their own granddaughter."

"But the house and all our work . . ."

"Don't give up on it yet. The Hideaway is a part of you," he said. "It's your past regardless of what Sammy tries to do. And who knows, it could even be a part of your future." I nodded and he took my hand. "Now, let's get to work."

37

SARA

JULY

We spent the rest of the morning and most of the afternoon on the back porch, my laptop practically burning a hole in the cushioned ottoman and both of our cell phones buzzing with activity. While Crawford called friends in town he thought might be able to pull some strings, I researched eminent domain, property laws, and anything else I could think of that might give us a loophole. I even called Mitch.

"This isn't really my thing," he said when I told him the situation. "I mean, if you go to trial with it, I'm your guy, but I'm not sure I'm the right person to talk to about saving an old house."

As he spoke, Crawford paced the back porch with his cell to his ear and a notebook in his hand, scrawling notes as he listened. He'd postponed a morning meeting and canceled plans to attend an important

General Contractors Association meeting in Mobile.

"You know what? Don't worry about it. I'm sure things here will be fine."

"Are you sure?" Mitch asked. "I can probably ask around at the office and see if anyone is willing to take it on."

"I'll take care of it."

Crawford looked at me when I tossed my cell into the chair next to me.

"Was that a friend?" he asked.

I shook my head. "Just someone I thought might be able to help. Dead end."

He leaned against the door frame and crossed his arms. "That's most of what I've gotten too. Don't worry though, I still have a few people I can talk to." He looked at his watch. "I'm so sorry, but I've got to run. Missing my morning meeting wasn't a big deal, but I can't put off Mrs. Webb. She'll eat my apologies for dinner."

I laughed. "You've done enough. Thank you."

I walked him out and returned to my seat on the porch. Although the sun glinted off every shiny surface like a spotlight, without Crawford there to keep the sadness at bay, it crept back in. He seemed buoyed by the possibility of finding just the right loophole to fend off Sammy, but I wasn't as confident. Sammy may have been harmless years before, but it was only because he'd been busy laying the groundwork for what was happening now. I was glad Mags wasn't around to see it.

That evening, I found Dot at the dining room table. Bert puttered around in the kitchen behind her, putting away pots and pans from dinner.

"I'm turning in, girls," he said when he stuck his head in the doorway. He crossed the room to kiss Dot on the cheek. "Don't stay up too late, dear. We don't have to work it all out tonight."

Bert walked into the hallway and disappeared up the stairs. I looked at Dot.

"It's nothing," she said. "We're just talking about our next steps." She squeezed my hand. "It's been a big couple of days for you. It's a lot to digest."

I sighed and shook my head. "I think I've hit my limit, for sure."

"You'll figure out what to do. You're Mags's granddaughter. You have spunk running deep in your veins."

I bet William had some of that too. Maybe it came from both of them, their DNA mixing and marrying, passing on down the line to me.

Dot closed the magazine she'd been flipping through and pushed her chair back from the table. She stopped on her way out of the dining room. "I almost forgot to tell you. Bob Crowe called today."

I shrugged. "Who?"

"Bob Crowe? The Roving Reporter? Honey, you have been gone too long. He breaks all the big stories. From the *Mobile Press-Register*?"

I shook my head.

"It's a big deal for him to call." She seemed disappointed that I didn't hold him in the high esteem he obviously deserved. "He said he wanted to talk to you about The Hideaway. I wrote his number down — it's by the coffeepot in the kitchen. Maybe he can help you with Sammy. That's what he does — he finds dirt on people that no one knew was there."

"I'm sure there's plenty of dirt on Sammy, but I don't see what a reporter can do to fix this mess."

"Just call him. See what he has to say."

In lieu of responding, I smiled, which satisfied her.

After she left, I picked up a few stray mugs from the dining room and carried them into the kitchen, the weight of the last couple days bearing down hard on my shoulders. I made my way toward the stairs but stopped when I saw light coming from the reading room in the back of the house. I walked to the doorway and peeked in.

Glory was asleep on the couch, her legs propped up on an ottoman. Her glasses had slipped down her nose, and she held a half-empty mug of tea that tipped precariously. I reached over and took the cup from her hand, careful not to wake her. I picked up the magazine lying facedown on the cushion next to her and saw the title: *Georgia Land and Real Estate.* She'd underlined several houses for sale and made notes in the margins. *Could make this work. Part-time job at the armory?*

Everyone in the house was scrambling. I thought of what Crawford said earlier, that The Hideaway was in me — it was my past, maybe even my future. Something clicked and the heaviness in my brain and body receded for a moment.

I grabbed Bob's phone number off the counter in the kitchen and took it upstairs with me. Before crawling into bed, I called and left a message at his office.

"Mr. Crowe, this is Sara Jenkins from The Hideaway. I'd like to talk."

38
SARA

I woke a few days later to the sound of
excited voices and footsteps in the downstairs hallway. The house didn't usually have
that kind of activity until at least midmorn-
ing when Bert would flip through recipes
for the evening meal and Major would chide
him for whatever choice he made.

I dressed quickly and headed for the
noise, but the doorbell rang before I reached
the first floor. As I crossed the foyer to the
front door, I saw the newspaper lying on
the console table. "A Sneaky Deal in Sweet
Bay?" the headline blared. I smiled. Mr.
Crowe must have done his job.

"I hope you don't mind that I spoke to
that reporter," Mrs. Busbee said in a rush
as soon as I pulled open the door. "I've got
to get up to the diner, but I just had to talk
to you first. When Mr. Crowe told me this
place might be torn down because of

Sammy, I couldn't help myself. Who does he think we are? The Sunset Strip?" She shook her head and glanced at her watch. "I'd hate to see anything along this stretch of the bay except The Hideaway. Please let me know if there's anything else I can do."

Neighbors came by and called throughout the morning, all of them offering their support. Mr. Crocker from the farm up the road shyly approached the house just as I was closing the door behind Norm Hammond, the town barber. Mr. Crocker said Mags had let him and his wife stay at The Hideaway for a long weekend soon after the birth of their fifth child.

"We needed some time away from the demands of the farm, not to mention the kids, but we didn't have an extra dime in our pockets. The next thing we knew, your grandmother was on our doorstep telling us to pack our bags. She knew we'd had a tough year with the drought and adding an extra mouth to feed, and she wouldn't accept payment from us. Not in money, anyway. I left her fresh milk and eggs every morning for a month after that. That was forty years ago and I still haven't forgotten. Your grandmother was a gem and this house was a lifesaver."

Later, Mr. Grimmerson stopped by and

told how after Hurricane Lorraine blew through in the seventies, Mags's home was one of the only places that didn't lose power — something about being on a separate power grid. "I had supplies in my store that people needed, but no one could drive anywhere downtown with so many trees down. Your grandmother rode her bicycle all the way to my store, helped me load supplies onto a wagon she pulled behind her bike, and then brought it all back to The Hideaway. This became my temporary outpost. She opened her doors to people who needed a place to stay or just needed batteries and flashlights. She was always helping people in the most unexpected ways."

During a lull in the action, Crawford pulled down the driveway with sausage biscuits from the diner for everyone in the house. "I figured you'd be busy, being famous and all," he said to Dot and Glory as they helped him clear the dining room table of newspapers so he could set out the food.

"Famous isn't what we want to be," Glory said.

"Yeah, but 'not homeless' is," Major said. "So if it takes Mr. Crowe and the *Mobile Press-Register* drumming up support for the house, I'll take the fame. I'll be upstairs shaving if anyone needs me."

"No one's coming to take your picture, Major," Glory called as he left. She turned to us. "I'd better go talk some sense into him. He'll be down here in his Sunday best before long." She hurried up the stairs behind him.

With the room blessedly empty, Crawford pulled me to him. "I've missed you," he said into my neck, his lips tickling my skin. He put his hands on the sides of my face and kissed me.

"You're in a good mood for someone whose hard work may be about to meet the wrecking ball."

"Not gonna happen. I have a feeling for these things."

"Oh, you do?" I asked.

"Mm-hmm. I also have a feeling we need to get out of here soon. I love your room-mates, but —"

Bert rounded the corner from the hall, his gaze down on yesterday's mail, and walked right into us. "Don't mind me," he said, disentangling himself. "I'll be out of your hair in a jiff."

"See what I mean?" Crawford whispered.

He kissed me again, soft and quick, then called out to Bert. "I brought enough food

to feed an army, Bert. No need to run off."
He handed me a cup of coffee, but before I
could take a sip, the doorbell rang again.
"No rest for the wanted," he said. "Better
see who it is."

I was just starting back up the front steps
after chatting with a man from the Baldwin
County Preservation Society when I heard
a rustling in the azalea bushes at the side of
the house. Clark Arrington pushed his way
through, carrying a pair of loppers in his
hand.

"Oh, hey," he said when he saw me. "I
always tried to keep these bushes from
growing too tall for Mrs. Van Buren. I just
figured I'd keep cutting them back until
someone tells me to stop. But if you'd rather
me not . . ."

"No, it's okay." Before, I probably would
have told him we could take care of the
bushes ourselves, but in light of everything
that had happened, I appreciated Clark's
desire to continue this trivial means of keeping The Hideaway in shape.

"I'm sorry about what's happening to this
old place," he said, his hands busy in the
bushes along the edge of the porch. "Sammy's been talking about it for a while, but I

didn't think he'd actually go through with it."

So this was what Clark had been dropping hints about on the dock. And I'd just thought he was being a nuisance.

"Thanks," I said.

"Yeah, I've been doing some work for him here and there over the last year or so. He wanted me to help him on this deal, but I just couldn't do it. Not if it meant tearing down your grandmother's house. I kind of liked the old bird."

I laughed. "I'm glad to hear it, Clark. I wasn't sure, to be honest."

"She was nice to me. She used to pay me in vegetables for my work around the yard. And if they ever had any leftover pie, she'd bring a slice across the street and leave it on the steps leading up to my apartment. She always covered it in plastic wrap to keep the ants away."

Clark bent down to pick up the branches he'd cut, then without saying good-bye, retreated through the space in the azalea bushes.

By lunchtime, a banner had been erected at the end of the driveway facing Highway 55. "Sweet Bay Supports The Hideaway!" it said. Several smaller, homemade signs dotted the grass: "Protect Our Town!" "Go

Away, Sammy!" and "Save Sweet Bay!"

The flood of neighbors and well-wishers slowed in the afternoon. I sank down in a chair at the dining table next to Bert, who was folding dish towels. "I can't even wrap my brain around what's happened today," I said.

"It's been a big day," Bert agreed. "I think it's been successful though. Maybe Sammy will pull the plug on the whole deal."

"Sammy won't do it, but if the mayor fears he's angered too many people, maybe he'll back off." I reached over and grabbed a towel to fold. "I never thought people in Sweet Bay cared anything about this place or even liked Mags that much. So many people made fun of her. I can't believe they're stepping up now and giving us — giving *her* — support."

"You don't have it quite right," Major said from the kitchen. He walked into the dining room. "If you hadn't been stuck inside that teenage head of yours all those years ago, you might have figured that out."

I opened my mouth, but he continued. "I'll be the first to say Mags was a little odd — she wore strange clothes, never picked up a mop for as long as I knew her, and she had a strange affinity for sitting in the garden late at night — but she left her mark

382

on Sweet Bay, and people won't soon forget that. Take me and Glory. We arrived here in south Alabama at the height of the sixties — two black faces in a whole town of white. She didn't bat an eye about opening her doors to us. Not only that, she talked us out of leaving when we thought we'd overstayed our welcome. She was a strong woman a step ahead of the times.

"Sure, some people made fun of her — small-minded people will do that. And kids — kids laugh at anything different from them. But most of the adults in town knew she was a necessary part of life here in Sweet Bay. A necessary part of our lives, for sure."

"Major's right," Bert said. "And like Mrs. Busbee said in that article, Mags was the town matriarch and she took care of people. She never seemed to have extra money to put into the house, but money would show up when someone needed help. I stopped trying to figure her out a long time ago. She is who she is — or was — and we loved her for that. End of story."

That was just it though — they had all known there was more to Mags than she let on, and the townspeople respected her for her help in times of need. I, on the other hand, took her for exactly who she was on the surface, never bothering to consider that a full, rich life had been waiting just underneath. I realized I loved her life, her spirit. I loved who she had been all along.

39

MAGS

1976

I wasn't normally a churchgoing woman. Back in Mobile, we attended the Episcopal church, although I always got a feeling it was more because of the beauty of both the stained glass and the congregation. The Methodist church right down the street would have been fine, but it didn't have glass brought in from Europe and couldn't claim the mayor of Mobile and the head of Bay Imports as members.

Dot and Bert had been going to Baldwin Baptist since they moved in, and they asked me to accompany them every Sunday. And every Sunday I declined. The house was quiet on Sunday mornings, and I usually spent those hours on the dock or in my garden. Why mess up a perfectly good morning with fire and brimstone and a healthy heap of guilt to go on top?

"You should try it just once," Dot said to

me one Saturday evening as I tiptoed through my garden picking bell peppers. "What can it hurt? It might even help."

"What makes you think I need any help?"

"Just think about it," Dot said. "No one's going to make you walk the aisle if you don't want to, and it may make you feel better to let go of — well, anything you may be holding on to."

Dot was many things, but subtle wasn't one of them. "Why do you think I need to feel any better than I do right now? I'm fine."

Dot moved closer to me, sidestepping a tall pepper plant. "I've been here for sixteen years. That's sixteen years of watching you walk around with a weight on your shoulders that you never talk about and pretend isn't there. And watching you love someone who is never coming back."

I drew in a quick breath and stepped back.

"Don't get mad, just listen to me for a minute. You are a strong woman in every area except one — William. You've told me a thousand times that you're over him, but it's just not true. I know he came in here and set your world on fire, but it was a long time ago, and life goes on. After all these years of being your best friend, I think I've earned the right to say this: You need to let him go."

So much for trying to look strong.

I wasn't ready to give up, but would it free me if I did? I wasn't sure if I even wanted to be free. What if, miracle of miracles, he did come back one day? If I'd already shut my heart off and let him go, I might not be able to kick it into gear again.

I put my arm around Dot. "I'll think about it."

Surprise crossed her face. "I thought you'd slap me for sure."

"Have I ever done anything to make you think I'm a violent person?"

She smiled. "Maybe not, but after Robert left, I told Bert to hide the oyster knife just in case he ever came back."

Not long after that conversation, I gave in.

"I won't even ask what changed your mind. Just be ready at eleven," Dot said. "And try to wear something normal."

I didn't tell her, but what made me change my mind was a simple question from Jenny that literally stopped me in my tracks. She and I had taken a stroll before dinner, and after chatting about her biology homework and the roses growing outside Grant's Hardware, Jenny took a deep breath. I knew something was on her mind, but I also knew just enough about teenagers to know if I came out and asked her what was wrong, she'd never tell me.

"Mama, how did it feel when you and Dad fell in love?"

I was so unprepared for that question, I stopped putting one foot in front of the other.

She turned. "What are you doing? We're in the middle of the street."

I followed her to the sidewalk, trying to come up with an answer.

"I know you don't like to talk about him," she continued. "I just — Mabel told me Mark Kupek is in love with me. She asked me if I'm in love with him, but how am I supposed to know? What did it feel like with you and Dad?"

Which one? The man she thought was her dad or the real one? I still hadn't given Jenny the letter I'd written on the beach in Gulf Shores, even though she was now approaching high school. Every time I gathered the courage to pull the letter out of its hiding place and take it to her, I lost the nerve. She'd be rocking on the back porch with a paperback in her hands, or laughing with friends on the end of the dock, or playing checkers with Bert. She was content with her life and the family she had at The

Hideaway, and I couldn't bring myself to shatter the peace.

Her question about love made me realize I'd put myself — and her — into a bind by not laying out the truth and letting her decide how to feel. Instead, I'd chosen the lens through which she'd view her family. But my daughter had asked me about love, and the only true love I knew was William, so I told her the truth.

"It was electric, like a thousand butterflies in my chest or a thousand balloons flying free. Sometimes being apart was even better than being with him, because I could anticipate seeing him. When we'd finally see each other again, the air between us would crackle and snap, and I couldn't cross the room fast enough to be next to him."

It had been a long while since I'd thought of those first weeks with William. Was that all love was? Electricity, excitement, and anticipation? No, not all.

"That's how it felt, but love is a choice you make in your head too. I knew I was in love with your father because I couldn't imagine my future without him. I didn't want to imagine it. He became such a part of me that I knew if he wasn't there, I'd lose a part of myself too."

"Did you? Lose a part of yourself?"

"A small part," I said. "But I had you, and you opened my heart up in ways I never expected. You, my dear, were a balm for that wound. So were our house and our friends. I have a lot of good things in my life. But I still haven't forgotten him."

We walked in silence a few moments before she spoke. "I'm definitely not in love with him." She might as well have said, "I'd rather not have chicken for dinner tonight." My Jenny, so uncomplicated.

"Who is Mark Kupek?" I asked.

"Just a boy," she answered.

I laughed and put my arm around her thin shoulders. *My sweet girl.* "That's how it is — they're always 'just a boy,' until they're not."

The church service was much like I expected it to be — lots of flowered hats, big smiles, hand-clapping hymns, and a good old fiery sermon peppered with "Mm-hmm" and "Preach it" from the congregation.

But something happened during the prayer time. After lifting up every injury and ailment in the congregation and the tribulations of every possible extended family member, the preacher stopped and called for a time of silent prayer. His voice lost its showman's edge and grew raspy and honest.

"I'm sensing there are folks here who need one-on-one time with God. No sweaty preacher up here spouting off about everything they should be thinking or feeling — just you and God. If that's you, I encourage you to close your eyes right now and listen." The organist started up with a melancholy tune that drew congregants to the front altar like a magnet. My butt stayed planted on the pew. "If you hear God's still, small voice, don't worry about me or anyone sitting around you. I just ask you to listen to what He might have to say to you this morning."

The church was quiet except for the organ. I closed my eyes and tried to listen for that voice. Since the day Jenny asked me about falling in love with William, I'd been more aware than usual of his shadow trailing me. He'd been gone for years, yet he was still a very real presence in my life. Dot let me know in no uncertain terms that the weight I'd thought I'd hidden well still sat on my shoulders in full view of everyone around me.

I wasn't always on the best terms with God, but I was thankful He had given me William at all. If William hadn't been living at The Hideaway when I moved in, there was no chance I'd still be there now. I would have stayed a few nights, felt the heavy weight of that fancy ring on my finger, and probably gone right back to Mobile and to Robert, continuing to scratch out an existence in the thing we called a marriage.

But William had been there. And my life was profoundly different because of him and my time at The Hideaway. I was thankful, but Dot was right. I was no longer the twenty-two-year-old I was when I met him. I was almost forty and my right to be a lovestruck girl had passed its expiration date. He was not coming back.

With my eyes squeezed shut and that organ droning on, I pulled my shoulders back and lifted my chin. *God, I know we haven't talked in a while, but —*

The preacher clapped his hands. "Thank You, Lord, for that time of prayer and silence. Can I get an amen? Mrs. Betty Jo, how about 'Onward, Christian Soldiers.' "

Betty Jo fired up the organ again. Mouths opened in song and hands lifted in praise, the time of prayer finished.

Fine then. I looked up at the rafters and winked. *I wasn't ready to let go anyway.*

40
MAGS

My Jenny found love at eighteen — too young in my eyes, but I quickly realized I had no need to worry. Ed Jenkins was no Robert Van Buren. Ed doted on Jenny, but he also pushed her to challenge herself. At his urging, she enrolled in a culinary program at the community college. She was always helping Bert in the kitchen, but I'd never thought of culinary school. Ed took a bite of her seafood gumbo one night and said, "You need to open a restaurant, Jenny."

The idea for Jenny's Diner grew out of that early evening dinner, consumed on the dock at sunset surrounded by our friends. Once darkness overtook the sun, lightning bugs popped out in the shrubs and trees. From the dock, they made the place look alive.

Jenny and Ed married less than a year later, and little Sara Margaret arrived ten months after that. Sara had the good fortune of loving, attentive parents and a multitude of "grandparents" who doted on her day and night. As Jenny's Diner grew in popularity, our job as stand-in parents grew in importance. Bert learned how to operate an Easy-Bake Oven, I became proficient in the rules of Go Fish, and Glory's knitting needles became fairy wands in Sara's little hands. Back then, Sara thought The Hideaway was a magical palace, and I never corrected her because, in a way, it was. Sara looked a little like Ed, but a lot like me. She had my skin coloring and dark, rebellious curls. That hair flew behind her as she ran from room to room through the house. She'd flee from anything resembling a brush or hair band, so her hair grew long and wild, especially during the summers when she was out of school and spent most of her time at our house. I sometimes tried to imagine what Sara would look like as a young woman or as an adult, but I couldn't see anything other than the carefree child before me.

I got to where I couldn't allow myself to imagine William coming back for me, or even Jenny, especially once she became a woman with her own family, her own roots. For some reason, it was easier to think of him coming for his granddaughter. Occasionally I'd allow myself the luxury of imagining Sara and William together. I'd give myself over to an afternoon's worth of a daydream about the two of them finding each other later in life and knowing immediately that something connected them — something potent and essential. They'd be drawn to each other, and they'd trust it, even if they didn't know why.

Jenny's death on the rain-slick highway shattered me. It was unspeakable. Not only had I lost my daughter, but I'd lost the last tie I had to William. I'd loved my daughter for the person she was, and she knew that, but I'd also loved William through my love for her. When Jenny was gone, it felt like he was finally gone too.

But the real truth was William was gone the minute he made the decision to leave The Hideaway all those years ago. I should have accepted that fact much earlier, but it was easier to hang on. After all, I hadn't decided what exactly I was going to tell him in his workshop that day. I wasn't going to ask him to leave — I don't think I was, anyway. I suppose I thought we'd figure it out together, like he'd said about so many things. I may have made the choice by not outright refusing my father all those years ago, but William took the decision out of my hands by leaving on his own. I don't know how he knew Robert was back in the picture, but I suppose he did what he thought was honorable.

All I had left of him were the few things he made for me during our short time together — the pieces of furniture, the bench in the garden, the tiny replica of the house — the one that should have been ours, built into a quiet cove on the bay, undiscovered by anyone but us. But life doesn't always work out the way it's supposed to, does it?

41
SARA

AUGUST

I called William at the number he gave me, and we made plans to see each other the next day. He said he'd make a day of it and visit some friends from his days at The Hideaway, Gary and Starla.

"Starla?" I asked.

"She gave herself that name back when she wore all black and smoked twenty cigarettes a day. It's a miracle she's still alive. I think her real name is Betty."

When he arrived in town, I directed him to The Outrigger for lunch, where we found a table on the deck overlooking the water. I wanted to tell him about the possible fate of the house — not to mention our family connection — but I was nervous about his reaction to both. To stall, I told him about leaving Sweet Bay, landing in New Orleans, and opening Bits and Pieces.

"But couldn't you have opened your shop

here? I've dreamed about Sweet Bay since I left fifty-some years ago. It's a special place, you know. And the house — it has a pull."

"I get it now," I said. "I think my time away finally showed me that. But after living with Mags for a decade, I guess I needed a break. Back then, she was a little odd."

"What do you mean, odd? Maggie was many things, but I wouldn't describe her as odd."

"I think it happened after you left. I understand more now, but as a clueless teenager, I just wanted out. And in coming back, I'm finding pieces of her life that I never knew existed."

He smiled, but it was halfhearted. "If it took her passing on for you to come back to your home and understand more of who she was — and who you are . . . well, maybe something good can come from something so sad."

I shrugged. "Maybe so."

Bubble gum snapped as someone approached behind us. "Y'all ready to order something?" the waitress asked without looking at us. I recognized her as the same waitress from my dinner here with Allyn.

William glanced over the menu and ordered a fish sandwich. I chose the grilled shrimp salad, and we both ordered sweet tea.

"You sure you don't want a glass of wine? Or three?" the waitress asked. I looked up at her and she winked.

"No, thanks. I'm fine."

"I'll have that out to you in a few." She snapped her gum as she wrote our orders on her little notebook and walked away.

I took a deep breath. "I left something out the last time we talked. I wasn't ready to tell you then, but I don't think I can keep it in any longer."

"Then you'd better tell me."

"That little girl you saw the day you came back to The Hideaway?" William nodded and I swallowed hard. "You're right that she was my mother. But she was not Robert's daughter."

William's brow creased between his eyes.

"Mags and Robert never shared a bedroom once he moved in," I said, making my point clear.

"Then who . . . ?" He turned his eyes to the water and clenched his jaw. "She . . . that little girl wasn't mine, was she?"

I nodded.

His mouth opened and closed, then he shook his head as if shaking away a dream. "Are you sure?"

"Yes."

"In those last couple weeks before I left, something about Maggie was different." William dragged his hand across his face. "She looked and sounded the same, but she *felt* different to me. I even wondered . . ." He shook his head again. "So all this time . . . and that day, behind the house wasn't . . ." He exhaled, blowing the air out with force.

I looked away. Whatever his feelings were, they were private. When I glanced back at him, his head was down and he'd put his hand over his eyes. Finally, he sniffed and pulled a handkerchief out of his pocket.

"I'm sorry," he said. "This is such a surprise. Where is she now? My — the little girl?"

I hated to deliver another blow. "Her name was Jenny. She and my father died in a car wreck almost twenty years ago."

William took his cap off and held it in his hands, pulling at the edges with his fingers. This man had lived most of his life under a wrong presumption, and I'd just thrown open the shutters, letting in the light of truth. Should I have kept my mouth closed?

He turned back to me. "Up until I met Maggie, I'd lived much of my life without a family. My parents died young, like yours did. When I met her, I thought that would all change, that I'd finally be a part of something bigger than myself, but it wasn't to be." He shrugged. "Not then anyway." He pulled the corner of his mouth up in a small smile as he wiped his eyes again. "This must be strange for you too. But I'm glad you're here — does that make sense?"

"It does. I understand."

The waitress brought our food and we ate mostly in silence. I began to dread the silent car ride back to the house, but then William began to talk about his life after he left Sweet Bay.

Despite the failed marriages, his life had been mostly good. When he left The Hideaway, he moved around for a while, finding odd jobs to support himself while he worked on his furniture.

"I was constantly on the road in my old truck, the bed filled up with planks and boards I pulled out of abandoned houses. I was always covered in sawdust. Still am, really." He looked down at his hands and dusted them off on his pant leg, even though they were clean.

He found a few shops that agreed to carry his pieces, and business took off. After coming back and seeing Mags and Robert together, he settled in Still Pond, a small farming community an hour north of Mobile, and had been there ever since.

"It's a nice town. I've had friends over the years, I have a church, people who look in on me. Most of the town eats at a dining table or sits on a bench I made for them or their parents or even grandparents. I know most everyone there. It's been a good life," he said, nodding. "Lonely at times, but a solid life."

"Sounds a lot like mine."

"You mean you don't have a fellow down in New Orleans waiting on you?"

I shook my head. "Not in New Orleans."

"Here?"

"For now, I suppose."

"I don't have much recent experience dealing with young people's relationships, but I can listen. If you want."

I wasn't in the habit of talking much about my relationships. Allyn knew most of what was going on with me at any given time, but it had taken me a while to feel comfortable sharing my life with him. For some reason, I felt okay telling William about Crawford.

Talking about Crawford naturally led to talk of the house and how beautiful it was becoming. I rounded it out by giving him the blow-by-blow of Sammy's plan.

"Sammy Grosvenor. The name rings a bell, but . . ." He shook his head. "Can he do it? Can he take the house?"

"I wish there was a way out, but Mags's lawyer has gone over it and checked with the mayor's office. Sammy has had his eye on the property for a long time, so once he convinced the mayor the time was right, he jumped on it."

William sighed. "All in the name of progress, I suppose."

I nodded.

"So much life in that old house," he said.

"Sammy used to come around The Hideaway every once in a while. He'd tell Mags he could set her up nicely for the rest of her days if she'd only sell. Every time, she'd practically chase him off the porch. I don't think Sammy ever understood what kind of woman Mags was."

William chuckled. "So she wasn't interested in passing her time with shuffleboard and sudoku?"

"Not quite. The only time I ever saw her sit down and relax was when she went to the garden at night to sit on your bench. Otherwise, she spent her time working on something — the boat motor, her vegetables, replacing a missing board on the dock."

"Sounds a lot like me," William said.

"Keeping busy — making things with my hands — is the only way I know to live. It's the only way for me to keep Maggie with me. Well, that and the keys."

"The engravings," I said slowly. "You made those."

He nodded. "It's my trademark. I've carved that key into everything I've made since I met her. But it's more than my mark, it's my inspiration — or more accurately, she's my inspiration. She held the key to my heart back then, as well as now. As much as it meant to me though, I didn't think she'd ever thought about it again. Seeing it carved into the marble on her headstone . . . Well, I wasn't sure what to do with that. I guess that's why I finally made myself come back and ask some questions. I sure am glad I found you."

"I am too."

We were both quiet a moment.

"Can I ask you a question?" I said.

"Of course."

"Why do you call her Maggie?"

He smiled. "It seemed like she was making a fresh start in her life, so I gave her a new name to go with it. And you call her Mags?"

I nodded. "I guess somewhere along the way it was shortened."

He sat back in his chair and crossed his hands over his middle. "So Sammy is taking the house."

I looked out at the water but kept an eye on William.

"Memory is a powerful thing," he said. "My memories of Maggie have kept me going all these years even though I hadn't seen the house, much less her, in decades. But the house isn't the keeper of memories for me. Mine are up here." He tapped his forehead. "You're different though. Losing the house will be a bigger blow for you, I imagine."

A year ago — six months ago even — losing the house probably wouldn't have even registered on my radar. But now? Everything about this new, unexpected chapter of my life was tied to the house in some way. Losing it felt like losing a part of my body I'd just learned how to use.

After lunch, William drove me home. We made no immediate plans to see each other again, but I wasn't worried. We had a lifetime of absence to make up for. I hugged him before I left his car, and he patted my cheek.

That night, long after Dot and the others had gone to bed, I walked through the house, dark except for the light in the kitchen. In the downstairs hallway, I paused in front of Mags's bedroom door. Dot and Glory had done a little cleaning out, taking bags of odds and ends to Goodwill and Sweet Bay United Methodist for their annual rummage sale. They told me they were leaving Mags's clothes and personal belongings for me to go through.

I turned the knob and the door creaked open. I'd requested that Mags's room be the last one to undergo renovation, so everything looked as it always had — single bed pushed up against one wall, a dresser along the opposite wall, chair and ottoman in one corner. Her vanity sat under the window that overlooked the backyard and the bay. I turned on a lamp and sat on the small stool in front of the mirror. A pot of Pond's cold cream sat on top next to a tube of Jergens lotion, a couple prescription bottles, and an old, silver-handled hairbrush. I twisted the top off the Pond's and inhaled. It was Mags's scent. Granted, the scent was usually mixed with something else — dirt, brackish water, motor oil — but the Pond's was always underneath.

The top drawer of the vanity held a variety of hairpins, travel-size shampoo bottles, a box of needles, and small spools of thread.

In the middle of all these trivial items, a pearl necklace gleamed in the lamplight. I smiled. Most people would have wrapped something like this in tissue and protected it in a jewelry box, but not Mags. She just dropped it in with everything else.

The bottom drawer appeared to be empty, but when I pushed it closed, I heard something inside skid across the wood. I pulled the drawer back open and leaned down to peer in. Way at the back was an envelope. I reached in and pulled it out. My mother's name was written on the front. I turned the envelope over — it was still sealed, never opened.

I moved my fingers over the envelope and felt a folded piece of paper inside. It wasn't for me, but it had been for my mom, and for some reason, she'd never read it. *Should I?*

I slid my finger under the flap and opened the letter.

My dear Jenny,
    As I write this, you are a lovable nine-year-old running around the beach with salty air in your face. The thought of telling you what I'm about to share on paper is unfathomable — that's why I plan to give this to you when you're

much older. Hopefully by then you'll be able to better understand the complexity of the human heart and how it can clutch both hope and pain in the same tight fist.

Up until now, you've been told that your father, Robert, died of a heart attack years ago when you were a toddler. It is true that a man named Robert Van Buren died when you were three, and of a heart attack, but this man was not your father . . .

When I finished the letter, I ran my fingers across my mom's name on the front of the envelope. Then I wiped my cheeks and replaced the letter inside. It was late, and I was tired, but instead of going upstairs, I lay down on Mags's bed. I slid the envelope under the pillow and closed my eyes.

42
SARA

Despite the signs and pleas from Sweet Bay, Sammy and Mayor McClain did not relent. The mayor sent a firm but apologetic note explaining that we would be compensated for the value of the house, which none of us cared about. Sammy showed up on the doorstep two days later with a court order in his hands.

"You have thirty days to vacate the premises. You don't want to be here after that."

He backed down the steps and walked to his car, but he stopped before he opened the door. "Miss Jenkins, this doesn't have to be all that bad. You'll get on back to New Orleans and go about your business. I'll set things in motion here and move on to my next acquisition." He opened his car door and sat down. "Life goes on."

Later that evening, hours after Sammy had dropped off his court order like an unwanted fruitcake, the five of us sat in the living room together.

"I'm proud of you," Dot said. "You turned this house into something magnificent, which is exactly what Mags wanted. You should be proud of yourself too."

"What are you going to do?" I held a mug of Lady Grey tea, but it had long grown cold.

"We're moving down to Florida," she said. "We should have done it years ago. If you'd told me when I first moved in here that I'd outlive Mags and still be here at this age, I'd have told you to go jump in the bay. This place gave us a wonderful life, but everyone has to join the real world sometime . . ." She paused and shook the ice cubes in the bottom of her glass. "I suppose our time has come. Almost fifty years later."

"Just like that?" I asked. "It's such a quick change."

Dot looked at Bert and he nodded. "It's not so quick," she said. "We've talked about it off and on for years, but just never put the plan in motion. But it's time now. And we're okay with it. Don't worry about us." I thought I heard a wobble in her voice, but her face remained calm, almost cheerful.

"What about you?" I searched Glory's face for any indication of panic or sadness.

410

If I'd seen even a hint, I'd have crumbled.

"Major and I have had our eye on some property back in Georgia for a while. It's still on the market, so I think we'll put up a nice little house and dig in roots. We may even try our hand at farming."

"Farming?" Major laughed. "A trendy chicken coop is not a farm, my dear."

"We'll start there and see what happens." Glory winked in my direction.

"Your turn," Dot said. "What's next for you? For a little while, we thought you might stick around here." She glanced at Bert. "We weren't sure at first, but it seemed like you and Crawford . . ."

"What she's trying to say is it was nice to see some young love under the roof again," Bert said. "And he seems like a gentleman. Knows how to treat a lady. That goes far in my book."

"I'm sure she can rest easy knowing she has your approval," Dot said. "Crawford put a lot of work into this house. He must be devastated that it's all going to be for naught. How is he handling everything?"

My mind went back to something he'd said in the dining room the day the newspaper article came out. We'd finished breakfast and he was about to leave.

"Most of the houses I work on are just

jobs to me," he'd said. "Occasionally I get asked to work on some great old house and it becomes more important, but when I finish the job, I move on to the next one without a hitch. This one was different from the start."

"That's probably because you had your eye on the owner before you even saw the house," I said.

"I got lucky. I heard she almost went with Earl and his overalls." He smiled. "The thing is, I've come to love the house too. When I first saw it, I loved that you weren't taking the easy road and unloading it as quickly as possible, which probably would have put it right into the hands of someone like Sammy. Yet here we are staring demolition in the face." He ran his hand through his hair, leaving it sticking up in tufts, and leaned toward me, his elbows on his knees. "Regardless of the house, you come first. I can find another old house to fix up, but I don't want to lose you."

Dot looked at me, still waiting for an answer. Crawford was so kind and good. He'd probably never left anyone in the dust, as I had with Mags. He wouldn't know how to do that. I shook my head and answered the question she hadn't asked. "I don't know what's going to happen."

■ ■ ■ ■

In the last weeks, I spent as much time as I could soaking up the essence of the house and Mags — I walked down the long, curved driveway, watched the sunset from the dock, rocked on the porch, and sat in Mags's bedroom. I wanted to pack up the memories and take them with me, even if only in my mind.

My last night in the house, I found myself in the garden at dusk. Cicadas serenaded me from their hidden places as I sat on Mags's bench, my fingers automatically finding the skeleton key on the underside. A light breeze blew in from the south, the sky darkened to a range of purples and pinks, and I let my tears fall without holding them back.

I stayed in the garden long after darkness fell, covering everything like a warm, thick blanket. Sometime later, the screen door creaked open. "Sara, honey?" Dot asked. "You okay out there?"

I pulled myself up off the bench and took one last look around. In the dark, everything was a little out of focus. I saw myself as a child, scrambling through the garden, trying to snatch up as many strawberries as I could before Mags came around with her basket. Then as a teenager, sitting next to Mags on the bench, not understanding why she came out here every night in the dark to do nothing but think. Then me at eighteen, packing my suitcases and pulling away from The Hideaway, leaving a smiling, waving Mags behind.

It seemed everywhere I looked — every surface I touched, every sound I heard — reminded me of how I'd misunderstood perhaps the bravest woman I'd ever known. With my mind and heart full to overflowing, I turned and left the garden.

The next morning, I stood in the driveway packing and repacking the trunk of my car. It all fit fine, but I kept rearranging items so I wouldn't have to look Crawford in the face. Everything William had made, and as many other pieces as we could haul, sat in a storage facility in Fairhope. The box containing Mags's most precious items sat up front on the passenger seat.

Finally, Crawford put his hand on my arm. "I think it's fine." His voice cut through the quiet.

Thunder rumbled in the distance, but the sun shone brightly. I exhaled and leaned my forehead on his chest. He wrapped his arms around my back and his hands went to my hair, lifting the curls off my neck. I raised my face toward him and he pressed his palms to my cheeks.

"I'll miss you," he said.

I nodded, not trusting my voice to speak.

"I'm going to give you some time to get back in the swing of things at work. Pull Allyn back in line, get your shop in order, whatever you need to do. I'm not going to bother you, but if you decide you want me there, I'll hop in the truck that minute. I mean it. I'll even bring Popcorn if you want."

"I don't need Popcorn." I leaned my cheek on his chest. "Besides, who would take care of Charlie while you're gone?"

"Good point."

We were both quiet, then he cleared his throat. "I could say so many things right now, but I'm not going to. You know how I feel about you, and I think I know how you feel about me."

"You think?"

He sighed. "I can't help but think if you felt the way I do, you wouldn't be about to drive back to New Orleans."

He's right. What am I doing?

"But my shop, everything . . ."

His shoulders tensed.

I closed my eyes to keep the tears from falling.

I want my life to be here. I'm more me here than I've ever felt before. My life has changed and it's because of you and Mags and this place. I wanted to say it, but I couldn't push the words out of my mouth.

Crawford squeezed my shoulders and I turned to open my car door. I didn't want to hurry away from him, but I needed the silence of my car to let my emotions go. I could feel another storm coming — it was lodged somewhere in my throat — and I preferred that it happen in private.

I faced him for one last good-bye. His now-familiar smell of cedar and fresh laundry, and something else vague but distinctly Crawford, filled my senses and muddied my thoughts. His lips were warm and soft, his faint stubble tickling my skin. I put my hand to his face and turned to climb in. He leaned down to the open window.

"Sara? Please don't wait too long."

43
SARA

SEPTEMBER

Later that day, I opened the door to Bits and Pieces and inhaled the familiar scent of gardenia. I walked through the shop, running my fingers across chair backs, plump down pillows, and dustless tabletops. Allyn had been hard at work.

I walked behind the counter into our makeshift office. Allyn was hunched over the laptop with his head in his hands. The glow from the screen made his face appear pale and sickly.

"Hey," I said.

Allyn jumped, almost toppling his can of LaCroix on the table. "I didn't hear you come in. I've been trying to figure out all this QuickBooks stuff. Couldn't you just use a notebook and a calculator?"

He nudged a chair out to me with the toe of his boot. I sank into it. "So, you're back," he said.

"I'm back." I laid my head down on the table in front of me. He patted my shoulder, then reached into the mini fridge and pulled out a beer.

"It's only two o'clock. Is this what you've been doing since I've been gone?"

"Calm down, Boss. It's not for me."

He opened the bottle and handed it to me. I hesitated, then took a long swallow.

"William?" he asked.

"He's back home in Still Pond, swimming in all the memories I dredged up for him. He wants me to come visit him one day." I smiled. "He still makes furniture, you know."

Allyn nodded. "Maybe you can sell some here."

I pushed back from the table, but Allyn stopped me with a word. "Crawford?"

"He's giving me some time to get settled in. He's waiting on a phone call telling him I'm ready for a visit."

"That's a phone call that'll never happen," he said, partly under his breath.

"What?"

"You'll get back to work here, pick up some new clients, take off on salvaging trips, do what you do — and just not be able to find a free weekend for him to come."

I shook my head. "No, I don't think that's

what will happen at all. I —"

"You and I both know how this will go." Allyn cut off my babbling. "The same thing happens every time you meet someone."

I thought of Mitch and others before him. Mitch had lasted longer than most, but our mutual understanding got us both off the hook when our lives were too busy to connect.

"Am I talking to Allyn the therapist or Allyn my friend?"

"They're one and the same. I just know you better than you know yourself, so I'm obligated to warn you of what's to happen."

We sat quietly until the bell on the door announced a customer and voices filled the room.

Allyn took me out onto the floor to show me some new mercury glass vases he'd brought in and a line of hand-painted ceramic dishes. They'd already sold out once and he'd had to place a second order. Allyn moved confidently through the shop, picking up a stray feather, brushing off a cushion with his hand.

"Allyn, this is . . . Thank you for taking care of everything. I appreciate it. And you."

"Don't mention it. Anyway, I didn't expect you to come back, and I didn't want to be the reason it went under without the captain at the helm. Bits and Pieces is your baby, but you know how I feel about this place. It feels partly mine too."

"You didn't think I'd come back?"

He shook his head. "In all our years together, I always thought if you ever left New Orleans, it would be because you finally answered the call from that old house. Once you got settled there, I heard something different in your voice. You didn't sound like the girl who plans her day out to the last second and chafes when something interrupts the schedule. You sounded happy, and not in an 'I just scored a table for Mrs. Broussard' kind of way."

"I don't chafe." My voice betrayed both my irritation and guilt. "And I guess you don't know me as well as you think you do. I didn't stay, did I?"

"No, you didn't."

I sighed and stretched my arms over my head. "You obviously have things under control here. I'm going back to the loft to unpack. I'll see you in the morning?" I turned and headed for the door.

"Oh, no you don't. For better or worse, you're back in New Orleans, and we're going to celebrate. You're not sitting home and pouting on your first night back. Let me make a few phone calls. I'll pick you up at eight."

I didn't bother arguing. I knew I wouldn't win.

At eight on the dot, Allyn picked me up on his motorcycle. He handed me a helmet and I climbed on, hitching my skirt up to my knees. I felt awkward back in my usual clothes. I thought I'd relish straightening my curls into submission and slipping my feet back into summery wedges, but my toes were cramped, and my work with the flat iron was no match for the thick humidity in the air. I missed the cutoffs, T-shirts, and air-dried hair that had become my staples in Sweet Bay.

We sped through the Quarter's tight streets and back alleys until we reached the restaurant. Allyn's friends waited outside for us, a colorful menagerie of laughter and hugs. On the way in the door, Allyn pulled me to the side. "Are you sure this is what you want?"

"Sure. It'll be fun."

"I don't mean tonight. I'm talking about this — New Orleans. Leaving Sweet Bay. Coming back."

"I — yes. I went to Sweet Bay for Mags. She's gone, the house is gone. This is where

I belong."

As I said the words, I thought of all I was giving up, but something told me I'd made my decision. I didn't let myself think of the implications.

"Whatever you say." Allyn took my hand and led me inside.

Dinner was as raucous as I'd expected it to be. After several rounds of after-dinner shots, most of which I politely declined, someone touched me on the shoulder. "You're back."

Mitch.

Under the table, Allyn nudged my knee.

"I didn't hear from you after you called about the house," he said. "Did everything go okay?"

"It was fine. I actually just got back today. I stayed a little longer than I expected."

He nodded, unbothered by the fact that I'd been gone for more than four months instead of a week as I'd originally planned.

The lively conversation at the table carried on without me, and no one looked our way — except for Allyn, who kept one eye on us as he bantered with the group about a recent photo of Lady Gaga dressed as a drag queen.

Mitch sat in the chair next to me, emptied

when the previous occupant excused himself to go to the ladies' room.

"You look good," he said. "Rested."

Of all the things I looked, I knew rested was not one of them. Maybe it was what he thought I wanted to hear. He was the one who looked good. Sleek charcoal suit, white shirt unbuttoned at the throat, confident smile. It wasn't Crawford's torn khakis and wrinkled cotton, but it was nice.

Just then, a wispy blonde with legs too long to be real sauntered over from the bar and put her hand on Mitch's shoulder. "Your drink is ready, baby." She gave me a once-over, then glided away to a small table in a dark corner. Mitch and I both watched her as she settled herself in her chair and gazed back at us with a look of amusement on her smooth face.

"It's not what it looks like," he said.

"It probably is. And it's okay."

"I'd love to call you. Or better yet, what if I stop by later tonight?"

"I don't think that's a good idea," I said.

"Tomorrow then. I'm free after three. I can pick you up and take you somewhere quiet. I know you don't like places like this."

I thought about it. I could slip back into my life like nothing had changed. Go back to the shop, back to fancy dates with Mitch every two weeks, back to my routine. It was tempting, if only because I knew I could bury myself in it. But everything had changed, and I'd be cheating everyone — Crawford, William, Mags — to pretend otherwise.

I looked up at Mitch. His body was turned toward me, but his eyes were on the blonde. I cleared my throat and he turned back to me.

"What do you say?" he asked.

"Go on." I nodded toward his date. "Enjoy yourself."

He kissed me on the cheek and followed his date's path to the corner table, leaving a musky scent in his wake.

Allyn pushed my drink closer to me, but I nudged it away.

"Sad to see him go?" he asked.

"Not really."

"So small-town Alabama woodworkers are more your thing now, huh?"

I smiled. That covered both Crawford and William — sort of. "Something like that."

Allyn dropped me off at my loft past midnight. I'd let him and his friends talk me into a dash to the revolving Carousel Bar at the Hotel Monteleone after dinner. Thankfully, Allyn whisked me away after one round, much to the dismay of the rest of the group.

I dismounted at the curb in front of my loft and handed Allyn the helmet.

He was about to pull away when I stopped him.

"Was there a part of you that hoped I wouldn't come back? You would've been the 'captain at the helm' after all."

"No, I —"

"Don't worry, I'm not mad," I said. "In fact, I totally get it. You can run Bits and Pieces with your eyes closed just like I can. It's your baby too."

"I'd never wish for you not to come back. Understand that first. But if we're being honest, sure — I thought it'd be fun to have the run of the place. That is, if you even left it in my hands. You could just as easily have sold the shop and gotten a nice chunk of money out of it. I wouldn't have blamed you a bit."

"I couldn't sell the shop. There's too much of me in it. And you."

"Same thing with The Hideaway," he said. "You could have sold that, but you didn't because there was too much of you and your family in it. You're funny that way — you hang on to things that mean something to you, but you have a hard time hanging on

425

to the people who do the same. Other than me, of course. I know you could never let me go."

I pinched his shoulder. "You're right. We're stuck at the hip, lucky for both of us."

"But unlucky for Crawford." He revved his engine, but before he pulled away from the curb, he pulled his helmet back up. "You may think you have nothing left in Sweet Bay, but you're wrong. You do have something, regardless of the house. You have love. And you have family now — William, Dot and Glory and their old men. You can't tell me that's nothing."

He snapped his helmet back into place and sped off.

44
SARA

The next day began like so many others before it. I had my usual breakfast of yogurt and fruit, showered and dressed, and was out the door at nine fifteen. The last time I'd left my building on a regular workday, it was a crisp April morning. Now it was early September, cloudy and so muggy you could almost wring the air out like a sponge. I hopped into my car and zipped through the Quarter and down Canal toward Magazine. Along the way, other shop owners opened their doors, swept the detritus of the previous night from their sidewalks, and watered thirsty window boxes.

I jiggled my key into the lock at Bits and Pieces, holding on to my purse and to-go cup of coffee. Allyn roared into the driveway behind me.

"Morning, Boss." He tucked his helmet into its place under the seat.

Inside, I flipped the lights on, powered up the computer, and switched on the Keurig in the back. When I checked the dish for pralines, I found squares of dark chocolate. The CD player held Michael Bublé rather than the usual Madeleine Peyroux or Diana Krall.

"Just small changes," Allyn said, noticing my tension. "You can handle it."

And I did. That day drifted into the next, and before I knew it, I'd been back a week. My skin prickled anytime I thought of Crawford, but I tried to get through each day without thinking too much. I still felt restricted in my heels and smooth hair, but I fit my surroundings, and the shop was thriving. Nothing — and yet everything — had changed.

The Saturday shoppers came early, reminding me why I loved retail in a tourist town. Whether they were from Louisiana or Minnesota, they all wanted to buy something embellished with New Orleans's famous fleur-de-lis. Thankfully, Allyn had amped up our supply of pillows and knickknacks featuring the symbol.

I was blessedly busy all morning, my mind occupied with customer questions and client requests. I visited the site of Mrs. Broussard's new house to ensure the builders remembered to include the east-facing bay window in her walk-in closet/dressing area — at her special request — and I squeezed in a quick trip to an antique mall in Metairie. Allyn and I passed each other in the back hallway once, both hurrying to meet a demand somewhere.

"Glad you came back to this?" he asked with a smile.

"I haven't sat down since I ate my breakfast this morning and my feet are killing me, if that tells you anything."

"Do you still love it?"

I nodded. "I think I do. I just may have to take these heels off and go barefoot."

"That's the Sweet Bay coming out in you." He continued down the hall to a waiting customer.

Early afternoon business slowed enough for me to take a short break on the front porch. I sat in the swing as folks passed by on the sidewalk. I was fine until I saw the little girl. She was probably four or five, with dark curls and still-plump arms. Her daddy grabbed her and spun her around, her delighted squeals making everyone around them smile. When he brought her back to the ground, she ran straight into her mother's outstretched arms.

All the sadness and longing I'd packed into the most remote pocket of my mind when I left Sweet Bay came flooding back. I thought of Mags. Of William's old, gnarled hands and Crawford's sturdy, capable ones. Of The Hideaway and all that had taken place there. The force of my longing almost doubled me over.

Allyn chose that moment to stick his head out the front doorway. "You okay?"

I managed a nod. He kept his eyes on me a moment longer before closing the door.

Back on the sidewalk, the little family was gone. I stood and peered over the edge of the porch rail for a better view, but I didn't see any sign of them. I ran shaky hands over my hair and straightened my dress, then opened the door and walked back in.

After a quick snack, consumed in stolen moments in the back office, my cell rang. I was busy with a customer, so Allyn answered.

A moment later, he mouthed something to me from across the room. I shook my head in confusion. He crossed the room and whispered, "It's Vernon Bains. The lawyer?"

I took the phone and left the customer in Allyn's care.

"Mr. Bains, this feels like déjà vu with you calling me here at work," I said as I stepped into our tiny courtyard and pulled the back door closed behind me. "Last time you had bad news."

"Ah, Miss Jenkins, a common misconception. A lawyer on the phone doesn't always mean bad news. In this case, I have very good news for you. At least, I think it's good."

"I'm listening."

"It appears Mr. Grosvenor has withdrawn his plan to take over The Hideaway's property."

"Excuse me?"

"He called me early this morning and said he was going in a different direction. When I pressed, he said he bought another piece of property near Mobile Bay. He's scrapping the boardwalk idea and building his condos there instead. For better or worse, it appears Sweet Bay is destined to remain the secluded town it's always been."

"I — but I don't . . ."

"I know," Mr. Bains continued. "I was speechless too."

I forced my brain into gear. "So if Sammy isn't taking it, does it just . . . ?"

"Everything goes back to normal. I can't say the mayor won't one day try to run with the plan again, but without Sammy badgering him about it, and seeing as how most of the town of Sweet Bay was against it, hopefully he'll let the idea die."

Allyn stuck his head out the door. "Everything okay?" He walked into the courtyard and sat next to me. *What is it?* he mouthed. I shook my head.

"I don't know what to make of Sammy's change of heart," Mr. Bains said. "I'll let you know if I find out anything else."

"Tell me," Allyn said as soon as I put down the phone.

"Sammy isn't taking the house."

"What happened?"

"I have no idea."

Allyn sat back in the wrought-iron rocker and crossed his arms. "You said you needed something to make Sammy go away. I guess that something happened."

A grin pushed at my cheeks. I couldn't wipe it away.

"You're excited," Allyn said.

"I don't know what I am." I stood and took a deep breath. "But I think I have to go."

"Of course you do. Get out of here."

"Wait." I sat back down. "I can't do this. Mrs. Girard is coming at four and I have a shipment —"

"Don't worry about it. I'll take care of everything," he said.

"But what about — ?"

"Stop. It's fine. You can go."

"I don't even know what I'm going there to do."

"Yes, you do. You've already started a life there. Now you're going to go back and pick up where you left off."

"You make it sound so simple," I said.

"Things aren't always as difficult as you make them out to be. Sometimes you just have to turn your brain off and dive in. This may be the last time Sweet Bay tries to pull you back."

I chewed on the end of a fingernail. "Crawford?"

"Only one way to find out."

I hugged Allyn and went inside to grab my purse. On my way through the shop to the front door, I trailed my fingers on tabletops and chair backs. Pausing at the door, I turned to look through the room. Two women stood in the corner near an armoire, contemplating the big purchase. Allyn joined them, and within seconds he had them laughing and moving toward the register. Bits and Pieces would be just fine.

On my way out of the city, I rolled my windows down as far as they'd go and dropped my heels on the floorboard next to me. I didn't know exactly what I'd find in

Sweet Bay when I returned, but I wasn't going to let my last chance slip away without a fight.

I called Dot from the car and told her I was on my way home.

"Well, it's about time. I guess Vernon called you?"

"He called this afternoon. I was going to give you the news, but it sounds like you already know."

"Oh yes." She chuckled. "A lot has happened since you've been gone. Let's wait and talk when you get here though. I need to make a phone call."

She hung up before I could ask what was going on.

A couple hours later, I pulled down the long driveway and shaded my eyes from one last sharp ray of light. Two people sat in rocking chairs on the porch, and one of them stood as I approached the house.

Crawford. But it wasn't him.

When my eyes adjusted to the shadowy light on the porch, I recognized William's slightly stooped figure. Dot sat in the chair next to him. I parked under the big oak and climbed out. Without stopping to grab my bag, I headed for the porch. William and Dot were both smiling.

"What in the world is going on?" I asked. "How do you two . . . ?"

"It's been busy around here," Dot said.

I looked at William. "I took care of Sammy," he said.

"You — what?"

"A long time ago, I bought a piece of property down at the mouth of Sweet Bay. I didn't think much about it until I decided that's where I wanted to build a house for me and Maggie one day. It doesn't have a name — we just called it the cove." I glanced at Dot. She winked. "I never built the house, but I kept the property all these years in the hopes of — I don't even know. I just couldn't bear to part with it."

"And you're giving it up now? But how did you know . . . ?"

"It was Crawford," Dot said.

William nodded. "He worked hard for this house after you left. He found me after digging through old land records looking for anything that could fend off Sammy. He was the one who put it together that the cove could be the thing to save the house."

Crawford did it?

"But why would Sammy want the cove?" I asked.

"He visited me years ago and asked me about it. Turns out it's quite a coveted piece of property. I told him back then I'd never let it go, but now that Maggie . . . Well, once I met you, I realized I have no reason to hang on to it. All it took was a phone call. Sammy bought the property from me on the spot and signed The Hideaway back to you."

"I can't believe you sold it," I said.

"I hope it's okay." His face clouded with concern. "I could tell how much you loved this house, and I hated to see you lose it."

"Okay?" I laughed. "It's more than okay." I didn't have the right words, so I hugged him, and Dot too.

"William and Crawford just couldn't give up on this old place," Dot said. "Or you, it seems."

"I don't know about that. We haven't . . . I haven't talked to Crawford since I left."

Dot arched an eyebrow. "And yet he's been here doing all this work. Honey, he didn't do it for us."

"I got to know him a little this past week," William said. "He builds things, you know."

I nodded. "I know. You have that in common. And you two." I pointed at William and Dot. "Looks like you've sparked an unexpected friendship."

Dot looked over at William. "We had a lot to catch up on, that's for sure." Then she turned to me. "Let's get you inside. I apologize in advance — it's a mess in there."

I followed her through the front door where boxes and suitcases spilled in disarray all over the sparkling hardwoods. Despite the mess and the remaining old furniture, the house felt new. Even unfinished, the open floor plan, extra space, and fresh paint gave it life and new legs. Excitement fluttered again in my chest.

"We meant to be all packed up by now, but it's taking longer than we expected," Dot said.

I put my hands on my hips and inhaled deep. "Maybe you should just stay here then."

Openmouthed, Dot stared back at me. "What?" she asked, just as Major called down from the landing on the stairs, "Thank the Lord. We're all old. Our kids can come visit us."

I smiled and patted Dot on the arm, then headed for the kitchen to look for a celebratory bottle of wine. "Go ahead and unpack your bags. You're not going anywhere."

45
SARA

DECEMBER

I stood in The Hideaway's gleaming new kitchen pouring a cup of coffee when Major stomped down the stairs.

"Sara! Where's my Gillette? And my toothbrush? I can't find anything in this blasted house."

"It's all in your new bathroom, the one attached to your room. You know you don't have to keep using the hall bath. That's why I built you and Glory your own."

Major trudged back up the stairs, grumbling the whole way, until Glory called out to him. "Stop your whining, Major, or you'll be brushing your teeth on the dock."

I took my coffee into the light-flooded dining room and sat at our new heart pine table. I ran my hand across the top, my fingers finding the indentations of the skeleton key at the edge.

"See? You'd have missed all this if you'd

438

stayed in New Orleans," Bert said from across the table, working on his second apple scone. "What would you do without Major's presence in your life?"

"For one, I wouldn't have someone yelling at me about a toothbrush at seven in the morning."

I heard a tentative knock and looked up to see Mr. and Mrs. Melman.

"Breakfast is at seven, right?" Mrs. Melman asked.

"Yes, please come in and make yourself at home," I said. "Scones and coffee are just in the kitchen there, and muffins and fruit are on the table."

"Thank you. This place is wonderful," she said. "Has the house been open long?"

Bert and I looked at each other.

"It's recently reopened," I said.

Mrs. Melman touched her husband's elbow. "We'll have to tell Maylene and George. They just love quaint places like this."

As the Melmans shuffled into the kitchen, Bob Crowe and his wife entered the dining room. Bob booked a weekend right after we opened for business. "You've outdone yourself." He pulled a banana out of the basket on the table. "I know I talked this place up in the newspaper article, but I still had doubts it would make it."

"You and me both," I said.

"How'd you get Sammy to back off, anyway?"

"It wasn't me. Someone offered him a better piece of property and he took it."

"You sure got a lucky break. There's no chance anything Sammy could build would be half as classy as this."

The Crowes followed the Melmans into the kitchen in search of steaming coffee and pastries. The air smelled of cinnamon and apples mixed with a tang of salty air from the open windows. The sky was bright, the sun sparkled, and my heart was full. My new Hideaway. My new life.

It wasn't lost on me that if it weren't for Mags drawing me back to Sweet Bay, I wouldn't have had any of this. I'd still be churning away in New Orleans, thinking I'd found all I was to do with my life. I'd thought I was done with The Hideaway forever, but family was the magnetic pull that drew me back. I may have given up on Mags a long time ago, but in her own unorthodox way, she was the one who saved me in the end.

The phone in the hall rang, and I jumped up to get it. "The Hideaway, this is Sara." I loved the words as they left my mouth.

"Hey, babe," Crawford said.

"Hey, yourself. Why didn't you call my cell?"

"I know you love answering the house phone."

I smiled even though he couldn't see me.

"You're out early this morning," I said. The background noise told me he was in his truck with the windows down.

"I'm on my way to the McCaffertys' house in Lillian to meet the floor guy. You'd love this place. It's a rambling old Creole full of antiques. I mean *antique* antiques."

"What are they doing to the house?"

"Adding on. Again. They need room for the grandkids. Although I don't know how kids and all these antiques will mix. How did the night go? Was Major on his best behavior?"

"I didn't hear a peep out of him until he got feisty this morning about his toothbrush. But he's fine. It's all perfect, actually." It had been a few weeks since the last construction worker left, but the newness had yet to wear off for me.

"I can't wait to see you," he said. "I have a few more stops to make, then I'll head your way. Need anything?"

"Just you."

441

At ten, after giving the Melmans a map of the Eastern Shore of Mobile Bay and suggesting a few places they could grab lunch, I went next door. It was a beautiful thing, my business being forty feet from my home. Sometimes I missed the clattering streetcars and morning "rush" of traffic in the Quarter, but you couldn't beat walking next door with your coffee mug to flip the Open sign around and begin the day.

In the three months I'd been back in Sweet Bay — for the second time — renovations on The Hideaway had wrapped up, and Crawford and his team built a small cottage on the empty lot next door. We were fortunate to have a long stretch of good weather in early fall, and the builders made quick work of the cottage. It now housed my new shop, Lost and Found. Allyn was the one who'd convinced me I could do it.

"You started the first shop from scratch. Why can't you do it again? Alabama surely has just as many estate sales and old barns to salvage as Louisiana does. They'll eat your stuff up, just like they do here."

Crawford was on Allyn's side, of course. They met when Crawford and I drove to

New Orleans to pack up my loft and bring a few things back home from the shop. Allyn insisted on taking us out to dinner. I picked a sidewalk café near Jackson Square, a place I thought would be just noisy enough to distract us from the fact that Crawford and Allyn would have nothing to talk about. But I was wrong — I could hardly get a word in between them bantering back and forth, first about farming and motorcycles, then about me.

"You're the lucky one who gets all of Sara's pent-up romantic yearnings," Allyn said to Crawford, nudging me with his shoulder.

"That makes me sound like I've been locked up in a tower somewhere."

"You basically have," he said, then turned to Crawford. "No one has been able to break down that wall she built around herself."

"You did the hard work," Crawford said. "All your advice at least convinced her to give me a shot."

"Do I even need to be here? I can scoot out if you two want to keep talking about me and my wall."

Crawford smiled at me. A candle flickered on the table between us, right next to a red glass vase holding a plastic rose. His knee touched mine under the table.

The truth was, I'd had to convince him to give *me* a shot when I got back to Sweet Bay. I drove to his house after I told Dot and the others they didn't have to move out. He didn't believe I was there to stay.

"I can't do this twice," he said. "How do I know you're not going to skip town again?"

"I'm not going anywhere. This is where I need to be — where I *want* to be. Everything has changed."

Crawford leaned against his kitchen counter, hands in his pockets, and smiled, but it wasn't his usual smile. "Of course it has. You have the house back."

"Yes, I have the house, but it's more than that. I'm sorry for not calling, for not explaining myself to you. Once I got back to New Orleans, it didn't take long to realize I'd made a huge mistake." I stepped closer to him and put my hand to his face. "There's nowhere else I want to be, and no one else I want to be with."

He covered my hand with his own but still didn't speak. Finally, he gave me a real smile. "You're back?"

"I'm back for good."

Despite being a week into December, it was a warm day. Sunlight flooded through the bank of windows facing the bay. Not long after I propped open the front door, a gaggle of ladies entered the shop, all fleshy arms and laughter.

"You'll have to forgive us if we're too loud, dear," one of them said. "We're just excited to be here on a girls' weekend. Our husbands are out hunting and we have a lot of shopping to do."

"You've come to the right place. I have a little bit of everything, so make yourselves at home. Let me know if you have questions."

They were still puttering and gossiping when Crawford walked in. It may sound crazy, but I could have sworn the sun blazed brighter and the breeze turned warmer when he entered. Or at least that's how it felt to me. He walked through the room, stopping to chat with the ladies and make them blush with nothing but his charm and easy smile. It was hard to believe I'd even considered leaving him — and everything else — for my overloaded life in New Orleans.

"This is perfect." One of the women touched a buffet table in the back of the shop. "I'm looking for something just like this to go in my dining room. I love the rustic look. Where did it come from?"

"A woodworker up in Still Pond made it," I said. "He's been making pieces like this for most of his life. He can't handle the workload he used to, so he only makes a limited number of pieces now. I have two tables in here and another handful next door that are also for sale. He does custom orders here and there, if you ask nicely."

She chuckled and smoothed her hand down the length of the table.

"You won't find another table filled with as much love as this one. Look here — see this key engraved into the wood? He cuts the key into every piece he makes. He started doing it fifty years ago when he fell in love with a girl named Maggie. He said she held the key to his heart."

"Well, you don't hear that every day," the woman said. "What happened to them? Tell me they married and lived a happy life together."

"They didn't marry," I said, "but they should have. I'm pretty sure she loved him until she died earlier this year, and he still very much loves her."

"Sounds like you know this woodworker well."

From across the room, Crawford caught my eye and winked.

I nodded. "I do. He's my grandfather."

■ ■ ■ ■

That night, long after the last customers found their way out of the shop, most with shopping bags rustling around their knees, Crawford and I relaxed in the rocking chairs on the back porch of The Hideaway. The Crowes were getting ready for a dinner I'd booked for them at the Grand Hotel in Point Clear, and the Melmans were at the Outrigger. Another group of guests wasn't arriving until the next afternoon, so I had the evening off.

I sipped my wine and settled farther into my chair. My legs rested on a blanket in Crawford's lap and he gently squeezed my bare feet.

A scuffle in the house behind us made us both look up to the open doorway. Bert stood with one hand on the door frame, the other caught in Dot's firm grasp.

"Bert, give them some privacy," she scolded, then turned to me. "I'm sorry. I told him you two wouldn't be interested in his silly games, but he's being very pig-headed."

Bert shook his hand free from Dot's and walked out on the porch. "I picked up this new game at Grimmerson's today. George said it's popular with the young people."

"It's *Pictionary,*" Dot said, exasperated.

Crawford grinned. "What do you say?" he whispered.

"I can draw a mean crawfish," I whispered back.

"Let's do it," he said. "Here's to another night in paradise."

46
MAGS

MARCH, NINE MONTHS EARLIER
I often went back to the cove. I went on days when I couldn't bear the loneliness of missing William — or maybe I just pined for that short, sweet time in my life when he would hold me, touch me, make me feel as alive as a power line, shooting sparks and electricity out into the universe. I'd sit along the edge of the water and imagine what it would have been like if things had turned out differently. If Robert hadn't had that first episode and landed himself in the hospital, or if I'd never cashed that check, leading Daddy to The Hideaway, William and I might have still been together. We would have spent every evening out on our porch overlooking the water, dumbstruck at our love and how lucky we were to have found each other.

Or maybe that's not true at all. Maybe we would have fizzled as quickly as we began.

A bright burst of fire at the beginning and another, dimmer burst at the end, like a firework that never quite made it off the ground. We could have hurt each other a thousand ways, both of us eventually needing more and offering less than we had to give. I would have always wondered if he stayed with me out of a sense of duty, because of Jenny, while he'd worry that I'd only stayed with him to defy Robert and my parents.

I could dream all day long, but at its core, the truth of my life is that I am a lucky woman. I've known real love and true beauty, two things not given to every person. Without Robert, I never would have found my way to The Hideaway or William, and without William, I wouldn't have known the delight of both Jenny and Sara.

While I'm thankful for both of these men in my life, I'm more thankful for the woman they showed me I could be on my own. Not to mention the people they brought into my life. The Hideaway was always full of friends and lovers, mothers and daughters, secret keepers and secret spillers, straight talkers and soft shoulders. We had hurt and we had joy, but I wouldn't have had it any other way.

Things could have turned out better or

worse, but I don't dwell on any of that. I have a tarnished old house to live in, a garden to keep my hands dirty, and sunsets to watch. Sitting here on my old cedar bench, my toes dug deep in the earth, herons swooping low over the water, and the sun an orange ball of fire slipping below the horizon, I figure I've had it just about as good as it gets.

ACKNOWLEDGMENTS

Thank you to my agent, Karen Solem, for your patience, kindness, and enthusiasm for this story. Thank you to everyone at Harper-Collins Christian Publishing and Thomas Nelson for taking a chance on me and *The Hideaway.* It's an honor to be welcomed into the family with such open arms. I especially want to thank Daisy Hutton, Karli Jackson, Becky Philpott, Kristen Golden, Amanda Bostic, Kristen Ingebretson, Jodi Hughes, and Paul Fisher. Additional heartfelt thanks to Karli, who believed in and championed this book from the very beginning. I truly believe you were just the right editor at just the right time, and I'm so thankful my manuscript landed on your desk. Thank you also to Julee Schwartzberg for her editing prowess and another huge thanks to Kristen Ingebretson for the gorgeous cover. I've spent way too much time just staring at it, wishing I could sit on those rocking chairs in the warm breeze.

I'm grateful to have stumbled on Denise Trimm and her fiction workshops, first held under the Continuing Ed program at Samford University, then under her own Alabama Writers Connect. The encouragement, feedback, critiques, and laughter have been such a thrill these last several years. There have been various incarnations of the group, but the biggest thanks for help with *The Hideaway* goes to Denise, Barry DeLozier, Anna Gresham, Alex Johnston, and Chuck Measel. I'm also thankful for and indebted to The Cartel, of which we will not speak . . .

Thank you to my friends and family who read various drafts of *The Hideaway* and gave heaps of encouragement and confirmation that the time I spent writing it hadn't been wasted: My mom Kaye Koffler, my husband Matt Denton, friends Sara Beth Cobb, Thames Schoenvogel, Carla Jean Whitley, and Ella Joy Olsen.

Additional thanks to Sara Beth Cobb of Nimblee Design for creating such a beautiful website and logo for me so *The Hideaway* would have a place to hang out online. Thank you too for being so excited about this story from the beginning and for encouraging me in myriad ways. I'm thankful for our friendship.

Thanks to my dear friend Anna Gresham for unending support, laughter, rambling texts and e-mails about how HARD this writing thing is, and long car rides where we never run out of things to talk about. You're a kindred spirit and I'm thankful to be "Anna's friend Lauren."

Thank you to Angie Davis for the beautiful photos and for making me more comfortable than I expected when having someone take pictures of me!

It's a beautiful thing when writers help other writers. A huge thank you goes to author Patti Callahan Henry for launching me from the slush pile to the desk of Ami McConnell, then editor at Thomas Nelson. Thank you for reaching out a hand to help and for thinking enough of my story to pass it along to your friend, and thank you to Ami for handing it off to the fabulous Karli Jackson. Thank you to authors Anne Riley, Carla Jean Whitley, Ella Joy Olsen, Emily Drake Carpenter, and Karen White for being generous with encouragement, support, and advice. Author Carolyn Haines responded to an out-of-the-blue e-mail from me and, over the years, offered encouragement and support as I worked toward publication of *The Hideaway*. I'm a member of the Women's Fiction Writers Association, a group of generous and talented writers who are always quick to offer advice, commiseration, encouragement, and shared excitement. Writing can be a lonely pursuit, and it helps to be able to jump online and within seconds, have friends jumping into conversation.

People smarter than me offered tidbits of info that helped make the details in this book more authentic: Elisa Munoz for insider information on New Orleans levees. Julie Gulledge and David Wallace for help in finding information about Mobile Mardi Gras balls in decades past. Aaron Dettling for lending his legal expertise in the area of eminent domain. Any mistakes are mine alone.

My family is my heart, my biggest and most profound blessing. Thank you to my hardworking husband, Matt, who never complains when I escape to the library to write and come home long after I say I'll be home. Thank you for believing in me and for loving me more than I deserve. I'm so glad I get to do life with you. Thank you to Kate and Sela, my lovebugs who make me want to be better every day and who had such blind faith that my book would be AWESOME! My sweet Kate was the only one whom I was brave enough to take to the D section of the library and point to where I hoped my book would go one day. Kate was on the receiving end of many of my hopes and dreams — dreams that seemed too far-fetched and naïve to say out loud to any adult. She took those dreams at face value and never doubted that they'd come true. Thank you to all the Kofflers, Dentons, and other extended family members and friends who have shared my joy and excitement as if it were your own. I love all of you.

Every day as I sat down to write *The Hideaway,* I asked God to guide my hands (and words) and to give me continued inspiration. I loved the characters and I was devoted to telling their story, but I was constantly plagued by fears that the inspiration would dry up and this would become one more unfinished story in my overloaded file of unfinished stories. By His grace and some kind of blind naivety on my part, I was able to not only finish this story, but (with much help) hone and polish it into something I am immensely proud of. So, thank You, Lord, for the inspiration, for guiding my words, for allowing me to bear Your creative image through my writing.

DISCUSSION QUESTIONS

1. Sara fled Sweet Bay and The Hideaway as soon as she was able. Do you think that decision had more to do with her parents' death and the pain associated with that time in her life or because of Mags's mystery and eccentricities? A combination of the two?
2. After leaving her parents, husband, and former life, Mags makes a new life at The Hideaway. In essence, her friends at the B and B become her new family. Have you ever found yourself in a situation where you've had to make a new life and family with the people around you?
3. Mags's parents expected her to marry a man from a respectable family who made enough money to keep her in the life she was used to. They also expected her to look the other way when Robert strayed and to wait for him to return to his senses and his marriage. How are marriages in

general different today? How are they the same? Do you — or someone you know — have experience similar to Mags's?

4. As Sara peels back the layers and hears stories from Mags's friends, she learns Mags had a full, rich life before becoming the unconventional grandmother Sara knew. Have you ever been surprised to learn something about a family member you thought you knew well? How did your childhood view of this person differ from your opinion once you grew into adulthood? Did the new revelations change the way you thought about the person?

5. In a sense, Mags uses The Hideaway as a way to hide from her life and difficult situation in Mobile. In what way are other characters in the book hiding? Think of Sara in New Orleans, Allyn at Bits and Pieces, and Dot's friends at The Hideaway. Do you have any experience with hiding in a comforting or safe place when things in your life feel out of control?

6. Sara comes to regret that she never took the time to get to know who her grandmother really was. Do you have experience with familial regret? Has someone passed away or otherwise passed out of your life whom you wish you had taken a chance to ask key questions, whether

about the past or some event that person had experience with? How do you deal with or make peace with that regret?

7. When we first meet Sara, she is fully devoted to her work and doesn't make much extra time for friends, family, or extra pursuits. How does Sara evolve over the course of the book? What did you think about her decision to return to New Orleans and Bits and Pieces after spending the summer at The Hideaway? Do you understand her?

8. Sammy Grosvenor has a vision of Sweet Bay as a tourist destination. Those who live in Sweet Bay want it to remain the sleepy town it's always been. What do you think of the tension between progress and the desire to keep things the same? Do you know of a place that has undergone a similar fight with progress?

9. Mags left her parents and husband to escape a life that was suffocating. Would you have had the courage to make a decision so opposite your family's expectations? Do you think Mags made the right decision to leave her home? What about her decision to stay at The Hideaway?

10. If Sara had been able to meet Mags as a young woman, do you think they would

have been friends? Would they have agreed with each other's life choices?

ABOUT THE AUTHOR

Born and raised in Mobile, Alabama, **Lauren K. Denton** now lives with her husband and two daughters in Homewood, just outside Birmingham. In addition to her fiction, she writes a monthly newspaper column about life, faith, and how funny (and hard) it is to be a parent. On any given day, she'd rather be at the beach with her family and a stack of books. *The Hideaway* is her first novel.

Website: laurenkdenton.com
Twitter: @LaurenKDenton